## "Mr. McH... out of here . . . !"

. . . Captain Calhoun shouted. "We're going to try and shake that thing loose."

McHenry didn't move. He was staring, stunned, at the blackened screen.

"McHenry!"

"I . . . I can't," McHenry said.

"What do you mean, can't?" Calhoun was out of his command chair, standing next to McHenry, looking down at him in surprise. "I've seen you fly this ship virtually blindfolded. You piloted her without instrumentation. You're the one who's constantly in tune with his environment. This shouldn't be any different for you."

He had never seen McHenry look so lost. "Sir, something about its motion . . . it's disrupting space/time. I feel completely disoriented. I'm not sure why it's happening, but I can't get any sort of . . . mental lock on where we are and where we should be. I don't know which way to take us. I could fly into a star and kill us all . . ."

# STAR TREK®
# NEW FRONTIER

## #8

# DARK ALLIES

## PETER DAVID

**POCKET BOOKS**

New York   London   Toronto   Sydney   Singapore

An *Original* Publication of POCKET BOOKS

POCKET BOOKS, a division of Simon & Schuster Inc.
1230 Avenue of the Americas, New York, NY 10020

ISBN: 0-671-02080-3

First Pocket Books printing November 1999

10  9  8  7  6  5  4  3  2  1

# *TWENTY YEARS*
# *EARLIER . . .*

ROLISA WAS THE GREATEST WORLD in all of the known
galaxy.

It had started slowly, and certainly when one looked
at the world's earliest years, no one could possibly have
seen it coming. The Rolisans seemed a rather unre-
markable people. Rolisa was not particularly lush nor
attractive. It was not strategically located. It had no resources that anyone found attractive, and the Rolisans
were mostly known for being of somewhat sturdy
stock, but not much else.

Who knew?

Who knew that there would be a woman named Tara
(that was as far back as the ancestry could be traced)
who would sire a child named Arango, who in turn
begat Izzo, who begat Faicco the Small. Faicco the
Small turned out to be not only one of the greatest

thinkers of Rolisa's history, but in fact one of the greatest thinkers in the history of the quadrant. She took to lecturing, putting forward philosophies and directions on how to live a good life that were so pure, so unique in all of recorded history, that strong men wept and women would dissolve in paroxysms of ecstasy. Word of Faicco spread; eventually Faicco had two children, a boy, Milenko, and a girl, Blaymore, who shared Faicco's gift. They went throughout their home sector, and word of their teachings spread, carrying across the spaceways like glittering dust.

Soon, races from all over the known galaxy were flocking to hear their words. Means of communication being what they were, their words reached places that never would have known such thoughts and concepts were possible.

Different races fell over each other to show their gratitude by making pilgrimages to Rolisa itself, the birthplace of the greatest sages known in the history of sentient life. Rewards, technology and gifts were rained upon the citizens of Rolisa. Unlike other instances in the past where races were overwhelmed by such advancements, the hardy folk of Rolisa rose to the task. They built upon what was given them, taking things in new and unexpected directions. Rolisa grew in stature, wealth and power—but power used always for the common benefit, never for destruction. Rolisa became the model of civilization for all, likened to such ancient and lost realms as Atlantis and Ko'norr'k'aree. But Rolisa was not legendary; it was real, gloriously real.

Once begun, the wave of glory rolled over the known galaxy, unstoppable, and who would have wanted it stopped? Within two hundred years, as the descendants of Faicco, Milenko and Blaymore continued their ancestors' great work, it was a time of unparalleled peace and prosperity. Unthinkable, unbelievable as it seemed, there was no war, anywhere. All races, from the least to the most advanced, had simply outgrown it. And no one knew that it was only the beginning. Well . . . no one except such elevated races as the Organians, for they knew that soon (soon being reckoned as Organians reckoned such things) all of that which was considered mortal would rise to their level.

And many millennia hence, that was exactly what happened.

And lo . . . there was glory everlasting, forevermore.

In another universe.

"Universe" is a misnomer, for all of creation is, in fact, comprised of a vast and wondrous multiverse, where many possibilities can occur. In one universe, the humble world of Rolisa was the birthplace of a great and transcendent fate for all of life . . .

. . . because, by an evolutionary quirk, the Black Mass did not exist in that universe.

Here is what happened in a universe where it did exist . . .

Tara let out a screech as her stomach swelled almost to bursting. The doctor crouched next to her, clutching her dark blue hand tightly, and said, "Now breathe steadily . . . that's it . . . that's it . . ."

She groaned. "It's easy for you to say I should breathe easily. You're not the one who feels as if a million needles were being jammed into every pore of the body. You're not the one who has been carrying this gradually growing lump of flesh in your belly for the past eleven months. Who in Krod are you to say breathe steadily?" She tried to sit up, couldn't, and fell back like a beached fish. "I'm trying to remember just why in the world I ever thought this was a good idea, and nothing immediately comes to mind. Where is my mate? Where is he?" she demanded.

"He would be here if he could," said the doctor soothingly.

"Why isn't he?"

"Because he wanted to be somewhere else," the doctor told her, and then let out a yelp as she squeezed his fingers so hard that it threatened to snap them off. The vents in his throat flapped quickly as he sucked in air to prevent further unprofessional vocalizations of pain. He forced a grimace and said, "Is that helping you . . . feel the pain less?"

"No," snarled Tara. "But making you suffer is helping me feel better."

"Whatever . . . works for you, then," he said gamely. "And if you break off some of my fingers . . . that's . . . that's fine. I can always . . . grow new ones. It's a long and . . . somewhat agonizing process . . . but I just want my patients . . . to be . . . unhhhh . . . happy . . ."

"Right now, I'm ecstatic—*arrrhhhhh!*"

That high-pitched scream signalled the final moments of the birth. Her outburst echoed to the sky, which was not surprising considering they were outdoors. That was the traditional and preferred venue of a Rolisan birth, since it was felt that if a child is coming into the world, then the child should actually be exposed to that world as soon as possible. Tara had picked a rather nice area, actually, a peaceful wooded site not far from her house. The doctor had had no trouble finding it, which was rather fortunate. He was also grateful that there was nice weather for this birth, since births in the rain or snow were always such an unpleasant chore. Indeed, Tara could not have picked a finer day, or a more glorious moment in that day. The hottest part of the afternoon was already gone. The sun was lowering on the horizon, but there was still plenty of light, with just enough shade to add to the coolness. He had hardly had to dab any sweat from her forehead.

The vent across her belly widened for the last push, and her body trembled in the labor throes. One more shove and then the newborn child popped out of the birth sac at the usual high speed. In this case, the doctor nearly missed the child completely, since one of his hands was still in Tara's grasp. But he snagged the speeding infant at the last moment. "Got him!" he called, the traditional exclamation that a doctor gave when the newborn had been successfully snagged.

The declaration penetrated some of the haze in Tara's poor brain, the pain only just subsiding. "Got him . . . ? Your . . . your hand! Oh, my Krod, I'm so sorry! I was crushing . . . and . . . and you needed . . . and I . . ."

"It's all right, it's all right. I'm used to it. Professional hazard." He shook out the newly released hand, restoring some of the circulation to it. "Actually, I suppose I should be grateful. I can assure you, I've been grabbed in far more delicate places than that."

"And it's a him? A boy? You're certain?"

"I don't pretend to know everything about everything, but even my medical training can distinguish that, yes."

She laughed, which was a surprising sound for her to hear from herself, considering the shrieking and string of profanity that she'd been letting fly moments before. "And his color? His color is good?"

"This is without question the most stunningly blue child I've ever seen. He couldn't be healthier."

"Let me see." She stretched out her arms, waggled her fingers. "Let me see . . . please . . ."

"All right, all right," and now he was the one who was laughing. "Here." He handed the child over to the eager mother and she took him in her arms with an almost ferocious attitude. The membranes on his neck were fluttering very nicely, and with a graceful, extended finger she traced the line of his face, his eyes which were not yet open (but would be within minutes). He made a small mewling sound and she jumped slightly on hearing it, and then laughed at her own reaction.

"Do you have a name picked out?" he asked.

"Arango," she said immediately. "I shall call him Arango."

"A very nice name. Rather popular this year, too, I believe."

"That doesn't matter," was her firm reply. Her agony of a short time ago already forgotten, she tried to prop herself up. He eased her to sitting as she drew the child closer into her lap. The stressed vent in her stomach had already sealed itself up, the automatic healing process commencing reliably on its own. "I had visions, doctor."

"Visions?" he asked. "What sort of visions?"

"He's going to go on to great things," she said. "And not just him. His children, and his children's children, and . . . oh, doctor. I just know it."

"Of course they are, Tara."

"You're laughing at me," she said with a slight pout.

"No, I'm not."

"You are," she remonstrated. "Let me guess: you've heard this from more mothers than you can count. We

8

all speak of how wonderful and incredible our children are going to be, and we're all fools because we're setting ourselves up with such high expectations that no children can possibly live up to them."

"Well, now, Tara, you said that. I didn't." He glanced toward the sky, mildly surprised. It was getting darker earlier than it usually did.

"You didn't have to. And I admit, doctor, that most of the time ... you're right. All those new mothers, they are being unreasonable. They don't know what they're talking about."

"But you do."

"Absolutely. Little Arango ... he has a place in things. It may not be a big piece of the puzzle, but it's a piece nonetheless. And it's going to have ramifications beyond this world, I'm telling you."

"Oh, now, Tara, let's not start that again," he said scoldingly. "I've been your doctor ever since you were a little girl, and we've always had these discussions." As he spoke, he tried not to sound distracted, because he saw that he wasn't imagining it. It really was getting dark far too early to be normal. An eclipse, perhaps? But such an event would certainly have made the news, and there had been no word of such. He tried not to be alarmed about it, though. There really was no reason to be. It's not as if it was the end of the world, just because the sun was setting faster. "As much as I would like to indulge your fantasies about meeting up with alien life forms some day, I have to admit I'm somewhat the skeptic."

"There are the legends ..."

"Yes, yes. The Red Gods. They who come from the sky and return to the sky at will." He shook his head. "As you say ... legends."

"Or visitors from outer space," she said insistently. She tickled under Arango's chin. The baby scrunched it up automatically. "Perhaps Arango will find out. Arango or one of his children's children's children, right, my precious? My love?" Then she gasped in delight. "Doctor!"

"What? What?"

"His eyes! They've opened. Aren't they beautiful? Quickly, what's he looking at? They say the first thing a child looks at will be a tremendous influence in his life."

"The 'they' who say that are mothers, and the reason they say that is obvious, don't you think?" said the doctor.

"You," she said archly, "have no romance in you at all. No sense of wonder, no . . ." Her voice trailed off and with clear disappointment, she said, "Ohhh . . . he isn't looking at me."

"And here I thought you said mothers weren't the ones who came up with that superstition. So where is he looking?"

"Skyward. Just straight up, at . . ."

Once more she lapsed into silence, but this time it wasn't simply tapering off into quiet. This time her voice sounded more choked off. Confused, the doctor looked up to try and get a feel for what the child was looking at.

"The sky . . ." she whispered in low, uncomprehending horror. "The sky . . . it's . . . it's moving . . ."

The sky was darkening, faster and faster. Something huge was blocking out the sun . . . no. No, beyond huge. It enveloped the entire horizon. And the reason that Tara had said it was moving . . . was because it was.

Something dark had entered the skies above Rolisa, something very dark. The rays of the sun were trying to punch through, but were failing. And in the few areas where sunlight was visible, they were quickly closing up, as if the planetary curtain being drawn over Rolisa was getting tighter and tighter. Day was becoming night without the usual niceties of the planet turning on its axis. Something, some . . . thing . . . was eating the sky.

And it was indeed moving. Not just moving . . . undulating. It was still miles off, but it was drawing steadily closer, and whatever it was looked—even from this distance—like a huge mass of intertwined threads. The light was completely gone now. There was only the mass, drawing closer, becoming blacker, and eerily silent. It seemed as if such an occurrence should be accompanied by some sort of noise, but there was nothing. Only the silence.

The threads were continuing to move, twining and untwining, slithering, pulsating . . .

"Oh my Krod . . . it's alive," she whispered. "Whatever it is, it's alive."

"That impossible," said the doctor with a distinct lack of conviction. "Whatever that is, it's not part of nature. It can't be alive. It has to be a . . . a . . ."

"A what?" she demanded. She didn't sound as if she was being challenging. Instead, more than anything, she sounded like someone who desperately wanted some sort of explanation that made anything remotely resembling sense.

"Let's get back to the house," he said urgently, not trying to answer. What purpose was there in endeavoring to come up with a reply. He had none to give, no real clue. The only thing he wanted to make certain of was that they weren't in the open when it hit. And it was going to hit, of that he was quite certain. What it was going to do once it got there, he had no clue, but he knew he didn't want to be outside to find out.

"Hurry. Hurry!" he urged her. Normally he would never have dreamt of speaking so to a woman who had just given birth, or forcing her to stand. But now he took one of her arms and draped it over his shoulders, hauling her to her feet as she held her baby tight with her other arm. He didn't give her any opportunity to delay or drag her feet. Instead he half-pulled, half-carried her along the ground, hauling her toward her unassuming house.

The mass drew closer. Its individual components were becoming more and more evident. It was unquestionably creatures, individual creatures, interlaced with one another. His rational, scientific mind told him that was not possible. Because science had made far too convincing a case against there being any such things as creatures from outer space. And if this cloud was what it seemed to be, then it was something extraterrestrial. Something beyond the understanding of everyday science.

The notion that there might be anything beyond that which was already known was utterly terrifying to him.

He had no intention of letting her sense his fear. For her, he was going to be brave and determined and fixed on the not-inconsiderable task of getting them to safety.

They made their way to her house, and the mass was coming faster. He wouldn't have thought it possible, that something that far away could approach that quickly. The house was just ahead. There, there would be safety and explanations. There he would put on the vidnews, and they would explain the nature of this . . . this mass hallucination, yes, that had to be it. A trick of light, or swamp gas, or some similar rational explanation would be put forward, and they would all laugh about it by tomorrow and go on with their lives.

He shoved her into the house, barred the door, just in case it wasn't something completely laughable. "Let's watch the vidnews," he said quickly. "See what's happening."

She tried to turn it on. Nothing happened. The vid remained silent. There was a visual, but it was a sign that just told them that there were technical problems which were being dealt with as expeditiously as possible.

"Don't worry. They'll get it fixed shortly," said the doctor with an impressive amount of certainty, all things considered. "These things always work out in the end."

There was a sudden rushing of air, and for some reason that the doctor never quite understood, there was a sense of heaviness all around. He turned to her, was about to speak . . .

. . . and then there was a fierce rustling in the trees nearby, as if something was pushing down on the treetops. There was a sound of bending and breaking, and branches being splintered . . .

. . . and suddenly the roof caved in. Everything was shaking them from all around, and there was the very quick flash of blackness.

Arango looked up from his mother's arms. He heard the shriek from his mother as the Black Mass descended, but was unable to process the information as being anything other than a loud noise. As for the Black Mass, there was something attractive, even beautiful, in the way that it was slithering, and Arango burbled happily just before the Black Mass dropped down on him after having eaten through his mother in less time than it took him to make a cooing noise. He didn't have time to comprehend his fate before it was upon him, and as he vanished into the maw of the Black Mass, his descendants who would never be cried out in protest, and somewhere the Organians wept for the future of all life in the galaxy.

Si Cwan had no idea where to look first. He was so excited that he ran back and forth on the bridge of the cruiser until finally his uncle, the noble Sedi Cwan, fed up, grabbed him firmly by the wrist and shook him. Si Cwan's feet lifted clear of the deck and his body snapped about like a whip being jiggled. "Stop it! Stop it!" Si Cwan cried out, his protestations and slightly shrill voice garnering amused glances from others aboard the bridge. "Sedi! Let me go!"

"You let yourself go," he said sternly. Sedi Cwan was not especially tall, but he was wide and beefy and his strength was almost as legendary as his temper. The weight of Si Cwan did not daunt him at all. Nevertheless, he opened his thick fingers and allowed his nephew to thud to the floor. "You let your emotions go. That is not the discipline one wants to see in a young nobleman, Si Cwan. Even one of your tender years."

Si Cwan stumbled to his feet, rubbing the posterior that he'd been dropped on. "I was just excited," he said with as much defiance as he could reasonably muster, given the circumstances. "I think it's understandable."

"Anything is understandable. One understands why an infant messes itself. One, however, can still be offended by the stench of immaturity. You should not be acting like a child."

"But I am a child!" protested Si Cwan, which was true enough. He was not quite eight years old.

"Have you ever seen a drunken man?"

Si Cwan blinked, not following the question. "Yes."

"As have I. Many more than you have, I fancy. Most of them, however, have the good decency to at least try and act as if they are sober. It may be obvious to anyone seeing them what their true condition is, but one at least gives them points for effort. You are a young prince and noble, Si Cwan. Do you think it unreasonable that you be held to the same standard as a drunken man?"

The young man sighed heavily. "I guess not."

"You guess not?"

"No, it's not unreasonable."

The corners of Sedi Cwan's mouth twitched ever so slightly, but from long practice he prevented it from becoming anything more pronounced than that. "This is my flagship, Si Cwan," he said gravely. "How you behave yourself becomes a reflection upon me. Do not embarrass or disgrace me."

"I won't, Sedi Cwan."

"Good." He nodded approvingly. "The Thallonian Empire has a grand and glorious tradition. We have never lost a battle. Such a rich tradition stems from equally rich discipline. I know that I can trust you to uphold it."

"Thank you, Sedi Cwan."

"Sedi Cwan!" The call came from the officer manning the tactical station. Sedi Cwan crossed the bridge, and Si Cwan followed, appropriately, in his footsteps. In his heart, Si Cwan had mixed feelings. On the one hand, he was embarrassed that he had allowed himself to get so rambunctious. On the other hand, he was so excited to be on a ship for the first time—and the flagship of the great Sedi Cwan at that—that he could understand why he might be a bit out of control. And if it was understandable to him, why couldn't it be understandable to Sedi Cwan? Well . . . perhaps, Si Cwan realized, it was just that Sedi Cwan had so many other things on his mind.

Si Cwan tried to peer unobtrusively around Sedi Cwan to see what the readout was on the tacticals. Sedi noticed from the corner of his eye that his nephew was trying to get a better view. He reached out, got a grip on Si Cwan's shoulder and eased him around to another angle so that he could see. Si Cwan tried to understand what he was looking at, but much of it was a jumble of indecipherable readings. Nevertheless, he made as serious a face as he could and nodded as if comprehending everything that he was seeing.

Sedi Cwan, on the other hand, clearly understood it all, and didn't like what he was seeing. "How is it possible?" he demanded. "How could they have gotten so far, so fast? Where were our observation stations? Our early warning facilities?"

"Our facilities are state of the art, Lord Cwan," one of his men said. "And they were entirely within keeping with the time required, based upon the Mass' previous attack, to alert us as to movement."

"So what went wrong . . . ?"

"The Mass . . . moved faster . . ."

Sedi Cwan made a rather angry-sounding noise in his throat. Si Cwan, knowing that he should simply remain quiet, was unable to help himself. "Is it the Black Mass, Sedi? As the instruments said?"

Happily for Si Cwan, Sedi did not remonstrate with the boy for speaking out of turn. Instead he said very gravely, "Oh, yes. Yes, it is most definitely the Black Mass. And the situation is worse than we have imagined. Are we in visual range?"

"At extreme magnification, yes, Lord Cwan."

Sedi Cwan turned and faced the viewing array. "Let's see it," he said. It seemed to Si Cwan that Sedi was steeling himself, preparing for a sight that he did not particularly want to see.

The viewing array shifted from the starscape that was before them, and then a world appeared on the screen that was so black, it appeared to have been covered with some sort of thick liquid. Si Cwan couldn't believe it. His understanding had been that, for a world to be that dark, it had to be situated so far from its sun that light never reached it. But this was . . .

Then he gasped as he realized that the planet . . . was throbbing. At least, its surface was. Like a great heart, it pulsed, the covering around it writhing about as if it were having . . .

". . . a feeding frenzy," he whispered. Si Cwan had been on a hunt once, less than a year before, and he had seen a pack of beasts running. One of them had been wounded by a shot from one of the hunters, and Si Cwan had expected that the pack would simply leave it behind. Instead, several members of the pack, sniffing the blood, had turned on their wounded fellow, and proceeded to tear him to pieces. Consequently, the hunters made a larger capture than they would have, previously, as the attackers were so busy devouring the wounded one, they forgot about their own self-preservation. Si Cwan had been told that the term was a "feeding frenzy."

Now Sedi Cwan nodded when Si Cwan spoke. "You're very right," he said, and although under normal circumstances Si Cwan's little chest would have swollen with pride over being told that he was right about something so grown-up, in this instance all it did was sicken him. "The only difference," continued Sedi Cwan, "is that other creatures lose their heads and give in entirely to instinct during such a time. The Black Mass is . . . something else again."

"Where did they come from, Sedi? Where is its ship? Are they animals? Or a sentient race? Or . . . ?"

"Not . . . not now, Si Cwan," Sedi said. There was no anger in his voice, but instead focused concentration. Then he turned to several of his men. "Toth. Bring weapons on line. Prepare to fire."

The one known as Toth looked confused. "Fire at what, precisely, Lord Cwan?"

"I'll tell you in a moment. Sanf, put me in communication with the other ships."

Within moments, Sedi Cwan was in touch with the four other vessels that had accompanied them to the site of the Black Mass' migration, and had—in quick, straightforward terms—outlined a plan of attack calling for a simultaneous assault at different points on the planet upon which the Mass was feeding.

As the ships moved into position, Si Cwan couldn't remove his eyes from the undulating sheet of parasitic life that had enveloped Rolisa. "The people," said Si Cwan. "The people of Rolisa . . . where are they?" he asked suddenly. "Where are their escape ships? Where are—"

His voice trailed off as he saw the look in Sedi Cwan's eyes. "No," he whispered.

"They are gone," Sedi Cwan said flatly, making no effort whatsoever to sugarcoat the truth for the boy. "As we speak, they are in the belly of that . . . whatever it is."

"All those people . . ." Si Cwan could barely grasp it. One death, he could understand, he could relate to. Two deaths, three . . . these were simple quantities for him to grasp. But there had been hundreds of millions of people on Rolisa, according to what he had heard Sedi Cwan say when they first launched.

Sedi Cwan's voice hardened. "It means nothing," he said.

"Nothing?" Si Cwan couldn't fathom whether his uncle was saying these things because he believed them, or out of some belief that it was necessary to toughen the boy up in some manner. "It's lives. It's people. How can you say it's nothing . . . ?"

"You're embarrassing me, young noble," Sedi said sharply, and Si Cwan immediately fell silent. "In the Thallonian Empire, all that matters, truly matters, are we Thallonians. That's it. That's all. You should know that. If your tutors have not made that clear to you, then I am going to be having some serious discussions with them."

"Yes. They've made that clear," said Si Cwan. "But they have also made it clear that waste is a sin. This is a waste of lives, and therefore a great sin."

"They were nothing, Si Cwan. Rolisa was an unadvanced planet with an unadvanced people who were never going to make the slightest difference to anyone except themselves. Whether they are here or gone matters not in the slightest. The Black Mass, on the other hand, presents a threat. A threat that we shall deal with . . . now. Toth . . . ?"

"All ships are in position, Lord Cwan," Toth informed him.

"Excellent. Attention, all vessels: When we fire upon the Black Mass, it will come after us. The plan is simple, but effective: Divide and conquer. The Mass will not know which ship to attack first and—theoretically, at least—will split up and come after each of us. When they do . . ." and his voice dropped to a deadly tone, "then we simply fry the bastards. Prepare to fire, on my order."

Si Cwan watched the flurry of activity on the bridge as they prepared to go to war with an unknown, and unknowable, opponent. He wished that there was something he could do, but realized that there are times when one simply has to stand by and let others who know their business attend to things. He couldn't wait, though, for a time when he would be old enough to become involved in a great and glorious battle against an incredibly bizarre foe.

"Three, two, one . . ." Sedi Cwan paused a moment—dramatically, it seemed—and then shouted, "Fire!"

And the ships cut loose with everything they had.

They used disruptors, they used plasma cannons, they used controlled fusion and thermite bombs . . . they used, in short, every weapon of mass destruction they had in their arsenal.

The Black Mass ate it.

Si Cwan couldn't believe what he was seeing. In fact, he was certain that what he was perceiving—what he was believing to be the case—had to be just flat out wrong. There was no way, simply no way, that the Black Mass was somehow absorbing their assault. But that was what it seemed as if they were doing.

"This isn't possible," Sedi Cwan said, and the fact that he was clearly so stunned by what he was witnessing was probably the most upsetting thing of all for Si Cwan. As far as he was concerned, his uncle was unflappable, a rock, a pillar of strength who had endless war stories through which he swaggered with confidence and gusto, overcoming all manner of opponents with equal ease and facility. "Is it . . . is that thing . . . absorbing it somehow?"

"It . . . appears so, Sedi Cwan," said Toth. He was looking at his instrumentation and he appeared as thunderstruck as his commander. "The Black Mass is completely ignoring us. We haven't . . . sir, we haven't even really gotten its attention."

As humiliating as it was to admit, that was indeed the case. The Black Mass had not the least interest in departing the world upon which it was feeding. Instead it simply ate . . .

. . . and ate . . .

. . . and ate.

The Thallonian fleet fired again, and again. They used everything they could think of on the Black Mass, every weapon, every tactic. But it was simply impossible to make any sort of effective attack upon an enemy that doesn't even seem inclined to acknowledge your existence. For over an hour it went on, as Sedi Cwan consulted with his scientists, his fellow commanders—even, in desperation, his personal fortune teller, who intoned that the day would be long remembered in the annals of Thallonian military history, but refused to say just what it would be remembered for. This was, of course, less than useful.

In the meantime, the planet which had once been Rolisa continued to shrink, the Black Mass converging upon itself as its feast diminished in size.

Sedi Cwan walked right up to the viewing array, staring at it intensely. Si Cwan watched in silence from nearby. And then Sedi Cwan leaned forward, his hands flat against the screen, and he hung his head and shook it in a most dismaying fashion.

"Sedi . . . ?" whispered Si Cwan. He had not spoken during the entirety of the assault. "Sedi . . . what are you going to do now?"

When his uncle looked at him, it was with darkened and haunted eyes. "Do?"

"There has to be something else . . . there has to—"

Sedi Cwan sighed deeply, and called out, "Stand down all weapons. Withdraw to a safe distance."

There was a collective gasp from the bridge crew which was quickly smothered, and they worked smoothly to carry out their orders. Si Cwan stood bolt still, transfixed to the place where he had just heard his renowned uncle give an order for retreat. "Withdraw? You mean . . . we're going to run away?"

"No, Si Cwan," said Sedi Cwan softly. There was a sound in his voice that Si Cwan had never heard before. It took him a moment to hazard a guess as to what it might be: It was the sound of defeat. "No . . . we are going to remain . . . and we are going to watch. So that we will be able to sear into our brains the memory of this day. The day when the collective might of the Thallonians . . . was utterly useless."

Si Cwan shook his head in disbelief as he stared at the feasting Mass. "What . . . are they?" he asked finally. He had asked the question before, but the answers he had received had been terse, tossed at him in an off-hand fashion as if the question were going to be moot in short order, since the Black Mass certainly couldn't hope to stand up to Thallonian supremacy.

"They swarm from the Hunger Zone, Si Cwan," his uncle told him, "an area of space that no Thallonian has ever been. That is, indeed, forbidden to all. If anyone ever has been there, then he has not lived to return and speak of it."

"Why is it called the Hunger Zone?"

"Because . . . it is where the Black Mass resides until such time that its hunger becomes overwhelming. At which point, the migration begins." He shook his head, obviously still barely able to believe it. "The Mass migration can be in any one of an infinite number of directions out of the Hunger Zone, and no one ever knows when it will be. It depends, I suppose, on how much they consume during their time out of the Zone. They have not been seen for over fifty years before this day; the time before that, however, was only a ten-year stretch . . . before that, ninety. There is simply no way of telling. They may return during your lifetime, Si Cwan. I pray, for your sake, that they do not."

"Is it one creature? One being? Or millions, or billions, or—"

"I don't know, Si Cwan!" and Sedi Cwan made no effort to hide his frustration. Considering his formidable powers of self-control, there was no greater indicator of just how utterly dismayed he was. "I don't know. Nobody knows. If we knew something about it, perhaps we could defeat it. It is not like a traditional enemy . . . it's not like any enemy at all, it's . . ." He stared at it with a combination of horror and awe. "It is like a force of nature."

"Lord Cwan!" Toth said suddenly. "It's on the move!"

"Are you certain?"

"Positive, milord!"

He was right. The Black Mass was moving away from the world around which it had swarmed. And in its place was . . . nothing. A few stray bits of rubble; that was all that remained. The Mass began to re-form itself, then, slithering about and reshaping into something that Si Cwan fancied looked a bit like a ship. It seemed vaguely symmetrical, with downward scoops that rippled as the ship moved.

"Wait. . . . look!" Si Cwan said, excitement growing. "Look where it's going! It's killing itself! Our problems are over!"

Sedi Cwan, unlike the overenthused Si Cwan, didn't immediately trust the evidence of his eyes. "Check its heading. Make sure that it's going . . . where we think it's going," he said with a glance toward Si Cwan.

"It is, milord!" said Toth. Clearly he was fighting to contain his own enthusiasm. He likewise couldn't believe that it was going to be this easy. "It's heading directly into the Rolisan sun!"

Technically, since there was no more Rolisa, it was wrong to refer to it as the Rolisan sun. But no one bothered to correct him, for the important thing was that the Black Mass had apparently decided to end its collective existence. It was angling, straight and true, toward the heart of a star.

"Track it," said Sedi Cwan. "Bring all the ships back to maximum distance. If there's some sort of disruption, some sort of nova, I want to make sure we don't suffer any casualties. Not when we stand on the brink of ending this."

The ships obediently retreated, watching as the Black Mass continued to head straight and true toward the blazing star.

"It cannot be this easy," Sedi Cwan was muttering. "It simply can't be. The Black Mass will veer off. That's the only answer. It will veer off and . . ."

It didn't. Instead it began to spread out, to become even larger as it approached the sun.

"Lord Cwan!" said Toth, "we're losing sensor readings on it!"

"What do you mean?"

"There's some sort of . . ." He shook his head in befuddlement. "Some sort of spacial distortion developing around the Mass, as if it's bending or warping space as it's moving."

"Impossible. It's biologic in nature."

"We're not getting a clear sensor reading of what's happening."

"We don't need one," Sedi Cwan said firmly, pointing at the screen. "See for yourself. It's only a matter of moments now before it—"

Then he went silent, as did everyone else.

The Black Mass enveloped the star.

It took several minutes for the light to cease reaching the Thallonian armada, but cease it did. The entire system was plunged into darkness, as black and unknowable as the Black Mass itself.

Si Cwan, in the entirety of his young life, had never known fear. Not really. Not the sort of fear that clutches at one's innards and simply will not let go, no matter what. But that was what he was experiencing now, and it was not a happy sensation.

"Adjust visual," Sedi Cwan said tonelessly.

The picture wavered once more, the technology of the Thallonian vessel making up for the lack of natural light, digitizing and reconfiguring the images so that they could see it again. And what they saw brought them all to stunned silence. One could almost hear the confidence seeping out of them, as if the Black Mass was vampirically draining their fighting souls.

The Black Mass devoured the sun.

It took quite some time, although the longer it feasted,

the faster it seemed to go. It was as if it gained strength as it went and consequently ate that much more vigorously. Every so often it would be visibly jolted, something exploding within the sun as if the star were fighting back. Either that or just writhing in its death throes.

And when the Black Mass was finished, it eased itself off the charred husk that had once been a star and re-formed itself into its ship formation . . . a formation that now dwarfed not only the planet that had been there and the star that had been there, but much of the area in between. The creature, if that's what it was, was thoroughly engorged.

It did not acknowledge the Thallonian fleet, which collectively seemed little more than a speck against it, any more than it had before. Instead it simply angled off, heading back toward the distant Hunger Zone, its migration completed, its appetite sated.

"It's moving at warp speed," Toth said in a voice that might well have belonged to a corpse.

"That is impossible," said Sedi Cwan for what seemed the hundredth time that day. "It has no warp engines or drive, it has no dilithium crystals, it has no . . . it can't . . . it . . ."

And then he stopped talking. Instead he simply walked to his command chair, eased himself down into it . . . and stared.

Si Cwan had never seen him quite like this. Sedi Cwan seemed . . . broken. Oh, the regal bearing was still there. The squared shoulders, the determined chin. But there was something in his eyes that had never been there before. A sadness, a sense that he had been . . . put in his place somehow.

"Sedi . . . ?" Si Cwan ventured. "Are you all right?"

Sedi Cwan looked at him and seemed to shake off

that which hung around him. "I am fine, Si Cwan. Fine. And this incident . . . was good for us. Excellent, in fact. This has been a good day."

"It has?" Si Cwan could not quite keep the incredulity out of his voice, which was a dangerous and inappropriate tone for him to take. This was, after all, Sedi Cwan, the great and noble Sedi Cwan. To doubt his word was entirely inappropriate, yet Si Cwan was concerned that that was precisely how it had sounded. Quickly seeking to perform damage control, he added, "I did not mean to give offense, Noble One . . . understand that, I did not . . ."

"I understand fully, young one. No offense was taken. In saying this was a good day, I have a very specific meaning. We Thallonians . . . we have believed ourselves to be the greatest force in this sector of space. We . . . were wrong. Clearly we cannot begin to approach the Black Mass for pure power. We are not even worth its time, nor capable of getting its attention. We have been put in our place. And that is a good thing. It is good to be reminded of one's respective place in the universe, so that one does not become too confident. For overconfidence leads to foolish mistakes, and foolish mistakes lead to disaster."

He rose then, looking more robust, his voice rising in timbre. "Remember this day, all of you. Remember how you feel, right now, in your proud Thallonian heart. Always remember the sense of disgrace and inadequacy that you are experiencing. Keep it close, so that when you face a foe another day—as you inevitably will—you do not automatically assume that victory is going to be granted you. For however powerful you believe yourself to be, there will always be someone or something . . . that is more so."

There were approving nods from all around the ship, and even Si Cwan felt a measure of pride in the words of his uncle. This had indeed been a humiliating day for not only the Thallonians aboard the ship, but all of the Thallonian Empire. And since it was Sedi Cwan who had commanded the fleet, it would be his disgrace to bear. But he had borne it with style, dignity and the warrior heart that he had been so long known for.

Si Cwan spent much time dwelling on his uncle's words during the voyage home. And when the proud flagship drew within an hour of the Thallonian home-world, young Si Cwan went to his uncle's quarters to ask him some questions about Thallonian philosophy, and also perhaps what new stratagems might be developed for the next time the Black Mass swarmed. For that next time, surely the might of the Thallonians would triumph. There could be a temporary defeat, certainly, but in the long run, the Thallonians were supreme. That was simply the way it had always been throughout Si Cwan's life, and would continue to be, forever.

He entered his uncle's quarters and stopped, the odd creaking noise being the first hint that something was wrong. The darkness of the room was the second. And then, as Si Cwan's eyes adjusted to the dimness of the chamber, he saw the distinct, bulky shape of Sedi Cwan's body hanging by the neck, swinging ever so gently. The chair upon which he had been standing had been kicked over once he had stepped off it.

There was a note on the floor next to his feet, which were dangling some distance from the floor. Si Cwan crouched next to the note, his senses numb, still unable to process that which his eyes were telling him. He picked it up. His name was written on it. Sedi Cwan's last thoughts were of him, and undoubtedly an explanation was contained therein as to why he had just deprived Si Cwan of his continued wisdom and intelligence.

Si Cwan crumbled the note without reading it, turned on his heel and went to contact someone so that they could cut his uncle down. Since Si Cwan was the ranking noble, despite his youth, and also Sedi Cwan's closest relative, he was asked what he wanted done with Sedi Cwan's body.

His terse answer stunned them. "Blow it out a torpedo tube. It's all he deserves."

The protests began. One look from Si Cwan—formidable, even at that age—silenced the protests. And so Sedi Cwan was ejected into the hostile vacuum. Moments before his body was hurled away into space, Si Cwan shoved the note into his uncle's pocket, still unread. He turned away and never looked back as he walked out of the torpedo room, leaving the crewmen to their job.

Upon learning what Si Cwan had done, his father—Sedi Cwan's brother—publicly congratulated the young noble on his handling of the situation. In private, he beat the boy so soundly that he was unable to move for the better part of a week.

In the entire hideous misadventure, the one thing that Si Cwan kept clinging to was the likelihood—as Sedi Cwan had said—that Rolisa was a largely irrelevant planet that would never have been of much use to anyone.

And the Black Mass returned to the Hunger Zone . . . there to wait until the hunger called it once more.

# NOW . . .

# I.

MORGAN LEFLER HATED THE COMMON COLD, for it was the one thing that even her immortal immune systems couldn't shrug off. Every terminal disease known to humanity, those meant nothing to her. But the damnable cold that she was currently suffering through was hammering her, and Morgan was not a particularly good sick person, since it happened to her so rarely. She tended to become somewhat fetal, lie about and complain incessantly. When she was sick, she felt as if she were in a deep hole that she would be trapped in the rest of her life. And considering the fact that she was—to the best of her knowledge—virtually immortal, the rest of her life tended to seem a very long time.

She could have consulted with Doctor Selar about it, but in many ways, being sick was preferable. Ever since she had reached the final weeks of her pregnancy,

Selar—never exactly renowned for her bedside manner—had become more distant, unfeeling and cold than ever before. It was not as if she were incapable of carrying out her duties; she was as capable of diagnosis and treatment as ever. She was just . . . so damned unpleasant. Her speech pattern had become flat and mechanical—even more mechanical than the computer. It was downright chilling just to be around her. Morgan didn't know whether all Vulcans were like that in the last stages of pregnancy, but if they were, then she pitied Vulcan husbands everywhere.

"No wonder Spock's father married an earth female," she murmured. "Probably went a long way toward saving his sanity." She hated the way her voice sounded. She hated the way her head was pounding. She hated herself.

At least Robin wasn't around to see it. She was busy at the banquet, which was enough to make Morgan insanely jealous. Here she was, flat on her back, and her daughter was organizing a wonderful, semiformal get-together designed to welcome the long lost sister of Si Cwan to the good ship *Excalibur.* All of the senior officers were going to be there and, frankly, it was going to be a good opportunity for Robin to impress her superior officers with her organizational skill. In a way, it seemed a rather trivial exercise. All the solid duties that Robin carried off in the course of a day should have been more than enough to warrant attention and promotion from the rank of ensign which she currently carried. Yet the simple truth was that people could be impressed by the damnedest things, and Captain Mackenzie Calhoun and Commander Elizabeth Shelby might be just as likely to find her duties as hostess as memorable as anything she did at ops. It didn't make any sense, but people were just funny that way.

Morgan could see the gathering in her mind's eye. There would be Calhoun and Shelby, bantering over brisket or some such preparation. Their attraction for each other was electric, and their knack for short-circuiting that same attraction was just amazing. And there would be Si Cwan, tall, noble and proud, with his young sister, Kalinda, next to him. Morgan had only caught a brief glimpse of her, having contracted her illness right after Kalinda ("Kally" as he called her) had come on board. The girl had looked older than she had originally envisioned her, equivalent to an earth child in her late teens instead of the very young girl that Si Cwan had always described. Morgan reflected that perhaps the way he described her was the way he saw her. She couldn't help but wonder whether that attitude might cause problems down the line.

This new fellow, Xyon, she hadn't seen at all. Supposedly he was the son of Captain Calhoun, but no one seemed to know quite what to make of that. Well, whatever the situation between them was, certainly it could all be worked out. Calhoun was nothing if not innovative when it came to the realm of personal relationships.

The door to the quarters slid open and Morgan, using what little energy she had, half propped herself up in her bed as she called out, "Robin! How did it go . . . honey . . ."

The term of endearment died in her throat as she saw the dishevelled condition of her daughter.

The front of Robin's dress uniform was covered in what appeared to be frosting. There was a small bruise on her forehead, and her hair—which had been neatly arrayed in a very becoming 'do—was hanging down around her face. Her expression was carefully stoic.

"It could have gone better," Robin said.

"My God! What happened?!"

Robin said nothing at first. Instead she walked across the room to the closet, from which she withdrew a towel. She used it to start wiping away the frosting from her uniform and the ends of her hair.

"Robin! Tell me what happened!"

"This," Robin said slowly, tapping the frosting which was now covering the towel, "was the welcome aboard cake. It had Xyon and Kalinda's names on it. Apparently, however, the cake also had my name on it."

"What do you mean?"

"I mean I was the one who wound up wearing a good deal of it, so that's why I said it had my name on it."

"I still don't understand . . ."

Robin sighed deeply as she peeled off her uniform to toss it into the ship's laundry. "There was some friction."

"Seems to me more like there was total combustion."

"Xyon," continued Robin, as if her mother had not spoken, "is having a bit of difficulty working and playing well with others."

"What others?"

"Captain Calhoun. Oh, and Si Cwan."

"What happened?" asked Morgan.

Robin sagged into a chair as she pulled on a short bathrobe. Her hair was still a mess, and the bruise was getting darker. She ran her fingers sadly through her hair and shook her head as she looked into a mirror and apparently wondered whether she was, in fact, the individual in the reflection. "It started nicely enough," she recounted. "Everyone was standing about, chatting. Everyone except Xyon. He didn't seem especially happy to be there. I went over to him and asked him if something was bothering him. He told me all he really wanted to do was get his ship fully repaired. Apparently his ship sustained some damage in escaping the nebula surrounding Star 7734, and there were some other repairs made to it that were simply stopgap in nature to begin with. His ship really needed an overhaul, and Captain Calhoun was more than happy to offer it since Xyon had been of such help in the entire Kalinda affair."

"So?" prompted Morgan.

"So he was spending the party keeping in a corner off to himself. In retrospect, if he'd just been left there by everyone, allowed to stew in his own juices and maybe be sociable on his own terms, then maybe matters would have turned out differently.

"But no, not our crew. First there's Captain Calhoun, trying to engage the boy in conversation. Now Xyon, he's making it clear to the captain that he's not interested in talking to him. Apparently there was some sort of falling out, or Xyon felt that Calhoun hadn't been much of a family, or something like that. In any event, Xyon was brushing him off. Everyone saw it. It was openly disrespectful. But it was obvious to everyone that the captain didn't want to make a big deal about it. That his attitude was, 'If this is how Xyon feels, I'm not going to fight with him about it. Let him work it out on his own.' Which was pretty sporting of him, if you ask me, considering that the first time they met each other, Xyon hauled off and slugged the captain."

"Yes, I know. Word of that spread rather quickly," Morgan said with a dry sense of irony. "Xyon was fortunate that the captain simply rubbed his chin and turned the other cheek, so to speak. I have no doubt that the captain could put him through a bulkhead if he were inclined to do so."

"Well, he almost had the inclination," said Robin. "After he brushed off the captain, Xyon started to leave the party."

"Did he have any of the buffet before left?"

Robin stopped talking and stared at her. "The what?"

"The buffet."

"Mother, who cares?"

"I do. You worked very hard to set it up."

"I don't know if he did. I don't care. The point is, he started to leave . . . and then Kalinda stopped him. She seemed very anxious to talk to him. She sat down with him and soon they were laughing and having a grand time."

"Oh! Well, that's good," said Morgan.

"No, that was bad," Robin corrected her. "Because apparently Si Cwan decided to become overprotective of her. So he rather politely asked Xyon to stop monopolizing her time."

"Oh. That's bad."

"No, that was good," said Robin. "Because at least he was polite about it. He was nothing but civil to Xyon."

"Oh. So that's good."

"No, that was bad, because Xyon took offense anyway. I believe he said, 'After everything I've been through to save your sister, I can't believe that you would try to prevent me from having some private time with her.'"

"Oooo . . . that is bad."

"No, that was actually good. Because Captain Calhoun overheard, and stepped in on his son's behalf, telling Si Cwan that Xyon was absolutely right, and Si Cwan should give them some distance."

"Oh! Well, that's good."

"No, that's bad. Because Xyon told the captain that he could handle the situation himself."

"Well, that's . . ." Morgan stopped, frowned, and then shook her head. "I lost track. Are we up to bad or good?"

"It doesn't matter. The point is that Xyon put his arm around Kalinda and tried to walk out of the room with her. I don't know whether he did it in order to show that no one told him what to do, or in order to annoy Si Cwan, or what. But Si Cwan grabbed him and pulled him away, telling him that no one manhandles a princess of Thallon. And then Xyon shoved Si Cwan, and Si Cwan shoved him back, and the captain got in the middle and there was more shouting . . ." She shook her head in disbelief. "It's hard to understand how it spiralled out of control, that quickly. One minute I was standing there chatting with Shelby about something perfectly innocuous, and the next thing I know, someone is slamming into me—"

"You were attacked!" Morgan's voice bordered on outrage.

"Not exactly. More like, I got hit on the rebound. And I fell into the cake. And there was more shouting, and anger, and security showed up as Lieutenant Kebron restored order pretty quick, but they needed a cleanup crew and . . ." She put her face in her hands. "God, what a mess."

"Robin, it wasn't your fault . . ."

"And if everything had gone swimmingly, Mother, that would have been something I'd get the credit for, right? So when it turns into a debacle, as this did, who are they going to blame?"

"You're being much too hard on yourself." She coughed several times to try and clear out her lungs.

"Maybe I deserve it. I mean, look at the way things are going, Mother. Maybe fate is trying to tell me something."

"Tell you what? I don't understand—"

"Well, first I decided to tell Si Cwan that I have strong feelings for him and that I wanted to accompany him on the mission to Montos . . . except by the time I did it, he was gone. And then I offered to conduct the entire reception, arrange everything, set it all up, mostly to make him happy . . . and it became a huge misfire. Maybe somebody up there," and she pointed, "is trying to tell me something."

Morgan looked up to where Robin was pointing. "Up there? You mean on the bridge?"

"No, Mother!" she said in exasperation. "I mean 'up there.' You know. Divine intervention may be trying to get a point across."

"You're overthinking it, Robin."

"No, I'm not. Nothing goes right for me."

"Now you're just dissolving into self-pity, Robin. I won't have it," Morgan said sternly. "You're made of better and stronger stuff than that. So instead of complaining about how everything goes wrong for you, just pull yourself together, and be the officer and the woman that I know you can be. Clear?"

Robin's jaw twitched in irritation, but finally she sighed heavily and said, "Clear."

She went into the bathroom and took a shower. By the time she came out, she was sneezing and her temperature was starting to climb. As she blew her nose, she looked daggers at her mother. "Thanks, Ma. I'm sure the cold you've apparently just given me will serve me as well as your advice."

Morgan rolled her eyes and pulled the covers over her head. As one, they sneezed.

Xyon sat in his quarters, chair tilted back, whistling softly. He was bare to the waist, having cleaned up after the debacle originally intended as a welcoming banquet for Rie—for Kalinda. He had to keep reminding himself that her real name was Kalinda. His long blond hair was newly cleaned and hanging around his muscled shoulders. There was a chime at his door. "You can't come in," he called. "Apparently I have misbehaved and am in isolation."

The door slid open and Mackenzie Calhoun was standing in the doorway. "Actually, what with being the captain and all, I can come and go as I wish."

"That is what you excel at, isn't it? Going? As you went from Xenex after leaving my mother pregnant with me?"

Calhoun sighed deeply. "Xyon . . . grow up. Whatever disputes you have with me, they don't begin to excuse what took place at the banquet."

"I'm not looking to excuse myself to you, Captain. I don't care what you think."

Calhoun shook his head. "That's not true. If you didn't care what I thought, you would not have acted, and reacted, as you did. You would have ignored me, or brushed me off. You would not have taken a swing at me, certainly, and tried to hurt me."

"I didn't try. I did hurt you."

"No. You couldn't. Particularly if I'm ready for you." Xyon's eyes flashed. "Is that a challenge?"

"No. Simply a statement of fact."

Instantly, Xyon was out of his chair. It was an impressive burst of speed. Anyone else would have been very hard-pressed to get out of his way.

Calhoun sidestepped and drove his knee up into Xyon's midsection. Xyon gasped and Mackenzie slammed him in the back of the neck, sending Xyon to the floor. Xyon lay there, momentarily stunned. He couldn't understand it. He was as formidable a fighter as they came, and had handled any number of opponents with facility. So what in hell had just happened?

As if reading his mind, Calhoun sat down next to him and said, "You rushed it. Also, you were probably a bit daunted by the fact that I am your father."

"I wasn't . . . daunted."

"My mistake, then," Calhoun said, sounding oversolicitous.

There was dead silence in the room then for an uncomfortable period of time. "How is Catrine?" Calhoun asked finally.

"My mother is fine. I'm sure she hardly thinks of you at all."

"That's . . . good."

"How could you have done it?" He was shaking his head in slow disbelief.

"Xyon . . . certainly you must know the circumstances of your conception?"

"I know, I know. Mother wanted to continue the family line, her late husband had been dead a year, and you, as Warlord of Xenex, in keeping with tradition, accommodated her by producing me. Hurray for you. Hurray for tradition."

"You don't know . . . you can't understand what it was like for me, Xyon. It was not something I desired to do. But I had my duty—to tradition, to your mother, and to my title as warlord. Frankly, it should have been my brother, since he was the ranking . . ." He waved it off. "No, it doesn't matter. Because I also had a duty to myself. I was going to be leaving Xenex, attending Starfleet Academy. I couldn't put that aside because of—"

"Of a son."

"It was what your mother desired. She wanted to raise you on her own. She didn't want to hold me back."

"That may be what she told you, but it wasn't what she desired."

"What do you mean?" When Xyon didn't reply immediately, Calhoun repeated shortly, "What do you mean?"

"It doesn't matter."

"Obviously, it does. To you."

Xyon looked at him levelly and said, "She always hoped you'd come back some day. She could never ask you herself, tell you herself, because she didn't want to force you. But she hoped that someday . . . you'd return. Or send for us."

"I . . ." Calhoun looked stunned. "She never said . . ."

"Of course she never said. She felt it had to come from within you." Xyon leaned back against a wall, hands draped over his legs. "She has too much pride. And optimism: She hoped, sooner or later, your thoughts of us would become so overwhelming that you'd feel the need to return to her . . . to me . . . to us."

"That's not how we left it between us," said Calhoun tonelessly.

"Things are never as we think they are. But I knew. I am your son, after all," he said bitterly. "I know your

43

mind as well as I know my own. My guess is, over the years, you never thought of us. Did you? And the idea of returning, of being with her, with me . . . you never considered that at all. Did you?"

"No," was his soft reply. Then he looked over at Xyon with his hard, purple eyes. "I won't lie to you. The answer is, no, I never considered coming back to stay with her, not really. I had my own life to lead. I thought she was living hers."

"You said I had no idea what it was like for you," Xyon told him. "Well, you had even less what it was like for me. Living in the shadow of my father, the legend. The man who cared so much about his people that, by the time he was the age I am now, he had liberated an entire planet. Do you have any inkling what it was like . . . knowing that you cared that much about Xenexians in general," and he raised his hand, flat and horizontal, high above his head, "that you would do all that for them . . . and that you cared for me so little," and he placed his other hand just above the floor, to indicate the disparity in distance, "that you didn't come back to Xenex, or contact me, or . . . anything."

"I did come back . . . once. And I tried to find Catrine . . . but she had moved out of Calhoun. No one knew where she was."

"And you made oh-so-much endeavor to find her. Strain yourself mightily, did you? Use all your resources? Or was the challenge of finding one woman and one child on a small world too much for the redoubtable M'k'n'zy."

"I took her absence—her 'disappearance'—to mean that she did not want me as a part of her life," Calhoun told him.

"No. That was what you wanted to think. And what she knew you wanted. And deep down, you knew it, too. But pretending otherwise made it that much easier for you to go on with your life."

There was a long silence then.

"So what have you been up to?" Calhoun asked.

It caught Xyon off guard. Still on the floor, he angled himself around to look at the captain. "What do you mean?"

"It's a fairly straightforward question. What have you been up to? When you're not rescuing princesses. Or is that all you do?"

"Captain . . ." Xyon felt as if he were back in the nebula. "Didn't you hear anything of what I said? I don't like you. You're not someone I feel like discussing my life with."

"Yes, you've made that clear. And if all you want to do is dwell on that which can't be changed, then that is entirely your privilege. But I can tell you that the 'legendary' M'k'n'zy of Calhoun didn't help free his world from its oppressors by obsessing about what had been. Instead I thought only about what could, and would, be. If the only future you see for us is one of hostility, fine. We've gotten along just fine without each other to this point, and we can continue to do so, I would imagine. It's one thing to learn from the past; it's another to be a prisoner of it."

"Do you always speak in aphorisms?" Xyon asked.

"Depends on my mood. Aphorisms, riddles, rhyming couplets . . . whatever strikes my fancy at any given moment."

He headed toward the door and didn't even bother to look over his shoulder as he said, "I'm lifting your isolation to these quarters. Feel free to go where you choose, barring standard security protocols. Try not to slam anyone around. Oh, and you may want to tender an apology to Ensign Lefler; you made quite a mess of her little gathering."

"You mean that's it?" demanded Xyon. "That's all you have to say to me?"

This prompted Calhoun to turn and look questioningly at his son. "What else is there to say?"

"I don't know."

"What . . ." Calhoun actually looked astounded at the notion—"you're not . . . actually expecting me to say I love you or some such, are you?"

"Of course not," Xyon said stiffly.

"Good." Once more Calhoun started to leave, and suddenly Xyon said, "Did you love her?"

This time Calhoun did not turn quite as quickly. "You mean your mother?" he asked.

"Yes. Did you love her?"

"Xyon," he said heavily, "you probably don't know this . . . but your mother was the first."

"The first woman you got pregnant?"

"No. The first woman."

"Oh." Xyon cleared his throat uncomfortably. "I didn't . . . uhm . . . no. No, she never mentioned that."

"I love . . . that she was good to me. That she didn't make me feel self-conscious. That she understood that there could never be anything between us other than that. I love those things about her. But I don't love her. For the most part, I didn't even know her. I don't know you. You can't love someone you don't sufficiently know; it's just not possible."

"You know . . ." Xyon said with a touch of defiance, "I bet you've never 'known' anyone enough to love them . . . truly love them. Not ever. Because to get that close to them, you'd have to let them get that close to you. And you never have."

Calhoun appeared to be considering the concept. After a long, thoughtful pause he said, "You know what? You may very well be right. Then again, I should point out that, while you're busy judging me . . . I notice that you didn't feel compelled to remain on Xenex, with your mom, any more than I was. And I was about your age when I left. So before you're too quick to judge me . . . you may want to think about judging yourself. Enjoy the rest of your day, Xyon." With that, he walked out into the corridor and left Xyon behind, thoughtful, in his quarters.

## II.

MEDITA, THE AREA OF TULAAN IV wherein most of the Redeemers resided, seemed even less hospitable than usual. And considering that the temperatures there never rose much above freezing, and that during the night a steady wind called "monster breath" ripped constantly across the already battered ground, saying that Medita seemed even less welcoming than it usually was was going quite a ways in characterizing it.

In the Great Hall wherein dwelt the Overlord, the Overlord was not in his usual place—namely, his throne. Instead he was standing on the roof. The fact that he was doing so caught the attention of more than one of the Redeemers as they gathered at the bottom of the building, looking up and muttering to one another about the possibility that the Overlord had undergone some sort of mental breakdown and was contemplating hurling himself to his death.

He was, in fact, thinking about no such thing. His great black cape fluttered briskly around him as he stood at the foot of the statue representing the great God Xant, He Who Had Gone On, He Who Would Return. He knew in his heart, of course, that the statue was not divine in and of itself. It was simply a representation of the Great One himself, built by all-too-mortal hands of Redeemer acolytes many years before. It felt cold to the touch of the Overlord's obsidian hands, and his eyes glowed cold red in the chill of the night air.

"Great Xant," he whispered. "Help me in this . . . your followers' darkest hour."

Truthfully, he was not at all sure what he was hoping to accomplish. Nothing, probably. Anything that happened as a result of this impromptu "communion" with the great statue would come out of his own mind, rather than some actual link to the departed Xant.

He waited.

No response from Xant. No response from his own mind. Just the whistling of the wind . . . and the increasing volume from the nervous acolytes below as they obviously wondered whether their fearless leader had utterly lost his mind. He would have found it amusing if the circumstances were not so tragic.

He looked down upon his people one more time, and then stepped away from the statue and headed back to the door that led up to the roof. Several minutes later, he was in his throne room as the top Redeemers in his select council grouped around him. There were a dozen of them. None of them had names, or at least names that they discussed. The only one who had a separate designation was Prime One, the Overlord's second in command.

They stood silently and waited patiently for the Overlord to speak. At such times, that traditional wait could stretch for hours . . . even days, on one memorable occasion. This time, however, the Overlord spoke almost immediately. The fact that he did so was more than enough to add gravity to an already difficult situation.

"I will say now, for your mutual benefit, that which most—if not all—of you probably already know," the Overlord said. "The Black Mass is swarming from the Hunger Zone . . . and its target is this system."

The Redeemers did not quite manage to stifle the outburst of excited and frightened talk among themselves. It was an utter breech of protocol to do such a thing, to babble that way in the presence of the Overlord, and it was to their credit that the Redeemers realized this almost immediately and reined themselves in. But the Overlord could see it in their faces: They were afraid. They had no idea what to do, or what was going to happen, and they were looking to the Overlord for answers. Unfortunately, he had none to give.

"That is why you were speaking to the statue of Xant," Prime One said suddenly. "You were hoping that he would speak to you and give you guidance."

"Yes."

"And did he?"

"Did he?" "Tell us, Overlord, we beg you." The comments came from all over, the inquiries, the pleadings, and he knew at that point that he was in an excellent position. All he had to do was lie to them, tell them whatever wisdom Xant had "imparted" to him, and they would take it as gospel. They were so anxious to believe, so desperate to know that there was some plan, some alternative, that they would have swallowed whatever he tossed to them, gobbled it hungrily and begged for more. If he told them that Xant had said they should abandon their world, they would do it. If he told them that Xant wanted them to die, they would do that, too.

So much power he possessed.

And yet so little.

For he was bound by the truth. There were other religious leaders, he knew, who would not hesitate to say whatever was on their mind, to fabricate some sort of personal dialogue with their respective almighty for the purpose of guiding, even misleading the flock. Such leaders, however, were to be held in contempt. To be pitied. They did their followers no service, and they had no business calling themselves leaders. For it was their job to convey to the followers the true word of their deities. In the case of Xant, in many ways the Overlord was no different from the other Redeemers. He drew Xant's word and beliefs from the writings and teachings of Xant, back when the Great One walked among them in his mortal form. But that was the only true means of communication he had. It would be so easy . . . so easy . . . to make himself out to have more, for that was how eager they were to find options.

Not for the first time, the Overlord wished that he was evil and bereft of morals, so that he could make the lives of others that much easier.

"Xant speaks to me every day in his philosophies, as he does to you. But no more than that, I fear," said the Overlord.

The Redeemers took in that response without comment. Then one of the Redeemers stepped forward and said, "Overlord . . . we have no choice. None can withstand the might of the Black Mass. Even the Thallonians, at the height of their power decades agone, could not deter them."

"What would you recommend?" inquired the Overlord.

Emboldened by the quiet, open manner in which the Overlord asked his advice, the Redeemer said, "We must leave Tulaan IV." The others gasped once more, exchanged hurried comments. The Redeemer glanced at the others from the corner of his eye, and then gamely continued, "Our touch is upon dozens of worlds. There is no reason to cling to this one."

"No reason . . . save that this was the birthplace of Xant," the Overlord reminded him. "He departed from here to begin his great journey. It is to here that he will return. And does Xant not say that this world is sacred?"

"The Overlord is right," Prime One said. "It may very well be that this is a test . . . a precursor to the return of Xant. If we abandon this world, Xant might very well consider us unworthy of witnessing his return. We must have faith."

"But does faith mean that we are to simply sit here and wait to die at the hands . . . or the whatever . . . of the Black Mass?" asked another Redeemer.

"Of course not," Prime One replied. "Xant helps those who help themselves. We must try and take steps to forestall this horrible calamity. We must try to do what no one else has done: We must try and stop the Black Mass."

There were murmurs of approval, nodding of heads. It was hardly a plan, but at least it seemed like the beginnings of one.

The Redeemer who had advocated leaving, however, was not so quick to agree. "And if the steps we take fail, as—based upon the lack of success that others have had—they most likely will? What then? Do we remain on Tulaan out of some sort of loyalty to Xant? Or is it at that point that we leave for safety?"

"There is safety as long as we believe in Xant," Prime One said serenely. "For remember, no matter what else we may do to try and head off the Black Mass, the most important thing is our faith. As long as we maintain that, no harm will come to us. If we have taken every possible step, and nothing has averted them, then if we remain here, on Tulaan, to the last . . . Xant will protect us."

"We do not know that!" said the Redeemer.

"Yes. We do. For it is written that—"

"It is written that the Black Mass is unstoppable! I know! I have read the research, the abortive previous attempts. And we can argue about what Xant wants or doesn't want, tests he may or may not be making. But it is foolishness to simply stand here and let ourselves be devoured by the Black Mass! It would be idiocy to—!"

The Overlord spoke a word.

It was one of the more ancient words, and he directed it in such a way that only the one, protesting Redeemer heard it.

The Redeemer staggered back. The veins on his head began to throb, his eyes went wide, his entire body paralyzed in a rictus of shock as every muscle grew taut, and then his brain exploded. He stumbled back and fell.

"Now then," the Overlord said, not even bothering to wait until the Redeemer hit the floor. He hesitated only for a fraction of a second as the thud from the Redeemer's falling body reverberated throughout the chamber, and then he continued, "Prime One is quite correct. I did not require the spirit of Xant to speak to me . . . as comforting and convenient as that occurrence might have been. It is plain to any, aside from our deceased associate, that our faith requires us to remain here. But I do not believe that we must stay on this world, in the event we cannot stave off the Black Mass, and wait to see if the will of Xant saves us. For it is my belief that the saving of the planet itself is the test. That Xant will accept no less from us than the rescue of his birthplace. And I believe, my brethren, that we are up to this task."

"But how, Overlord?" asked one of the Redeemers, taking a half-step away from his fallen associate so that leaking brain matter would not get on his boots. "How are we to stop them?"

"Some of you are trained in a scientific bent," said the Overlord. "Which of you is the most trained, the most knowledgeable . . . in short, the most formidable scientific mind in our service?"

As one, all of the Redeemers pointed to the Redeemer who was on the floor.

"Ah. Hmm . . . that presents a problem, doesn't it? That is unfortunate. Oh well . . . there are alternatives."

"Such as, Overlord?" inquired Prime One. He had been more than happy to support the notion that Tulaan IV should not be abandoned. Beyond that, unfortunately, he was not going to be of much help.

The Overlord steepled his fingers thoughtfully. "Since the last time that the Black Mass swarmed . . . indeed, for the first time in recorded history . . . a new element has been added, introduced into what was once Thallonian space."

"What element is that, Overlord?" "Yes, tell us." "Tell us, Overlord."

So eager they were once more for any shred of hope. This time, however, he actually had an answer for them.

"The *Excalibur*."

There was stunned silence. "The *Excalibur?*" said one of the Redeemers. "The vessel captained by Mackenzie Calhoun, the false prophet of Zondar? The one that destroyed a Redeemer ship piloted by Prime One's illustrious predecessor? The one who recently aided a resistance in the M'Gewn sector to the degree that we were unable to spread the word of Xant there and were actually forced, for the first time in our history, to retreat?"

"The very same," said the Overlord with an air of confidence.

"But Overlord," began Prime One, and then he paused, obviously to choose the right words. Any sentence that began with "But Overlord" was one that had to be carefully considered and very judiciously phrased. "But Overlord . . . he is our nemesis. Our sworn enemy."

"That is correct, Prime One."

"He will not aid us."

"Ah, but perhaps," the Overlord said slowly, "perhaps he will. Perhaps that is the pure subtlety of Xant's grand plan. That we are to use this current state of affairs to take one who is a long-standing enemy, and use it to transform him into a helpmate. In this way, we can weaken his resolve. In this way, we can put him on the path to greatness that leads to Xant. For let us not forget, my brethren, that our mandate is not to kill. Not to annihilate. But to help. To teach. And there is quite possibly no one in this entire sector of space more in need of being taught than Mackenzie Calhoun and his crew. To be blunt, my brethren, I have been considering this course of action from the first that I had heard of the Black Mass' imminence. It is my firm belief that we are to employ the resources of the *Excalibur* in order to serve us. They will cooperate."

"But how will we force them to do so, Overlord," asked one Redeemer. He glanced at the body of the fallen Redeemer and added hastily, "if I may be so bold as to inquire. You need not tell me, of course. This isn't—"

"I do not think it will require force," said the Overlord. "There are gentler means of persuasion. We can find ways, for Xant will bless us with the resourcefulness to do what must be done. Let us never forget that Xant is on our side. Praise Xant."

"Praise Xant," they intoned.

"Xant is vast. We are insignificant."

"Xant is vast. We are insignificant."

That went on for approximately ten minutes, the Overlord leading them in chants praising the greatness of Xant as opposed to the relative lack of greatness of the Redeemers. One would not have guessed, from the look of them, that their leader was capable of dealing punishment or death with a few well-chosen words, or that one of their High Priests could annihilate the population of an entire planet singlehandedly. In short, they did not appear threatening on the surface. But the fact was that the Redeemers, as a race, were the second most deadly force in Thallonian space. Another fact was that the most deadly force in Thallonian space was heading for them, with the destruction of their world inevitable unless they managed to do something about it.

And it seemed that the key to staving off their world's fate rested with an individual who might well be the third most deadly force in Thallonian space. The outcome of that very unlikely alliance would probably determine which, among those three, would end up as the deadliest force in Thallonian space . . . presuming that all of them were left alive.

# III.

Doctor Selar waddled down the corridor and wondered what she had ever done to deserve this.

She couldn't help but notice that most of the crew seemed to be steering clear of her. They would give her quick "Hello's" or such, but otherwise seemed more than happy to keep their distance from her. She wondered why that would be. She decided that it was just their concept of being solicitous; no one wanted to risk banging into her rather copious stomach.

Now if she could just get Lieutenant Commander Burgoyne, the child's father, to rein hirself in, that would go a long way toward solving her problems.

Intellectually, she knew that Burgoyne was just trying to help, just trying hir best. But the Hermat didn't understand that hir involvement in the pregnancy was purely on an as-needed basis. For reasons that completely eluded Selar, she had bonded on some sort of mental level with Burgoyne. It was probably some sort of random, unexpected development as a result of her experiencing a delayed, and extremely erratic, case of *pon farr.* It had been completely unpredictable, and frankly, somewhat embarrassing. If Burgoyne would simply realize that—

She came to a stop just outside her quarters. Her sharp hearing detected something moving within. That was, to say the least, unexpected. She had no idea why there would be any intruders . . .

Yes. Yes, she did. Suddenly she knew all too well.

She took a deep breath, readying herself for what was undoubtedly going to be a very unpleasant scene, and stepped in.

Immediately she noticed the candles. How could she not? They were set out, along with an elaborately prepared dinner, on the small dining table in the middle of her quarters. Seated on the opposite side of the table was Burgoyne, hir slender face flickering in the candle light. "Welcome home, stranger," s/he said. "Thought I'd prepare a nice dinner for you."

"Burgoyne—"

"Call me Burgy. It's about time you did."

"And it is about time you left, Burgoyne. These are my quarters. They are private. You cannot simply let yourself in . . ."

"Actually, I can," said Burgoyne cheerfully. "I am, after all, the Chief Engineer. With that job comes great power, and with that, great responsibility—"

"Which you are willing to toss aside at your convenience if it suits your purposes."

"You see?" Burgoyne was pouring soup into two

bowls. "You know me so well. Small wonder then that we belong together."

"Burgoyne, that would be illogical."

"Really? How can you tell? Your plomik soup is getting cold, by the way." S/he gestured to the bowl.

"What do you mean, 'How can I tell?' " She didn't sit.

"Well, you just carry yourself in exactly the same manner whether you have a headache, or a belly ache, or if your legs are hurting, or . . ."

"Is there some point to this, Lieutenant Commander?"

" 'Lieutenant Commander.' Great Bird, I was going for 'Burgy.' We're backsliding here. The point is, you have this whole stoic thing down so pat, I'd be amazed if you were in touch enough with your own body to know that you have a headache. Are you going to sit or am I going to have to bend your legs at the knees?"

Selar sat, very stiffly, very properly. She kept her hands placed on her lap. "This 'stoic thing' you refer to is a function of my training and my biology. It is my way of life. They are what make me who and what I am."

"Funny. Considering you're a pregnant Vulcan, I thought I made you who and what you are. The soup isn't getting any warmer, by the wa—"

"I do not desire soup."

"Straight to the entrée, then?" inquired Burgoyne, nonplussed.

"Burgoyne . . . I am obviously not making myself very clear. So I shall try to make this as simple and straightforward as possible," said Selar. She noticed that she was over-pronouncing her words with excessive formality and tried to tone it down. "I am someone who, every day of my life, has been in control of it. I knew what I wanted, I knew how to go about getting it. I answered to no master but myself. And I was proud of that. Very, very proud."

"And you have every reason to—"

"I am not . . ." the mechanical tone slipped back into her speech, but she mastered it and said as pleasantly as possible. "I am not finished. Consider, if you will, my situation. I am a doctor, a healer with responsibilities and skills that I have worked very, very hard to hone. Suddenly I find myself at the mercy of an unwanted biological urge that compels me to mate and spawn in a manner more suited to almost any lower order of life form, not excluding humans."

"That's cold, Selar, even for you."

"That is exactly my point. As pregnancy, and its attending discomforts, progresses, a Vulcan woman becomes . . . colder. Stoic. It is a reaction to how we are trained to handle annoyances in a logical, unemotional manner. That I am nearing term means this effect is at its strongest."

"So it's me."

She shook her head. "It has nothing to with you . . ."

"Oh yes it does," Burgoyne interrupted her. Hir lips were pulled back, hir teeth flashing slightly in the dim lighting. "You are linked, biologically and mentally, with a being that is as emotional as you are unemotional. I am the opposite of what you would like a child of yours to be. So, having partaken of my seed, you no longer wish me around."

"That is not what is happening."

"Yes, it is, and it hurts."

"I hurt as well," she said with force. "Lower back.

Spine. Breasts. Head. Calves. The child moves constantly—"

"S/he's moving?" Burgoyne said with interest. "Can I feel—?"

"No. To continue, my entire pelvis hurts. I am moving in a manner that makes a horta look like a gazelle. In short, Burgoyne, every physical aspect of me is in a monstrous amount of pain . . . and I deal with that by becoming what you call colder. I—ow!"

"What's the matter?" Burgoyne asked, coming around the table.

"More pain. I am in control again now," Selar said. "And do you know why I am in control. Because I am Vulcan. That breeding and discipline that you hold in such low regard is what will get me through this."

"I think as long as you deny what's really bothering you—"

"What is 'bothering me' " she said, making no effort to keep the ice out of her voice, "is you." Burgoyne would have stepped back except that s/he was alarmed to discover that Selar's hand was squarely gripping a rather tender area on hir body. Fully aware of the Vulcan's strength, Burgoyne didn't move a centimeter. Selar continued, her tone still frozen. "It is because of your seed within me that I am having these difficulties. Your presence therefore makes maintaining my control more difficult."

"That . . . must be very irritating . . ."

"To say nothing of the fact that a Vulcan mother forms a mental bond with her child while it is *in utero,* and the child in my belly has the most chaotic psi patterns any female in the history of our race has had to experience. Are you beginning to grasp the source of my difficulties?"

"Actually," Burgoyne said with remarkable restraint, looking down, "I think you're the one who's grasping the source. If you wouldn't mind . . ."

It took Selar a moment to focus on what Burgoyne was saying, and then with a grunt she released hir. Then Selar straightened her hair and said, in a more normal manner, "I suppose I should be grateful, to some degree. With my current condition—considering the previously unknown result of a mating between a Vulcan and a Hermat—in a way, I am providing a medical precedent. Thanks to you, my place in history is assured. So . . . thank you."

"You're, uhm . . . you're welcome."

"But as I said, I am experiencing difficulties that your presence exacerbates. Rightly or wrongly . . ."

"Logically or illogically," he said.

She inclined her head slightly in acknowledgement. "Your continued endeavors, therefore, to build an emotional bond between us are making things worse."

"But don't you see that this is the ideal time to . . . ?"

"No. I do not see that, Burgoyne. What I see is that you are not susceptible to reason. So I am spelling it out for you: Leave. Me. Alone. Is that clear enough?"

Very stiffly, Burgoyne said, "Yes. Perfectly clear."

"Good. Do not concern yourself with the meal; I shall deal with it."

"All right," said Burgoyne. "Good evening to you, then. I just wish to add—"

Selar rolled her eyes. "I knew it."

"I just wish to add that everything I've said is right. That . . . and I love you."

Selar came as close to laughing as she ever had. "Love me? Burgoyne . . . you do not even know me."

"That makes two of us," said Burgoyne who, apparently deciding that was a good exit line, chose to exit.

Selar shook her head, then looked down at the table Burgoyne had so lovingly prepared.

The hell of it was, she really did like plomik soup.

Mackenzie Calhoun sat in Ten-Forward, nursing a drink and hoping that everyone in the place would understand, without being told, that he just really wanted to be left alone at that moment.

"Ah. Good," said Si Cwan as he dropped into the chair opposite Calhoun. "Just who I desired to talk to."

"Uhm . . . Ambassador . . ." began Calhoun.

Si Cwan waved dismissively. "I know, I know," he said in his deep voice which always made him sound as if he were singing when he was speaking. "You hoped to sit here, giving off unspoken signals that you wished to be alone. However, if you truly wished to be alone, you could sit in your quarters or your ready room. What you are really seeking is interaction and, more specifically, someone interested enough in you to make the effort of breaking through your barriers."

Calhoun stared at him, trying to form words. "That's . . . very impressive, Ambassador."

"Thank you."

"And you are that interested in me, that you will make that effort?"

"In you as a person? To be honest, no."

"Ah. I appreciate your honesty." Calhoun took a sip of his drink. "Why, then, are you honoring me with your presence."

"Because you are the commander of this vessel, and

I would appreciate your cooperation in a formal request."

"All right. I'm with you."

"I need you to maintain noble propriety."

Calhoun blinked. "You just lost me."

Si Cwan shifted in his seat and leaned forward, elbows on the table. "I have been observing the activities of your son, Xyon. I believe that he has been showing an interest in Kalinda. More disturbing, I believe that she has been showing an interest in him."

"Ah. I think I begin to see," Calhoun said. "And you find this bothersome."

"That is correct. That is exactly correct."

"May I ask why, precisely?"

"Several reasons." He raised his hand, fingers extended.

"How did I know you were going to count them off?" Calhoun asked rhetorically.

"First, Kalinda is still trying to acclimate herself. Until fairly recently, she believed that she was someone else entirely, with an identity created artificially by my enemy Zoran. Thanks to some mental probes through the courtesy of your Lieutenant Soleta, her true personality has reasserted herself, her full memories returned. But that is still a great deal for her to assimilate."

"Could you possibly use a different word. It has rather negative connotations these days."

"Second," said Si Cwan as if Calhoun had not spoken, "there is a matter of positions to consider."

Calhoun stared at him. "Yes?"

"She is, after all, of the nobility . . ."

"Ah."

"And for someone of the nobility to become romantically involved with . . ." He drummed his fingers on the table. ". . . what's the best way to phrase it . . . ?"

"A commoner?"

"Yes. Exactly, thank you. A commoner. It's simply not appropriate. Third . . . well, there is no insult intended upon you, Captain, since I know you were not involved in the boy's upraising."

"You know this how?"

"Everyone on the *Excalibur* knows."

"Of course. For one foolish moment, I believed that such a thing as a right to privacy existed on this ship."

"It exists, but largely in theory. As I was saying, I know you had nothing to do with how the boy was raised, but the simple truth is that I'm concerned he can be something of a negative influence. On that basis, I would appreciate you sitting down with the boy and explaining to him why—during his presumably brief stay aboard—he should keep his distance from Kalinda. As captain of the ship, you would certainly have the authority to do so, and make it stick by instructing security to enforce it." Si Cwan laughed softly. "Certainly you can understand my concerns. Xyon has many commendable qualities, but he is very impulsive, acting with instinct instead of forethought. He is, to be honest, a bit crude, and he most certainly has an inflated sense of his own importance."

"I have no idea where he gets that from," said Calhoun.

"Kalinda is still a bit naive, despite all she's been through. I do not want her seizing on young Xyon as some sort of role model, or someone to aspire to."

"Despite the fact that he saved her life. Despite the fact that he essentially, to the best of my knowledge, passes his days trying to help people with no thought of remuneration or self-aggrandizement. Heaven forbid that you would want Kalinda to emulate such behavior."

"No," Si Cwan said, waggling a finger, "now you see, I think you're missing the point somewhat."

"Oh really. Then I will reiterate, to make certain all the points are covered." Now it was Calhoun counting off on his fingers. "First, you're worried because Kalinda is still getting her bearings. Understandable. And as her big brother, I'm quite sure you can be counted on to make certain that she gets them. Second . . . you're a snob."

"Now wait just a minute . . ."

Si Cwan's voice was raised, and Calhoun noticed that others in Ten-Forward were starting to look their way. He didn't care. Why should he? Everyone on the damned ship seemed to know everyone else's business. Why become faint-hearted about it now? Nevertheless, he dropped his voice to a low, intense level to afford at least an illusion of confidentiality. "Lord Cwan, I don't know if you've taken stock lately, but the planet upon which you reigned is rubble, and your empire has fallen apart. We continue to treat you with respect appropriate to your title as a courtesy to you, but make no mistake: It is courtesy, and nothing more. It's charming to consider yourself part of the ruling class, but considering you have nothing to rule over, you may want to rethink the possibility of pulling your head out of the dark area it's gotten stuck in."

Si Cwan flushed redder than he usually was. "How dare y—"

"Third, whatever Xyon's strengths and weaknesses of character might be, the fact is he doesn't have an inflated sense of his own self-importance. He has a streak of independence slightly wider than the Horsehead Nebula, and even if I lost all sense of reason and tried to order him to keep away from Kalinda, I can tell you with a reasonable amount of certainty that all such an action would do is increase his determination to spend time with her."

"Captain, you are being unreasonable . . ."

"I thought you were better than this, Si Cwan. Where's the nobility in this whining attitude?"

The muscles in Si Cwan's arms twitched as if he were containing himself. His teeth were tightly set. "I would strongly suggest that you do not insult me further, Captain, or I cannot be responsible for the consequences."

Calhoun felt a flush against his cheek, and was quite aware that his scar was burning red, the most reliable exterior sign that he was angry. "Are you implying that you would lose your temper and take some physical action against me?"

"I believe, Captain, the statement speaks for itself."

"Si Cwan . . . I have tremendous respect for you," Calhoun said, sounding so calm that one would have thought he was having a passionless discussion about gamma particles. "I know that you are trying to pull together the worlds in this sector into some sort of alliance that will enable them to function as one. I know that, to a certain degree, you have had to swallow your pride in your dealings with those over whom you used to rule. And you have been of tremendous use in the past months as we have gone about our business. All of this I freely admit. But lest you forget, we came to blows when you first arrived on this vessel, and I dropped you where you stood. So I think you have to understand that if you continue the direction of this conversation . . . or if you are foolish enough actually to swing on me . . . then I *will* be responsible for the consequences. Do we understand each other, Lord Cwan?"

Si Cwan appeared to be considering taking his chances. But there was something in Calhoun's dark, purple eyes that signalled him as to the lack of wisdom such a course would entail.

"Out of respect to your position, Captain . . . yes, I believe we do," Si Cwan said.

"Good." Calhoun sat back in his chair. "Would you like a drink?"

"No. I think not."

"Very well, then. Enjoy the rest of your evening."

Si Cwan rose from the chair, turned stiffly and walked out. All heads turned watching him go. The other patrons of Ten-Forward had not been able to hear what was being said between the two of them; they had made their voices too low for that. But everyone could tell that some rather harsh words had been exchanged, and there was even a general sense that something worse had only narrowly been averted. Practically in unison, everyone looked back at Calhoun. He raised a glass jauntily and downed the contents. "I wonder," he said out loud to no one in particular, "if this evening could possibly get any worse."

His comm badge beeped and he tapped it. "Calhoun here."

"Captain," came the brisk voice of Shelby, "sorry to contact you this late, but we've received a distress call from the planet Fenner. They're under attack by the Redeemers."

"That," Calhoun said, "will teach me to ask questions I don't really want the answers to."

"Sir?"

"Nothing. Alert the senior staff. We'll conference in the ready room."

"Not in the conference lounge, sir?"

"No. I don't feel like lounging. I feel like being ready. Calhoun out."

# IV.

IN THE READY ROOM, Soleta tapped the computer screen which had the specs on the planet Fenner. "Standard class M world," she said. "Populace is in early technological stages, having achieved space travel approximately one hundred years earlier. The people had a civil war relatively recently, but threw out the leadership that brought them to that state and since then have lived in relative harmony. Recently, however, an emissary for the Redeemers arrived on their world and informed them that they had been selected for conversion."

Around the room, Calhoun, Burgoyne, Shelby, Kebron and Si Cwan all nodded. They knew all too well the significance of that designation: the Redeemers had chosen the Fennerians for "redemption," to be converted in their beliefs to accept Xant as their savior and the Redeemers as their undisputed masters.

"They are aware of the *Excalibur*'s presence in the sector," continued Soleta, "and have requested our help to stave off this intended conversion."

"At warp six, we can be there in thirty hours," Burgoyne said. "Sooner if I squeeze a bit more out of the engines."

"Thoughts, people?" said Calhoun.

"I don't see that we have a choice," said Si Cwan. He was speaking in such a calm, businesslike manner, that Calhoun would never have suspected the cross words they'd had earlier if he hadn't been there. "We have to extend aid."

"It would seem," observed Soleta, "the logical thing to do."

"It may not be easy," Burgoyne said. "We took a bit of a pounding back in the M'Gewn system. All systems are running, but to be up to maximum efficiency, we could really use time in a starbase."

"I thought you told me you had a handle on it, Burgy."

"I do, Captain. But having a handle on it for normal operations, and taking this ship into combat against another of those Redeemer heavy destroyers . . . it's not something I'm looking forward to. For something like that, I wouldn't mind putting in some time for a major overhaul first. I'm not saying the ship is going to blow apart or anything from stress, but I certainly wouldn't mind skewing the odds in our favor a bit more."

"Time is of the essence," rumbled Kebron.

"I agree," said Si Cwan.

"We agree. Shoot me now."

Kebron's small joke drew a few smiles around the ready room. Calhoun looked to Shelby and said, "Commander, you've been rather quiet. Your thoughts?"

She didn't hesitate. "We help them, of course."

" 'Of course?' " Calhoun was clearly surprised.

"Yes, of course. We can't stand by and allow the Redeemers to subsume their culture."

"Actually," Calhoun said, "according to the Prime Directive, I thought that was precisely what we would have to stand by and do. As a matter of fact, in the M'Gewn situation, I seem to recall that you argued exactly that."

"Then, with all respect, captain, you do not recall correctly. M'Gewn was a different situation entirely. The M'Gewns were a warlike race who decided to take on the Redeemers, found themselves in over their heads, and called upon us to help them out. My contention was that they had brought their predicament upon themselves, and that it wasn't appropriate for us to bail them out."

"But there were strategic considerations," Si Cwan began.

Shelby put up a hand, cutting the conversation short. "It is pointless," she said, "to rehash something that is already done with. In any event, the situations are not analogous. I think we are obliged to help the Fennerians."

"Well, good. Good," Calhoun said. "All right . . . if we're all agreed. Mr. Kebron, have McHenry set course for Fenner. Inform them that we're on the way. Burgoyne . . . do what you can to make certain the ship is in the best possible condition, should we have to take her into battle."

"You'll have her fighting ready, Captain," Burgoyne said gamely.

"Good. The Redeemers," said Calhoun, interlacing his fingers on his desk, "have been our most persistent opponents since we arrived here. I suspect that matters are going to be building to a head. We have to be prepared for that. I want snap drills run in the various departments, just to keep everyone on their toes."

"You are assuming, then, captain, that however matters develop with the Redeemers, the only possible outcome will involve battle?" asked Shelby.

There was a subtle hint of challenge to her voice, so subtle that only Calhoun—from long practice—could detect it. "I think it likely, yes."

"Hmpf."

That was all she said. "Hmpf."

Calhoun looked at her through narrowed eyes, and then said, "All right. Everyone to their stations. Commander . . . a moment of your time, please."

"Of course, sir."

As soon as everyone else had cleared out, Calhoun sat back in his chair and regarded Shelby thoughtfully. "Elizabeth . . . I sense there's something on your mind."

"I'm simply wondering why you called the meeting, Mac."

"Why I called it? To solicit opinions, of course."

"All right. Fine." She shrugged. "Are we done?"

"No, we're not done. To be honest, Eppy, you've been acting strangely ever since Riker was in charge for a short time. What's going on?"

"I was just impressed by his honesty, that's all."

He stared at her. "I'm not following you."

"Riker," she said, "had total disregard for everything I had to say. But he wasn't polite about it, the way you are. He was straightforward about it. It was blunt and rude and, in some ways, refreshing." He started to voice a protest, but she kept talking. "You already decided that we were going to help the Fenner. I'm positive you did. So why did you waste our time discussing something you had already decided? For form's sake? Since when did you care about that?"

"Since when did you stop caring about the Prime Directive? We both know that an argument can be made that we shouldn't help with the Fenner. They're not a member of the UFP, and their being targeted by the Redeemers doesn't automatically mean they're entitled to our aid."

She laughed at that. "You must really think I have no compassion at all, Mac. You do, don't you? You think I'm just some sort of walking rule book, tossing around regulations and not caring about the conditions under which people are living."

"And you apparently think that I do whatever I want, whatever impulse seizes me, without caring about what could happen as a result." He came around his desk and leaned on the edge, barely a foot away from her. "Well? Isn't that true?"

"Of course!" she said reasonably. "That's exactly what you do. You do whatever, whenever, however. That's been your method of operation from the moment you took command. What, don't tell me you're denying it. Or starting to waver from that. The Mackenzie Calhoun I know would not only agree with my assessment, he'd consider it a badge of honor."

"That doesn't render me incapable of listening to what my officers have to say."

"Mac, you know what?" She put her hands up and rose from her seat. "I'm tired. It's been a long day as it is. And I'm getting worn out."

"From what?"

"From acting as your conscience, Mac, and being ignored. From acting as the voice of reason, and being steamrolled over. Or you go on the assumption that I'm going to disagree with you, and even express shock when I don't, as if we couldn't possibly ever be of a like mind, or I couldn't think of something beyond the edges of the Starfleet rule book. I'm tired from trying to ride herd on you, and from the fighting. Fighting with you, fighting with Riker, fighting with Jellico. I feel like I'm in a rut, Mac. Like we both are. That we just go around and around, and I don't know if I'm doing you any good as your second in command, and I sure know I'm not doing myself any good. The hell with command at this point; I'm starting to believe it'll never happen, because maybe I just simply don't deserve it. But I know what I do want: I want more from life than fighting. I want . . . I . . ."

Calhoun didn't even know he was going to do it before he did it. He stepped forward, grabbed Shelby by the arms, and pulled her to him. Their bodies pressed together and she gasped into his mouth as he brought his lips down on hers. For a moment, just a moment, her instinct prompted her to fight, and then she just seemed to melt against him as they kissed each other hungrily, giving in to something that had underscored their entire relationship, but which they had both been hell-bent to avoid acknowledging.

She pulled back from him, then, her chest rising and falling rapidly. For a moment more he held her, and then he let her go, and she bumped up against a chair. She held the back of the chair as if to steady herself, and they regarded each other as if seeing each other for the first time . . . or perhaps reacquainting themselves after a lengthy absence.

"Where the hell did that come from?" she asked. Her

breath was wavering and she sucked it in in order to steady it.

"I . . . don't know," he said. "It just . . . popped out."

"Mac . . ." Once more she took in a deep breath to steady herself, and when she let it out her voice still trembled slightly. "Look, I . . ."

"You don't have to say it. Bad idea. It was a bad idea." He had never felt quite so disoriented. "I just . . . I have a lot on my mind . . . and I was . . ."

"Looking for grounding?"

"Yes. Yes, exactly. That's all it was. Looking for grounding."

"Why?"

"It's not important. Nothing I want to discuss."

"Mac, perhaps it—"

"No," he repeated with more certainty. "It's nothing. Nothing I can't handle."

"It has to do with Xyon, doesn't it? Somehow, he—"

"Eppy," he said gently, placing his hands on her shoulders. "It's nothing. Really. I'm back to myself now."

"Are you sure?"

"Positive."

"That's good to know, because I—"

This time, when he kissed her, she was a bit more prepared for it even though he wasn't. It lasted longer and was more intense on both sides, and when they parted they didn't hurry to distance themselves quite as quickly as before.

"Mac . . ." she said steadily, smoothing her uniform jacket, "this . . . is inappropriate. You're the captain. I'm the first officer. We understood going into this . . ."

"I know. I know."

"I think we, and the ship, would be best served if we

acted as if this never happened. With your kissing me, twice . . ."

"You kissed me back."

"No. I didn't."

"Yes, you did, Eppy. I should know, I was there."

"Mac, I didn't . . ." She closed her eyes. "I'm not going to discuss this. I'm just not."

"That's probably wise."

"I'm going off shift now."

"That's probably even wiser."

"If this happens again, I will have to consider filing a report."

"I would understand," said Calhoun.

"Promise me you won't do it again. Ever."

He considered her request. "No," he said.

"No, you won't do it again?"

"No, I can't promise. Eppy . . ."

"Mac . . ." She took a deep breath. "Please . . . you've always been someone I could count on . . . even when what I was counting on was that I couldn't count on you. So don't disappoint me, okay?"

"Okay."

She exited quickly, and Calhoun sagged against his desk. What the hell had just happened? How could he . . . ? How could he have lost control that way . . . ?

Was it really that much of a fight for him to resist kissing her? Was he really still that drawn to her? Or was it what she had said . . . that the arrival of Xyon had triggered things within him. Regrets, doubts. Those things that Xyon had said about his not loving anyone, about never having let anyone get close.

"I don't doubt myself," Calhoun said firmly, as if someone was listening in on him. "Never." The words sounded hollow, though, possibly because he had never felt the need to say them out loud before. The fact that he felt the need now somehow undercut the sentiment.

He turned the computer screen around and looked at the information about Fenner. In doing so, he felt the hair on the back of his neck stand on end, which was generally his reliable indicator that there was danger hovering nearby.

He studied their distress message, tugged at his lower lip thoughtfully, and came to the conclusion that the entire thing might very well be a set-up. That the Redeemers either might be in league with the Fenneri-ans, or else were pressuring them to summon the *Excalibur* and force a confrontation on that basis.

Knowing this, however, or at the very least suspect-ing it, did not do Calhoun a great deal of good. He only had two choices: Go there or not go there. If he didn't go there, and the distress was legitimate, then Fenner would be overrun and the *Excalibur* will have done nothing to prevent it. That was unacceptable. But if he did go there, and the Redeemers were lying in wait, then things could get ugly.

The only foreseeable option was heading to Fenner and proceeding with as much caution as possible. Ex-pect nothing, anticipate everything. That had always been Calhoun's personal mantra, and he saw no reason to change it.

He poured himself a *raktajino* and was quite an-noyed to notice that his hand was shaking. He could still taste Shelby's lips against his.

"I think I'm losing my mind," he said. Then again, if he was . . . there were worse ways for it to go.

Shelby felt as if she were losing her mind.

Normally she never had any trouble sleeping, but

this night had been incredibly fitful. She thought that perhaps she had managed to sleep a few minutes here and there, but for the most part she had spent the evening staring at the ceiling, or the floor, or burying her face in her pillow. All in all, it had been one of her most wasted nights. She rolled over, looked at the chronometer and moaned softly. It was just past oh-four hundred hours, and she knew that closing her eyes was going to be pointless. She could have been on the bridge, in the middle of her shift during the height of a Romulan attack, and not been more awake than she was right then. She got out of bed, put on her exercise clothes, and headed for the rocketball court.

She figured that, at that time of night, it would not be occupied. So she was appropriately surprised when she walked in and found Katerina Mueller, the ship's executive officer, wielding a paddle and slapping the glowing ball around with ruthless efficiency.

Shelby had never quite known what to make of Mueller. In many ways, Mueller was still something of a mystery to her. She was a tall woman, with broad shoulders and an air of infinite superiority about her. Her body, outlined in the clinging tights she wore, was lean and hard. As she concentrated on the ball, her jaw was slightly out-thrust and her dark blonde hair—usually tied in a severe knot—was completely out of the way beneath a kerchief. She immediately became aware of Shelby's presence and turned to face her, her cobalt-blue eyes so intense that Shelby felt as if they were drilling right through her.

Mueller's most prominent feature remained her scar. It was not exactly like Calhoun's, it was on the left side of her face instead of the right, and thinner. The fact that she wore it, though, as opposed to having had some simple surgery to get it removed, spoke volumes of her. Shelby had heard that she had picked it up fencing at a university on Earth called Heidelberg.

Once upon a time, the rank of second in command, which was Shelby's rank, and executive officer, which was Mueller's, were synonymous. But about a hundred years before, it had been decided to split the two from one another, giving the ship the equivalent of two righthands to the captain. After all, in space the designation of day and night was purely arbitrary, a convenience for the crew and something that no potential enemy was necessarily guided by. Inadvertently wandering into hostile territory, the sleeping ship could venture smack into the middle of someone else's day. So although there remained one captain, it was felt that two people of identical rank directly beneath the commanding officer were required. But two individuals both referred to as "Number One," as it were, seemed confusing. After much debate, the First Officer/XO split was decided upon. It was a compromise that pleased absolutely no one, which was how everyone knew it was a good compromise.

So in essence, Mueller and Shelby were peers. However, since Shelby functioned during the day shift while Mueller had charge of the night, the two women almost never saw one another.

"Commander," Mueller said in her faint-but-crisp German accent. "You're up early, I see."

"More like up late, actually. I didn't know you played."

"Played?"

"Rocketball."

"Oh." Mueller looked at the small racquet in one hand and the glowing ball in the other. "Yes, I suppose some consider this play. To me it's more work, actually. Exercise. Keeping trim." She slapped her taut belly in obvious pride. It made a hollow sound. The woman was pure muscle.

"Absolutely," agreed Shelby, and slapped her own middle. It jiggled slightly and she muttered under her breath before forcing a smile. "Would you care to . . ."

"By all means. I so rarely have an opponent. Most people don't desire to compete. They find it disheartening."

"Do they?" Shelby said, her thin lips bright against her face. "How sad for them."

They lined up at the ready line and Mueller put the ball into play. It had been ages since Shelby last tested herself in rocketball, but she was pleased to see the old reflexes coming back to her. She moved gracefully to and fro across the court, handling each return and delivering it back against the wall with a smart snap of the wrist. She was rather pleased with her performance . . . until she noticed that Mueller barely seemed to be moving. She had absolutely no idea how she did it. The executive officer wasn't that much taller than she, her reach not terribly further. And yet she seemed to have no problem getting to every return of Shelby's with the most minimal of effort. For six straight returns, Shelby could have sworn that Mueller's feet didn't even budge from the spot. It was as if her damned arm just stretched somehow to get the racquet there.

Shelby, for her part, was constantly on the move. Consequently, she began to wear herself out. As the game progressed, she missed more and more returns. Soon she was panting, and at one point she missed the ball so completely that she stumbled. Just before she fell, however, one of Mueller's strong arms was around her, stopping her from hitting the floor. "Thanks," Shelby managed to gasp out.

"You're playing excellently," said Mueller.

"Sure I am," Shelby said, pausing for breath by leaning against a wall. "You're kicking the crap out of me."

"Perhaps. But I play regularly, and my body is accustomed to functioning at this hour. You're in an unfamiliar sport at an odd time of day. If I were not kicking the crap out of you, there would be something seriously wrong with me."

Shelby laughed. "You make it sound like I should be proud that I'm losing."

"You should be. There are others I've played who would have left the court by this time, or even earlier. Then again, I haven't played many women. Mostly I've played against men." She shook her head, sounding a bit annoyed. "I know that, by and large, they are the weaker sex, but one would have thought they would have a bit more intestinal fortitude than that. Come." She gestured for Shelby to follow her, which she did. Mueller crossed to a food slot and said, "Two Mueller specials."

After only a moment's pause, the slot door slid open and two small glasses of some sort of colored liquid were inside. Mueller took one and sipped it, extended the other to Shelby. "Here," she said. "Only drink a little. It goes a long way, plus you wouldn't want to fill up with liquid. You'll cramp."

"What is it?" It didn't smell particularly inviting to Shelby.

"My own special blend. Very high in electrolytes. Just what you need."

Shelby braced herself and took a sip. It smelled

worse than it tasted. And she had to admit that Mueller knew what she was talking about; just a small bit of it reinvigorated her. "This is excellent. Thank you."

"Odd, isn't it?" said Mueller philosophically. She sat on a small bench nearby, the racquet dangling from a loop around her wrist, squeezing the glowing ball absently in her hand. "Humanity considers itself so advanced. We look to our ancestors, see the racism, the hatred, the pointless wars, and we pat ourselves on the back over how far we've come. And yet, the male ego remains a universal constant, after all this time. Men get much more upset when I beat them than women do."

"Well, to be fair, there are other universal constants besides the male ego," said Shelby.

"Female superiority?" Mueller suggested, which drew a laugh from Shelby.

"Yes, that. And stupidity. Stupidity is a major universal constant. Despite what scientists say otherwise, stupidity is probably the most common element in the entire universe. And there are others."

"There certainly are. Another round?"

"Why not?" said Shelby gamely, slapping her thighs as she rose.

Shelby fared slightly better the second time around. She still wasn't Mueller's match in technique, but she started watching Mueller more carefully and saw that it wasn't so much that Mueller wasn't moving. It was that, through a combination of patience and practice, she was anticipating where the ball was going to go. So instead of playing catch up, trying to make it to where the ball was (as Shelby was doing) Mueller was moving to where the ball was going to be and heading it off before it could take additional bounces or build up more speed to stay away from her. So Shelby started imitating the style of play. Naturally she wasn't quite as deft at it as Mueller was. But every now and then she managed to get to the ball earlier than she had been, and send it off in unexpected directions that would surprise Mueller and make her work a bit more than she had anticipated. Mueller smiled in grim appreciation and approval. "Very good," she said after one particularly invigorating and lengthy volley that Shelby had won.

"Thank you."

"You're watching me and learning. A very good practice."

"Thank you."

Another sip of Mueller's brew, and then Mueller said, "So why the difficulty sleeping? I assume that's why you're here."

"Oh, it's nothing. Stupidity. Nothing of any real significance."

"Ah. I see. It's a man, then."

Shelby laughed and shook her head. "Do you have a problem with men?" she asked. "You seem very critical of them."

"A problem? No. No, not at all," said Mueller. She removed her kerchief which was soaked with sweat by that point, and waved it about to dry it a bit. "Actually, I get along with most men quite well."

"Yet you seem to enjoy picking on them."

"Well," said Mueller wryly, "they are fairly easy targets. So this man you're losing sleep over . . . is he worth it?"

"Is he worth it? Yes. Is the relationship worth it? I don't know. Is the relationship smart? Definitely not."

"Ah. One of those," Mueller nodded knowingly. "Do you want to tell me who it is?"

"Nah. It's not really worth dwelling on." She looked at Mueller askance. "Have you ever lost sleep over a man?"

"Only during activities that make it difficult to sleep."

It was difficult for Shelby to tell when Mueller was joking. She said everything with the same deadpan. She either had a wicked sense of humor, or no sense of humor. Shelby couldn't quite make up her mind.

"I see. Ever had a shipboard romance?"

"Once. Probably it would be best if I didn't discuss it."

"Okay. I understand."

Mueller readied herself to serve again, and Shelby felt a wall going up between the two of them. She suddenly felt, not for the first time, a keen loneliness. The truth was that she didn't have many friends aboard the ship, and certainly no one who was her peer in rank. She felt as if she and Mueller were making tentative steps toward friendship with one another, but their mutual tendency toward internalizing and caution was now getting in the way of that.

The bottom line was, she liked Mueller. She wasn't sure why, but she did. She seemed dependable and forthright, someone whom she could count on. In many ways, they were quite similar, and there was a lot that they could build upon. The thing was, they could only go so far as long as they kept their guards solidly in place.

What the hell, thought Shelby. A little honesty won't hurt. Half the time everyone on this ship finds out everyone else's business anyway, so for all she knew, word would be out about her and Calhoun's unexpected romantic embrace. She didn't think Calhoun would broadcast it, but nevertheless these things somehow tended to leak.

So just as Mueller served the ball, Shelby said, "Calhoun. Captain Calhoun."

Mueller turned and stared at her, eyes wide open, clearly dumbfounded. "How did you know?"

"What?" Shelby saw the ball coming, returned it.

As if she were psychic, Mueller returned the serve without even glancing at it. "How did you know that it was Captain Calhoun I had the shipboard romance with?"

Shelby spun, gaped . . . and the ricocheting ball hit her in the head.

"Are you all right?" Mueller asked. She held three fingers up in front of Shelby. "How many fingers do you see?"

"Ninety," said Shelby.

"Here. Let's sit you down on the bench. Do you want me to call sickbay?"

Shelby took a deep breath and shook off her disorientation. "It's all right. I'll be all right."

"You didn't answer me. How did you know about me and Mac?"

Shelby steadied herself and forced a smile. "Well . . . it seems a natural fit, that's all. The two of you are a lot alike . . . and you've got the scars. As I said, natural."

"I didn't think it was that obvious."

"Well, when you know exactly what to look for, things become that much more obvious. So how long have you and the captain been . . ." She waggled her fingers while, at the same time, trying to fight down mounting incredulity.

She felt slightly relieved, though, when Mueller said, "Oh. It hasn't been here. On the *Grissom*. We were involved on the *Grissom*."

"Oh."

Mueller looked surprised. "What, you thought it was here? Now?"

"I wasn't sure . . ."

"Definitely not." She shook her head. "This was back before he was a captain. Not now. Oh, no, you'd have to be ten kinds of stupid to become romantically involved with a ship's captain."

"You think so?"

"Oh, absolutely. The captain has far too many responsibilities. The last thing he or she needs is to form some sort of romantic attachment to a member of the crew. It would totally affect the way he conducted himself. It would invite charges of preferential treatment, no matter how even-handed the captain was. And besides, let's face it: A captain is usually married to his ship, and he's got a thousand or so children he calls the crew to look after. Not that they necessarily need looking after, you understand, but that's the mindset they come from. Oh, involvement with a captain is just too much trouble. It's a huge amount of aggravation, and more than anyone could possibly need."

"So you would never become romantically involved with the captain now, despite what happened before."

"Never. Absolutely no way."

Shelby nodded and took a sip of Mueller's special brew.

"I'd sleep with him though," said Mueller by way of finishing a thought.

It was all Shelby could do not to cough up the liquid

through her nose. "What?" she managed to get out. "But you just said you'd never . . ."

"Become romantic, right. Sex isn't about romance. Sex is about exercise, relaxation, and letting off steam."

"You make it sound like rocketball," protested Shelby.

"It is a little," she admitted. "Although with me, sex is more of a game than rocketball."

Shelby leaned back and let her head thud against the wall. "You know, Katerina—"

"Kat."

"You know, Kat, in a lot of ways, I don't understand you at all."

"Good," Mueller said approvingly. "I value my mystique. So tell me—I've been candid with you—who is the man who's been keeping you up at nights. I told you, after all."

"You didn't tell me. I guessed. One guess is all it took."

"I see. So if I guess, then you'll tell me."

"This is a stupid game, Kat."

"It's simply seeking a bit of equity. Since—"

"Fine, fine," Shelby said impatiently. "Go ahead. One guess."

Mueller leaned back, her eyes appearing to search the inside of her skull. She chewed on her lip a moment, then leaned forward once more and looked straight into Shelby's eyes. "Captain Calhoun," she said.

Shelby did not so much as blink. Her face was a carefully maintained deadpan.

"Wrong," she said.

"Really? I was sure—"

"Wrong."

Mueller shrugged. "All right. Keep it to yourself, if it will make you happy."

It did not, in fact, make Shelby happy at all. And she was beginning to wonder if anything ever would.

Burgoyne was having trouble sleeping as well.

Unlike Shelby, however, s/he had no idea in the least what was causing it. S/he felt a vague uneasiness in hir stomach, but was at a loss to determine what was wrong. S/he reviewed the contents of what s/he had eaten that day, but it hadn't been anything unusual. So it likely wasn't food poisoning. It could be some sort of virus or bug, but the symptoms seemed so free floating. One moment there was a discomfort in hir stomach, the next it was an achiness in hir joints. "Computer," s/he said at one point, "am I running a fever?"

"Scanning," said the computer, and then after a moment, said, "Negative. Your present body temperature is well within Hermat norms."

"Atmosphere control: Room temperature at requested standard?"

"Affirmative."

Yet s/he felt clammy. It was nothing but confusing to hir. Finally some instinct prompted hir to sit up and say, "Burgoyne to Selar."

There was a long pause, with no response. "Burgoyne to Selar," s/he repeated.

"Burgoyne," came Selar's tired voice, "do you have any notion what time it is?"

"I'm not feeling well and I don't know why."

"You are in luck. There is this brand new invention called 'sickbay.' It is staffed with another new invention, called a 'night shift.' Go complain to them."

"I was wondering if . . ." Burgoyne wished that Selar

was with hir instead of simply being a disembodied voice over the intercom. "I was wondering if it might be connected to you somehow."

"That is very unlikely. Go to sickbay or go to sleep. Either way. But leave me alone."

"Selar, perhaps—"

"Burgoyne," and there was a faintly dangerous edge to her voice, "as much as you enjoy the pleasure of my company: If you make me come down there, I will kill you. Is that clear?"

The word "but" died aborning in Burgoyne's mouth. Instead s/he rather wisely said, "Clear."

"Excellent. Good night."

With Selar's voice gone, Burgoyne leaned back in hir bed, moaned softly as hir stomach ached, and then rolled over as best s/he could and went back to a fitful sleep.

## V.

CALHOUN LOOKED UP FROM HIS DESK in the ready room as Shelby walked in and stood there, her hands draped behind her. "You wished to see me, Captain?" she asked.

"Yes," he sighed. He took a deep breath, rose, and said, "Commander . . . I wish to apologize, formally and for the record, for my inappropriate behavior of the other day. Our previous relationship prompted me to act incorrectly in this relationship. If you wish to file formal charges or grievances with Starfleet, I will freely admit to the—"

"Oh, Mac, please, knock it off," she said. "Why are you saying all this?"

"Because it is the right thing to say in accordance with regulations when one has given offense in the manner that I believe I did," Calhoun told her, "and since you've always been someone with great respect for the regs, I knew you'd appreciate it if I attended to them in this instance."

She actually laughed softly. "Because you do it so infrequently, you mean?"

"Partly, yes."

"Mac," she said, "we have history. I took this position knowing that, and knowing that it might come up someday in our . . . interactions. And I know that you've been under a good deal of stress lately. You've held up under it well with your usual blend of stoicism and smart-ass remarks, but I know that Xyon's presence has been very difficult for you. Is it something you want to talk about?" she asked solicitously.

"At the moment I'm too busy being stoic," he said. "But when I'm feeling sharper, perhaps then I will."

"Okay. Well, the point is . . . I'm not dwelling on it."

"You're not?"

"No. I haven't given it a moment's thought since it happened. It's not like I'm losing sleep over it."

"Well, that's . . ." He smiled. "That's good to hear. I think we have a fairly solid working relationship here, Commander. I would hate to think I'd jeopardized it."

"You haven't. Don't give it another thought."

She extended a hand then, and he shook it firmly.

And that was when they heard the massive sneeze. They looked at each other and Calhoun said, "What was that?"

Suddenly Kebron's voice filtered through. "Captain . . . Kebron here. Your attention, please."

"Right there, Mr. Kebron."

"We're on final approach for Fenner," said Shelby as Calhoun came around the desk. "It's probably in regard to that. Let's hope it's not too big a problem."

"We can hope it, but let's expect that it is."

They walked out onto the bridge and Kebron said, without preamble, "Captain, long range sensors have detected—"

From his command chair in the center of the bridge, Calhoun put up a hand to momentarily quiet Kebron. "Let me guess," he said. "A Redeemer war vessel."

"Yes, sir."

Shelby turned to Calhoun and said, "Good guess, sir."

"It wasn't a guess. Are we close enough for a visual?"

"Puddin it onscreen, Cabdin," said Robin Lefler from ops.

Calhoun and Shelby both turned to Lefler, and Calhoun was mildly appalled at what he saw. Her eyes were puffy, the edges of her nose red and crusting. Her lips were chapped. "Good lord, what's happened to you, Ensign?"

"Nothin, Cabdin. Uhm fine."

"You're not fine. You look like an elephant sat on your face."

"Very colorful description, Captain," Shelby said, wincing.

"Ids juza liddle cold."

"Well, look at her, for pity's sake! The poor woman can barely breathe. Ensign, get down to sickbay."

"Uhm nod sick," she said stubbornly.

From conn, Mark McHenry said, "I've been telling her to clear out of here; she wouldn't listen to me, sir. If she were any more in denial, she'd be Cleopatra."

There were blank stares from everyone on the bridge.

"Denial. The Nile," McHenry explained. "Cleopatra was Queen of—"

"We get it, Lieutenant," said Shelby. "We're just not sure why you thought it was funny."

"Lefler, get out of here, now. That's an order," said Calhoun, having had enough. "Boyajian, take over at ops."

Lefler tried to protest, but momentarily choked on a wad of phlegm and thus was unable to put forward anything approaching a convincing argument. Giving in to the inevitable, she got up from her post and headed into the turbolift. Meanwhile, Boyajian eased into the ops station and moments later an image of Fenner appeared on the screen.

"Where is . . ." began Calhoun, but then he pointed. "I see it. Right there."

Moving in slow orbit around the planet, and coming into view from the other side, was a Redeemer vessel.

Calhoun gave a low whistle and said, "Big son of a bitch. If Burgoyne wasn't happy about the prospect of going into battle with a standard Redeemer warship, s/he's really going to hate this. Soleta, give me a full scan. Are there any others around?"

Soleta fed the tactical array through her science station. "No, sir."

"Any possibly hanging in warp space? Or with a cloak?"

"Not detecting any approaching vessels. No emissions outputs that would suggest a cloak."

"Still," Kebron added gravely, "anything's possible."

"I know."

"Captain, it's breaking out of orbit. Heading for us at a slow intercept course."

"Slow, Mr. Boyajian?"

"She's not moving in any sort of aggressive manner,

sir. We are not targeted, nor are they running weapons hot. They're just . . . heading this way."

"To let us know that they've spotted us," suggested Shelby.

Calhoun nodded. "And we've spotted them. So far, we're even. Mr. Kebron, take us to yellow alert. I won't take the first aggressive action, but I'm sure as hell going to be prepared."

"Going to yellow alert, aye," affirmed Kebron. Within moments, the entire ship was at a state of preparedness. The shields were on line, although none of the phasers or photon torpedos had been brought to bear.

"Scan their ship. Do they have sufficient fire power to overwhelm us?" asked Calhoun.

"Short answer: Yes," said Kebron after a moment.

Out of curiosity, Calhoun asked, "What's the long answer?"

"Yes, sir."

"Ah."

"Their weapons still remain offline," said Soleta from her station. "They're not doing anything threatening. In point of fact, we're taking the more threatening posture at the moment."

"Possibly because we feel more threatened," commented Shelby.

"Nor have they raised shields," said Soleta. "Thus far they've yet to take any offensive or defensive action at all."

"Sir," Kebron said abruptly. "We're being hailed by the Redeemer vessel."

"Are we now? How very interesting. All right, Lieutenant. Put them onscreen. Let's see what they have to say."

The screen wavered for a moment . . . and then Calhoun was looking at someone who had a face so dark it was almost obsidian, and red eyes that seemed to glow with an almost unholy fire. "Captain Mackenzie Calhoun," he said. He was speaking so softly that Calhoun had to strain to hear. He had a feeling that was the point.

"I'm Captain Calhoun. And you are . . . ?"

"I . . . am the Overlord of the Redeemers."

Shelby and Calhoun exchanged glances. There was clear surprise on her face. "The Overlord himself," said Calhoun. "You are the leader of the Redeemers, as I recall."

"That is correct."

"Should I feel honored . . . or worried?"

"A bit of both." Something resembling a smile actually passed over the Overlord's face. "As I'm sure your very capable instrumentation has already informed you, we are not approaching you in any sort of aggressive fashion. I was hoping that we might . . . talk."

"We are talking."

"In person."

Calhoun could feel all eyes from the bridge crew upon him. "In person?"

"Yes. Face to face. My shuttle vessel stands ready to bring me and my entourage over to you."

"It is my understanding," Calhoun said slowly, "that such an action can have a certain degree of risk attached to it. I seem to recall, for example, that if the blood of a Redeemer is spilled, that releases a virus capable of wiping out an entire planet's population in a fairly short time. How do I know that such a device wouldn't be brought aboard the ship. You may be simply endeavoring to destroy us in a new and simplified manner."

"I appreciate your caution and borderline paranoia, Captain."

"There's an old saying, Overlord: Just because you're paranoid doesn't mean someone isn't out to get you."

"I daresay. Indeed, I daresay. Very well, then. It is my understanding that your matter transport devices are equipped with an array of screens designed to detect and eliminate any such potentially hazardous contagions. Instead of coming to you in my shuttle vessel— as decorum would dictate—I shall allow myself and my associates to be brought over via your transporter. Before rematerializing us, you can scan our molecular make-up for any inappropriate viruses or similar contagions that could present a threat to you." He smiled once more. It was not a comforting facial expression. "I am bearing all the risk now, captain. After all, once I am in the grip of your transporter beams, I am entirely at your mercy. You could disperse our molecules over half the sector if you took a mind to. Deal the Redeemers a devastating blow by doing away with their leader with just the touch of a transporter control. If I am willing to incur risks, should you not be willing to as well? Particularly considering that—admit it—you are intrigued to know why I would want to meet with you."

"That is certainly true enough," said Calhoun. "All right, Overlord. I think a face-to-face meeting can be arranged. Provided you tell me, ahead of time, what the reason for the meeting is."

"That is simple. The reason is nothing less than the preservation of the Redeemer race . . . and it is entirely possible that only you can help us."

\* \* \*

"Let them die!"

It was the fifth time that Si Cwan had said that in as many minutes. He was walking down the corridor next to Calhoun, with Shelby on the other side of the captain. "Do you have any idea how much strife those obsidian bastards have caused the Thallonians? Going around space, converting people to worship of their precious Xant on pain of death. They're monsters! And if they're in some sort of trouble, then we would be monsters for helping them."

"And eighty years ago, the Klingon homeworld underwent an ecological disaster, prompting them to launch a major peace initiative," Shelby pointed out. "And there were lots of people in the Federation who were saying the exact same thing you are right now, Ambassador. But the Klingons wound up becoming the staunchest allies the Federation ever knew. And the lesson to be learned from that—"

"Is that you were all damned lucky. The Klingons could just as easily have used the respite to rebuild their empire and attack you with newer and greater aggressiveness. Just because you were fortunate once doesn't mean you should count on it again. Besides, it was one thing when the entirety of the Klingon Empire was approaching the entirety of the Federation. This is the entirety of the Redeemers, incarnated in their supreme leader, approaching a lone ship who has proven to be a source of constant irritation and embarrassment. There is no upside here, Captain. Either it's a trick that we're falling into, or else they really do need our help, in which case we'd be fools to provide it."

"I'm going to listen to them, Si Cwan. It's about time that you dealt with that fact. Just because I'm listening, however, doesn't mean I'm throwing caution to the wind. So calm down."

Si Cwan rolled his eyes. "Madness. It is madness."

They entered the transporter room and stopped. Zak Kebron was standing there, arms folded. "Lieutenant, how did you get here before us?" asked Calhoun. "You left the bridge a few moments after us." This was not unusual practice for Kebron; because of his bulk, he did not fit comfortably in the turbolift with others and avoided it if he could.

"I hurried," said Kebron.

Shelby cast a confused glance at transporter chief Polly Watson, who smiled and shook her head. "He contacted me from the bridge and asked me to beam him down here."

"She lies," Kebron said archly.

Calhoun didn't pursue it.

Standing next to Watson was Burgoyne, who inclined hir head in greeting. Burgoyne's presence didn't surprise Calhoun at all. Whenever there was anything unusual in the offing for a transport, Burgoyne tended to be present.

"Well, Watson?" asked Calhoun. "Have we heard from the Redeemers?"

From behind the transporter controls, she said briskly, "I have their coordinates, sir. Ready to beam them over."

"Where's Dr. Selar?"

The door hissed open and Selar stepped slowly in. Calhoun looked at her. She looked like an overripe melon. He did not, however, say that. "Thank you for joining us, Doctor." He noticed that although Burgoyne wasn't taking hir eyes off Selar, the doctor was barely glancing at hir. Trouble in paradise, it seemed.

She nodded, and then said, "Understand this caveat, Captain: I have had no opportunity to perform detailed research of Redeemer physiology. I can provide some degree of guidance, but there are no absolutes in this instance."

"You're saying that if somehow they trick us and, within minutes of their showing up on this vessel, we're all dead . . . don't come crying to you about it."

"That is basically correct, yes."

"Your 'caveat' is duly noted, Doctor. All right, Watson. Commence beam-over."

If she had the notion that she might well be beaming over something that would destroy everyone on the ship, she didn't give any indication of it. Instead Watson simply said, "Energizing."

The transporter beams hummed to life and the pads flickered in their customary fashion. And then, after a few moments, Watson said, "All right . . . freezing the transport, as ordered. They're in stasis." Burgoyne checked the readings and nodded hir approval.

Calhoun and Shelby stepped aside as Selar waddled to the pattern scanners. "All right . . . let us see what we have."

"Bio readings coming through now."

Selar's eyes narrowed as she took it all in. "There are three of them," she said after a moment. "Hmm. Interesting physiology. I will probably want to study these at my leisure. Their circulatory system is—"

"With all respect, Doctor, is this remotely pertinent to the issue at hand?" asked Shelby.

"Very likely not." She studied the patterns for what seemed a very long time. But no one was inclined to rush her. Not for a matter of such significance, at any rate. "Keeping in mind the cautions I presented to you earlier . . . I do not detect, anywhere in their bodies, any sort of organism or entity that could be interpreted as a virus. Not in any form, active or inactive."

"So you think we can materialize them here and be safe."

"No, I think you can reassemble them in the heart of the Fennerian sun and be safe. If you bring them on, there remains a risk of something that I have overlooked. Not that I do not appreciate your putting this much pressure on me, Captain, that the likelihood of whether everyone on this ship will live or die is resting largely on my say-so. That is, after all, why I have taken on this position. To provide expert advice while commanding officers try to determine whether they should risk the lives of all aboard."

There was dead silence for a moment. Calhoun glanced warily at Shelby. She shrugged.

"All right . . . thank you for your insight, Doctor," Calhoun told her. "Let's bring them aboard, Watson."

"Aye, sir."

The transporter beams shimmered to life once more after having kept the Redeemers in stasis, and the three of them appeared on the transporter pad.

For a moment, Calhoun thought that the time in stasis had had some sort of adverse effect on them, or perhaps Watson had simply screwed up. For the Redeemers had to be the shortest master race he had ever met. The Overlord barely came to Calhoun's chest.

"Greetings," said the Overlord. "Did you do as I suggested, Captain? Keep us in stasis and scan us?"

"Yes, we did."

"Impressive. For us the process was instantaneous. This," he indicated the Redeemer to his right, "is my assistant, Prime One. And this is a nameless retainer."

"I see. Well, we here on the *Excalibur* all have names. This is Commander Elizabeth Shelby. This is Doctor Selar, our chief medical officer. Zak Kebron, head of security. Chief Engineer Burgoyne 172. Transporter chief Polly Watson. And this is—"

"Lord Si Cwan." The Overlord had bowed slightly to each of them in turn, but to Si Cwan he bowed the most deeply. "We have had dealings in the past. I see that you have turned to this vessel for aid, Lord Cwan, just as we have done. On that basis, I imagine that you can be expected to be sympathetic to our cause."

"I would rejoice in the annihilation of your race," Si Cwan said.

Calhoun sighed inwardly.

"Your antipathy is understandable, Lord Cwan." The Overlord studied Selar for a moment. "By the distention of the middle of your body, can I take it to indicate that you are with child?"

"Yes."

"I'm the father," Burgoyne said, sounding rather cheerful about it. Selar remained stoic, as always, but Calhoun thought he detected a slight rolling of her eyes.

Then, to Calhoun's surprise, the Overlord suddenly put one hand on Selar's stomach and the other on Burgoyne's shoulder. Kebron took a quick step forward, clearly concerned over some sort of attack, but the Overlord closed his eyes and said mildly, "May the wisdom of Xant be given this child. May he bring pride to you in all his future endeavors." He removed his hands then and bowed once more in Selar's direction, then Burgoyne's, and then turned to Calhoun and said,

"What good comes from anything that we do . . . unless there is a new generation to do it for? Don't you agree, Captain?"

Thoughts of Xyon briefly crossed his mind, and then he pushed them away. "Absolutely," he said. "If you wouldn't mind coming this way, Overlord . . . do you have a name, by the way, other than your title?"

"We have no names, in that our individuality does not matter. All that is significant is what position we hold relative to our service of Xant. I am the Overlord. Prime One is my prime assistant. That is all that is required. And as for the individual Redeemers, nothing more is required than that they know that they are Redeemers."

"A simple 'no' would have sufficed, but I appreciate the insight. This way, then. Commander Shelby, if you wouldn't mind conducting our little group to the conference lounge on deck nine?"

Calhoun made certain that he hung toward the back with Si Cwan, and as they headed toward the conference lounge, he said in a low voice, " 'I would rejoice in the annihilation of your race'? What the hell was that about?"

"It is how I feel."

"*Grozit*, Cwan, I don't give a damn how you feel. Your function on this ship, such as it is, is as an ambassador of good will. No matter how much you may personally dislike the Redeemers—no matter how much I may dislike them—the bottom line is, Shelby is right. They represent, at the moment, potential allies, and our mission to provide aid and relief in this sector of space becomes that much easier if they're with us than if they're against us."

"You do not understand, Captain, and there is nothing more that I can say that will make you understand. But you will. Sooner or later—most likely sooner—the Redeemers will make you understand. Let us simply hope that it is not too late when that happens."

Shelby had to admit it; the Overlord certainly had a knack for looking imperial. He sat in a common, ordinary chair in the conference lounge in such a way that he made it look like a throne. And he, the imperious king, belonged there. Prime One and the nameless Redeemer stood on either side. When Shelby had indicated that they should sit, they politely shook their heads but said nothing else otherwise.

Grouped around the table were Calhoun, Kebron, Si Cwan (who never took his gaze off the Overlord, as if expecting him to pull a weapon at any moment) and Soleta. Soleta had actually had a brush with the Redeemers many years before. Of all the Starfleet personnel on the ship, only Soleta had spent any extensive time in Thallonian space, exploring the region surreptitiously back when it was still closed to outsiders. She had been on a world that was converted by the Redeemers and had had the opportunity to see them at work close up. To hear her tell of it, they had functioned with ruthless efficiency. The Redeemers in action, according to Soleta, were a terror to behold. Yet she was able to sit one seat away from the Overlord of the Redeemers and look at him with such a bland expression that Shelby couldn't help but admire her *sangfroid*. Sometimes she wondered if it wouldn't do her some good to go to Vulcan and study there for a couple of years.

"All right, Overlord," Calhoun said, leaning back in his chair, "you have all our attention. So why don't you—"

The door hissed open and Shelby, as did the others, looked up in surprise. Standing there were Xyon and Kalinda. Shelby noticed that Kalinda's hand had, a split second earlier, been brushing against Xyon's, but now they were simply next to each other.

"Hello," Xyon said evenly. "I was hoping, if it wouldn't be too much trouble, that we might be able to sit in on this meeting."

"May I ask why you feel your presence is necessary?" asked Calhoun.

"Well, it so happens that of everyone in this room, we had the most recent experience with the Redeemers . . . including this gentleman right here," said Xyon, indicating the Overlord. He was smiling in an excessively polite fashion . . . so much so, that Shelby immediately sensed danger. "As a matter of fact . . . he tried to kill me. Thought he did so, in fact. Left me for dead. Isn't that right, Overlord? And tortured Kalinda as well. That's right too, isn't it?"

There was a deathly silence and then the Overlord said, quite coolly, "Yes. That is right. Although the young lady was somewhat paler at the time."

"You torture my sister . . . try to kill the son of our captain. . . . and now you sit here looking for this ship to help you out of a problem?" said Si Cwan, barely containing his anger.

The Overlord never came close to losing his composure. "I did not know them for who they were . . . at least, not at first. Nor, obviously, did I know that I would at some point require your assistance. Had I been aware of any of this, then naturally I would likely had done some things differently. It is too late to go back. We can only go forward."

"Xyon . . . Kalinda . . . you may stay, if you keep in mind that you are here as guests," Calhoun said. "And you will be expected to conduct yourselves as such. Understood?"

They nodded and took seats as far from the Overlord as possible. Shelby imagined that she could feel the temperature in the room dropping a good thirty degrees. She wouldn't have been surprised if her breath started coming out of her mouth as mist.

"As I was saying," continued Calhoun, "why don't you tell us what this is about, Overlord, and we'll see how perhaps we can be of service to one another."

"I will come right to the point," said the Overlord, although coming to the point didn't stop him from pausing, possibly for dramatic effect. "The Black Mass is migrating toward our homeworld."

Shelby had the feeling that this was something that should have had a tremendous impact on her, from the way that the Overlord was saying it. Unfortunately, she had absolutely no clue what he was talking about.

But then she saw Si Cwan stiffen, looking as if he'd been stunned with a cattle prod. Kalinda likewise had a strong reaction, and even Soleta looked perturbed.

"All right," Calhoun said slowly. "Who wants to fill me in?"

"It is . . . a terrible thing," said Si Cwan, and from the gravity of his tone, it was clear to Shelby that he was speaking from first-hand experience. "I saw them . . . it . . . once, many years ago. It is horrible. I wouldn't wish it on anyone."

"On almost anyone," Kalinda said, firing a resentful look at the Overlord. The Overlord ignored it.

"And what would them, or it, be precisely?"

"Precisely, Captain . . . no one is quite certain," Soleta said. "The Black Mass is a 'thing,' for lack of a better phrase. It is either a single creature or millions of smaller creatures combined into one great creature; no one is quite certain, and descriptions vary. It resides in an area of space colloquially known as the Hunger Zone, situated in the outskirts of Thallonian space. Computer, Section Alpha Zed Eighty-three."

On the screen on the wall of the conference lounge, a sector of Thallonian space came up. Shelby was immediately struck by how little was charted.

"Think of it as the Marianas Trench of Thallonian space," continued Soleta. "Any endeavors to explore there have been unsuccessful. Probes have been disabled . . ."

"Eaten," said Si Cwan.

"Whatever," Soleta told him. "The point is, no scientific investigation of the nature of the Black Mass has ever been made."

"How big is it?"

"As big as it needs to be, Captain," said Si Cwan. "I saw it consume an entire world."

"An entire world?" said Shelby. "Si Cwan, you said you were a child at the time. Is it possible you're misremembering . . . ?"

"No. It is not. Nor will I forget when it ate the sun . . ."

There were outright sounds of skepticism then from Zak Kebron, and even Calhoun seemed incredulous. "A *sun?* You mean an entire star? Some entity actually ate an entire star?"

It was rare that Shelby saw Calhoun quite that doubtful, but she had to admit that she understood why he was reacting with such astonishment. The concepts that they were describing seemed not only beyond the realm of possibility, but beyond comprehension. "How can something eat a star?" Shelby said.

"If you come to Tulaan IV, you will be able to ask the Black Mass yourself," said the Overlord dryly.

"I must say that what we are hearing," said Soleta, "is in fact consistent with anecdotal evidence. Not only what others have said, but what I myself have observed. I went to one site that was allegedly assaulted by the Black Mass. My charts indicated that there was supposed to be a star there . . . but there was nothing. I think it difficult to misplace an entire star, don't you?"

"I'm sure that the vessel I was on as a youth recorded the event," said Si Cwan, "but naturally obtaining such records will be a bit problematic, considering my homeworld was devoured by a gigantic flaming bird. And might I add, captain, that since you witnessed such an unlikely event with your own eyes, you be a little less quick to question the likelihood of that which you consider 'beyond comprehension.' "

"Point taken," admitted Calhoun. "All right . . . just for the sake of argument . . . let's say this thing is real. It comes out of this Hunger Zone whenever it feels like it, eats whatever it feels like, and then disappears into the Hunger Zone for . . . ?"

"There is no set time. Years," said Si Cwan.

"We keep watch on the Hunger Zone, just as we keep watch on many things that have impact on our sector," said the Overlord. "We detected the Black Mass swarming from the Hunger Zone, and we tracked its trajectory. By calculating its present course, we found that it will make contact with Tulaan IV and, presumably, devour it—and, equally presumably, our sun—possibly within days."

"But I'm looking at where the Hunger Zone is . . . and I know basically where your homeworld is," said Calhoun. "Travelling at sublight speeds, it would take years for this—"

"Not years. It moves at warp speeds."

"Oh, come on!" Even Shelby was finding it impossible to deal with everything that was being tossed at her. "A biological creature travelling at faster than the speed of light? And yes, yes, I know, the damned Great Bird moved faster than the speed of light, but I would have liked to think that was a one-time occurrence, not something that was routine."

"You may think whatever you wish," said the Overlord. "The point is, this is what is going to be happening, and this is the difficulty with which we are faced."

"So you're saying that you want us to help prevent this Black Mass from destroying your world."

"Impossible," said Si Cwan flatly. "Nothing can stop the Black Mass. Nothing. I suggest that if your planet is targeted, you leave. Believe me, there are others who did not have such an opportunity. I watched them die."

"Now wait a minute," said Calhoun. "What happened then, and what might happen now, is not necessarily the same thing. Perhaps we can do something."

"We can't," Si Cwan said.

"We have been known to be fairly resourceful, Ambassador, from time to time," said Shelby, but she was starting to wonder. From everything she was hearing about this Black Mass, she was beginning to question just what one starship could possibly do. A fleet, perhaps . . .

"The Black Mass must be destroyed," said the Overlord. There did not seem to be any sign of compromise in his tone.

"Wait one moment," said Shelby. "If this is a sentient being, we can't just go in with guns blazing . . ."

"It wouldn't matter if we did," Si Cwan said again.

"We're not murderers," Shelby continued. "That's not what Starfleet is all about. We would—"

"You would what?" It was Prime One who had spoken. Then he hesitated, but a nod from the Overlord clearly encouraged him. "Try to converse with the Black Mass? Strike up a chat? Endeavor to talk it out of its intentions? Commander, with all respect, you speak thus because you have not witnessed the Black Mass in action. If you had, you would know that any such efforts would be doomed to failure."

"Starfleet has a Prime Directive, doesn't it?"

It was Xyon who had spoken, and all eyes turned to him. Kalinda looked mildly amused. "For someone who seemed to have no interest in Starfleet, you seem rather conversant with its rules," she said.

"A Prime Directive," continued Xyon, "that says you cannot interfere. Correct?"

"Yes," said Calhoun evenly.

"If this Black Mass is, in fact, some sort of sentient creature . . . I don't see where you can interfere with it, then. It's just going about its business. And if the Redeemers are having problems, why then, it's the Redeemers' problems. Can't interfere with that either. Way I see it, you don't have a choice. You have to stay out of it."

There were looks passed around the table. "He brings up a valid point," Shelby said.

"A valid point?" said the Overlord. "Nonsense. There is no rule that says Starfleet must stand by when there is an invasion of another world. That is what this is. An invasion."

"But Tulaan IV is not a world that we necessarily need care about," Calhoun pointed out. "It is populated—with all respect—by a race who has shown itself time and again to be very aggressive."

"And you have shown yourself, time and again, Captain, to be someone who does what he feels needs to be done, regardless of rules. I am aware of your activities, and any number of them fall outside the parameters of your Prime Directive," said the Overlord. "You can help . . . if you want to."

"And why should he want to?" Xyon said, and there was no mistaking the anger in his voice.

"It is not your concern, boy," said the Overlord. "And I suggest you hold your tongue, lest I be forced to teach you another lesson in manners."

Xyon's anger was clearly bubbling over. He was out of his chair and he took a step toward the Overlord. "You son of a—"

The Overlord spoke then. He said a word. Shelby didn't hear it.

Xyon apparently did. He staggered, grabbed at his ears, cried out and slammed back against a wall.

Shelby was half out of her seat, as was Kebron. Calhoun, however, never came close to losing his cool. Instead he was watching with keen interest.

Slowly, Xyon staggered to his feet. He brought his gaze up level with the Overlord . . .

. . . and then he laughed. The pain he appeared to be feeling, the agony that had supposedly thrown him around were gone, just like that.

The Overlord's face dropped in surprise. He spoke again, and once again, Shelby didn't hear him, which was odd because she was looking right at him. This time Xyon didn't move at all. Instead he made a fairly grotesque face and then uttered some odd noises.

"All right, that's enough, Xyon." Calhoun looked rather amused, both at his son's theatrics and also at the look of pure astonishment on the Overlord.

"Thank you for allowing me to test that, Captain. His expression upon realizing his impotence was very small payback . . . but it was something, nevertheless."

"Thank you, Xyon. And you, Lieutenant," he said to Soleta. Soleta nodded in acknowledgment.

Shelby was utterly clueless as to what had just happened. "Captain . . ." she began.

"The Overlord," Calhoun said by way of explanation, "has access to a most . . . curious form of offense, according to Xyon. Certain words, ancient words, that apparently trigger painful and aggressive synaptic responses. However, everything we hear the Overlord say, naturally, is translated for us via the instantaneous translators that are fairly standard issue throughout all of known space." He tapped his ear. "So once Xyon told me of this, I took the liberty of having Soleta reprogram all of the ones worn by *Excalibur* personnel—and by Xyon—through the central computer. The translator is essentially acting as a screening device. When it encounters a word that has no direct analog—one that is not known to modern linguistics—it disrupts the word's sonic frequency before it reaches your inner ear. As a result, the brain never hears it, and no damage is done. So you see, Overlord . . . whatever tricks you intended to pull, whatever pain you intended to inflict upon me or other members of this ship . . . it's not going to happen. Now then, Overlord," and he leaned forward, his hands on the table, his fingers interlaced, "what are you going to do to convince us to help you?"

Shelby figured that she should have been angry at Calhoun, perhaps even furious. She hated when he did this sort of thing: Embarked on some sort of strategy without bothering to let her know. She had complained about it to him repeatedly. He had always apologized, promised it would never happen again . . . and then had done it anyway. It was becoming tiresome for her, and she wondered whether she should just stop saying anything about it.

Or whether she should just quit.

She pushed the thoughts out of her mind as being inappropriate to the matter at hand.

"Convince you to help us?" asked the Overlord. "Do you need convincing? You were sent by Starfleet to extend humanitarian aid where needed. We are in need. Was there anything in your mandate that allowed you, or encouraged you, to judge who was, and who was not, worthy of aid in your eyes? Who are you to judge?"

"Coming from the Redeemers, that is almost amusing," said Si Cwan.

The Overlord did not even bother to continue looking at Si Cwan. Instead the level gaze of those red eyes remained entirely on Calhoun.

Shelby was, by that point in her career, quite accustomed to dealing with members of races other than her own. She did not habitually hold them up against humanity and set standards for them. That would have been inappropriate for someone who was a member of Starfleet. Nevertheless, she felt a chill in her spine as she looked into the eyes of the Overlord, for in them she saw something very, very inhuman.

"Well, Captain?" asked the Overlord. "You haven't answered my question. Who are you to judge?"

"The captain of the *Excalibur*," replied Calhoun, "with resources that are admittedly a bit limited, but discretion that is nearly unlimited. There's an old Xenexian saying that I think is especially appropriate at this time, Overlord: You plow my field, I'll plow yours. You want me to save your homeworld. All well and good. But it's not as if your people have gone from world to world, spreading good will and cheer. I don't reject the notion out of hand of saving your homeworld . . . but lives are not at stake. You could evacuate if need be."

"It is to our homeworld that Xant will return when he comes back from the beyond. We must wait for him there. We have no choice. If the Black Mass are not stopped, then we will be on Tulaan IV, waiting to the last. And if that last, for whatever reason, determines that we are devoured along with our world, then we will trust that Xant's will has been done. However, obviously living is preferable to dying. Given our choices, we would opt for the former."

"All right," Calhoun nodded. "I can respect that. But I, unlike you, have a choice. In terms of the Prime Directive, I think we're on shaky ground. An argument could probably be made for either side . . . correct, Commander?"

Shelby nodded. "I can provide both, if you wish, Captain."

"That shouldn't be necessary. Hopefully, the Overlord will be able to present the convincing argument."

"And how," the Overlord inquired, "would I go about doing that?" The edges of his mouth actually seemed to be turning up. Shelby was trying to figure out whether he thought the entire thing amusing somehow.

"Tell me why I should dedicate the resources of this vessel to saving the Redeemers."

"I am afraid I do not understand."

There were glances around the table, as everyone there knew perfectly well where the captain was going with the conversation. "Very well, I'll spell it out for you," said Calhoun.

"That might be best, yes."

"As much as you regard yourselves as some sort of religious do-gooders, forcing conversion upon unwilling worlds in order to prepare them for the return of your god, the fact is that most people—including me—regard you as little more than terrorists. So if you desire the aid of the *Excalibur,* and want to keep your homeworld in one piece, then you are going to have to change your way of life."

"Are we?" Something flickered in those red eyes that Shelby didn't like.

"Yes. You will have to cease and desist in your attacks on worlds in the former Thallonian space, now known as Sector 221-G. Those worlds which you have forcibly converted to your religion, you are to leave in peace. You are to withdraw your forces, your high priests, anything that poses a danger to those worlds and their populations, and allow them to go on about their lives in whatever manner they were pursuing before you got your hooks into them."

"Is that all?"

Calhoun said sharply, "This is a difficult situation—"

"I'm sorry, Captain, but I beg to differ with you," the Overlord said, interrupting. His hands were flat on the table, and he was smiling and shaking his head, with the air of someone who knows that someone else simply doesn't understand what should be an easily comprehensible set of circumstances. "This is not difficult at all. We of the Redeemers are not going to change our method of operation, our way of life, in the slightest. We perform holy work. We operate in accordance with the desires and writings of Xant. We can no more deviate from our mandated duties than you can change the pattern of your heartbeat."

"Actually, I can change the pattern of my heartbeat, if I'm of a mind to," said Calhoun, "but that's not the point."

Prime One spoke up once more. "Our dictates and rules are not quite as fluid as yours, Captain."

"It's not a matter of fluidity . . ."

"Ah, but it is. Your Prime Directive states that you must not interfere with the natural order of societies. Yet that is precisely what you would do with us. We do what our upbringing and teachings mandate that we do, and you would have us abandon those. For what? For self-preservation? Simply to save our lives, we must betray that which we hold most sacred? Not only do you have no familiarity with our way of life, but I begin to wonder if you have any grasp of your own."

And Shelby heard her own voice say, "Oh, go to hell."

Slowly all heads turned at the table, focusing on her. Shelby, for her part, couldn't believe she had said it. It was as if someone had told her id to blurt out whatever was on its mind. Because the fact was that the Prime One had a valid point. If they were going to adhere to the Prime Directive, follow the absolute letter of it, then they really should leave the Redeemers to their fate. But if they were willing to bend the Prime Directive to the degree that they were dictating policy to the Redeemers as to how they should live their lives . . .

. . . well, you couldn't have it both ways.

Her mind racing, she tried to analyze why she had said that which had just popped into her mind, and subsequently her mouth. And for the first time in a long time, Elizabeth Shelby spoke from passion, off the top of her head, rather than the careful and measured consideration that she usually gave to matters of such importance.

"Look . . . there are some things in this universe that are right, and some that are wrong," she said, thumping one hand down for "right" and "wrong" to emphasize them. "And going around to different worlds and forcing your views on them, under pain of death . . . it's just . . . just wrong." The Overlord was about to reply, but she kept right on going. "And if we save your world, your way of life, and you just go right on doing what you're doing, then every single world that falls prey to your self-styled messianic complexes, why, it's . . . it's as if we're endorsing what you're doing. Because we will have enabled you to keep on doing it. We'll be aiding and abetting you in doing something that we find unconscionable and that, sir . . . is also unconscionable. So you see our predicament here."

There was a long moment of silence, and then Calhoun slowly nodded, smiling. "Well said, Commander. You've summed up my feelings on the matter rather well."

"So what you are saying, then," the Overlord said thoughtfully, "is that you are lacking personal motivation."

"We're saying," Xyon cut in, "that you and this

Black Mass deserve each other. Why should we give any more of a damn about your fate than you gave about mine? Or Kalinda's?"

"The young man speaks accurately," said Calhoun. "Out of turn, but accurately. The fate of the Redeemers—to be blunt—is not my concern."

"Well . . . I appreciate your candor, Captain," said the Overlord. "Allow me, then, to be candid in turn. Let us discuss the people of Fenner a moment . . ."

"Let me guess," Calhoun theorized. "At the point where the Fennerians contacted us, you were already here. You promised them something in exchange for their summoning us."

"Very good," said the Overlord, and there was that frosty smile again. "To be specific, we promised them that we would never come to their world for the purpose of converting them. To be honest, the leadership of the Fennerians was so frightened of us, that they likely would have promised us their moons and star in exchange for whatever they asked. Odd, isn't it? Some individuals fear knowledge so greatly that they will do anything to remain ignorant."

"They don't fear knowledge. They fear loss of independence. Loss of themselves, and to be consumed by the 'greatness' that is the Redeemer worldview," said Calhoun.

"Be that as it may," said the Overlord, "and whatever it is that they may or may not fear . . . we will keep our word. We have no intention of redeeming them. However, we said nothing about allowing them to live."

There was another silence in the conference lounge, but there was an air of menace to this one.

"A high priest," guessed Calhoun.

"Very good!" said the Overlord, obviously impressed. "As of this moment, one of my High Priests is in hiding on the planet Fenner. At specific intervals, I will contact him and tell him that matters regarding the preservation of our species are proceeding apace. If he does not hear from me, he has orders to slit his own throat. This will, naturally, terminate his life. But if our world comes to an end, he would not want to live beyond us anyway. So predeceasing us is something of a mercy, you see. An honor. Once he takes his life in this violent manner, that will trigger the virus that all High Priests carry within them. Within hours, every one who lives and breathes on the planet Fenner will die."

"We can evacuate them," Si Cwan began, turning to Calhoun.

"There are, last I checked, two billion souls on that world," the Overlord said calmly. "I was unaware that your ship had sufficient capacity to accommodate two billion individuals. Nor, I fear, do they have such capacity. In any event, it is pointless. By the time any sort of evacuation plan was under way, one of the check-in times would have passed and the High Priest will have killed himself. Plus, the High Priest is not stupid. An evacuation could not occur without his hearing about it, at which point he is under orders, once again, to end his life. The result will be the same."

"Are you telling me that you are effectively holding all the people on that world hostage?" demanded Calhoun. Shelby could see that his scar was darkening red, which was never a good sign.

"Yes, Captain. That is precisely what I am telling you. And whether you doom those people or not is entirely up to you."

Now all eyes were upon Calhoun. Aside from the

scar standing out against the tan of his skin, his face was completely inscrutable.

Every word of the Overlord's hung there, like a dark cloud. "The Fennerians are, basically, an innocent race, Captain. They have done nothing to deserve extinction and genocide, I grant you that. But these are desperate times. Since you feel that the fate of the Redeemers is not your concern . . . then likewise the Fenner should be of no concern, either. In that event . . . your decision is a simple one . . . is it not?"

# VI.

SHE FOUND HIM, as she knew she would, in his ready room, pacing it like a caged animal. She had seen Calhoun in any number of moods, but she had never seen him quite this angry. He was boiling with barely contained fury, and when he turned and she saw the darkness in his eyes, it was the first time that she had an inkling of just what his enemies saw decades ago when he faced them on the surface of Xenex. She thought what it must have been like to see those eyes in a young face, covered with blood splattered on it by previous victims, a sword in his hand and a snarl on his lips.

Not for the first time, she was glad that Calhoun was on her side.

"This is Nelkar. It's Nelkar all over again," he said.

She knew what he was referring to, of course. "No.

It's not. It's completely different. The Nelkarites were holding, as hostages, people who wouldn't have been there except that they ignored your advice and went down anyway. So your first instinct then was to abandon them to the difficulties that they had gotten themselves into. But it's not the same here. The Fennerians are innocents, caught in between forces that they've had no part in unleashing on themselves."

"You're saying I should give in?"

"You're saying you're not going to?"

He stopped pacing and leaned against the observation window of the ready room. "This isn't one of those times when I know precisely what I'm going to do, Eppy, and I'm just looking for a rubber stamp. Or even a protest that I shouldn't do something just to spur me on to go ahead and do it. I'm at a loss here."

"Which is why you want to see me and only me, rather than all your officers."

He nodded. "That's it exactly. You know me well. Sometimes too well, I think."

"What's that supposed to mean?"

"Nothing."

"It obviously means something . . . but now is hardly the time and place to pursue it."

"I agree," he said readily. "If I help the Redeemers, then theoretically—presuming that the Overlord has been honest about the threat, and will also keep his word—I am saving the Fennerians. But I'll then be dooming whatever is the next race that the Redeemers attempt to convert. What makes the Fennerians more deserving, the next race less?"

"What's the alternative, though? Casting a death sentence on two billion people?"

"I wouldn't be casting it."

"You wouldn't be stopping it when it was within your power. Doesn't that basically amount to the same thing."

"Are you saying I should help them?"

"I'm saying, Mac, that you can make yourself crazy if you consider what could and couldn't happen as an outcome of every decision you make. Yes, it's possible that the Redeemers will then go after some other races. But who's to say that we won't help that other race, and put a stop to the Redeemers at that point?"

"We can put a stop to the Redeemers at this point," he observed.

"True. But only at the cost of two billion lives."

"And the saving of how many billions more?"

"Mac, I don't pretend to have all the answers here, or even *an* answer. What I do know is that the Overlord gave us a very short time in which to make up our minds."

"Yes, I know. And the notion of knuckling under to the dictates of that undersized—"

She raised a scolding finger. "Don't let this start playing to your ego, Mac. Don't let it be about that, because if it is, then I guarantee you you'll make the wrong decision, every single time. This has got to be about what's right and what's best, not what assuages your sense of self. How you feel about 'knuckling under' has nothing to do with anything. As difficult as it may be, you have to make a decision based on the merits."

"The merits aren't very meritorious."

"I agree. But they're all you've got."

Calhoun thought about it a long moment. The scar which had been standing out so brightly against his face, indicating his anger, was fading to normal.

Then he tapped his comm badge. "McHenry. This is the captain."

"Aye, sir."

"Set course for the Tulaan star system."

"We're giving in to them?" inquired McHenry guilelessly.

"To a degree," Calhoun said, unflappable. "Calhoun out." He turned to Shelby and said quietly, "Inform the Overlord that we will accede to his requests. We will accompany his vessel to the Tulaan system, and from there move on an intercept course with the Black Mass whereupon we will see what we can do. No promises, at least until we have some idea of what it is we're facing."

"Aye, Captain. And Mac . . . for what it's worth . . . I think you're making the only decision you reasonably can."

"Thank you, Commander. Oh, and Commander . . ."

"Yes, Captain?"

He leaned against his desk and said, with a very serious expression that gave away nothing he had on his mind, "Send Ensign Janos to me, would you? I have a little chore for him."

Si Cwan wasn't sure what to expect when he swung by Robin Lefler's quarters to see how she was feeling, but he certainly wasn't expecting to be screamed at.

He rang the chime and he heard Robin's voice from inside. "Comebin," it sounded as if she had said, and so he walked in.

Robin was lying on the couch in the middle of the room. Her closed eyes were puffy, her head clearly congested, her nose red from the combination of sneezing and blowing. "Didju gedduh med'sin fum sigbay, mudder?" she said in a voice so congested that it was barely recognizable as her own.

"No, I didn't get any medicine, and I'm afraid I'm not your mother."

Robin's eyes snapped wide open. They looked impressively bloodshot.

"Hello, Robin," he said, wincing at her ghastly appearance. "I thought I'd look in on my favorite aide to—"

That was when she screamed.

Si Cwan jumped back, startled at the volume and vehemence of the sound that was pouring from her throat. For someone who could barely breathe, she was remarkably vocal. Si Cwan backed toward the door, all the while trying to say something that would stop her from screaming. Something pleasant, something friendly. Either that or he could club her in the side of the head to silence her. With each passing moment, that seemed a better and better option.

The door hissed open and Morgan Lefler entered hurriedly. She was carrying something that Si Cwan correctly assumed to be some sort of medicine. "What are you doing here?" she demanded.

"I just came to see her, I thought, I—"

"Don't think! Just get out!"

Robin had, by that point, pulled the blanket over her head, and she was thrashing about, calling "Geddout, geddout, geddout!" while muffled beneath the covers.

Morgan quickly put down the medicine and took Si Cwan by the elbow. "Come along, Ambassador," she said. She likewise sounded a bit congested, but only a bit. She was far too busy hauling Si Cwan out of the room to care about her voice.

"What's the matter with her? Why is she acting like

this?" demanded Si Cwan as they stood in the corridor. "I was simply looking in on a co-worker, that's all."

"Perhaps she . . . never mind."

He looked down at her. There was a great deal of strength in her, he could tell. But he was nobility, and he felt that he had been ill-used enough in recent days. "Please do not say 'never mind' to me. Tell me what is in your thoughts."

"I was just going to say," said Morgan after a moment, "that perhaps she cares how you see her. Perhaps she attached a great deal of importance to that."

"I don't see why. Friends should not concern themselves about such things."

"I suppose you're right," Morgan told him. There was something in her voice that Si Cwan could not make out. As if she had something else on her mind but she was unable or unwilling to say it.

"What do you mean by that?"

"I mean you're probably right. I am agreeing with you."

"Oh. Then . . ." He frowned. "Why does it feel as if you're not agreeing with me?"

"Lord Cwan," she sighed, "I have enough trouble explaining my own emotions, and comprehending those of my daughter. Please do not ask me to explain why you feel a certain way."

"Fair enough," said Si Cwan, sounding quite formal. He bowed slightly and said, "Please convey my sincerest hopes to Robin that she recovers soon."

"I will. Hopefully, this medicine will get her back on her feet."

"I share your hope."

Deciding that he wasn't going to be having much more to do with Robin Lefler that day, Si Cwan headed in the direction of Kalinda's quarters . . . but stopped as he passed the guest quarters he knew had been assigned to Xyon. Perhaps he had been hasty in his treatment of the young man at that. Not that he would admit it, of course, to anyone. He had a certain status to maintain, after all. But the fact that Xyon was the son of the captain—even an estranged son—certainly required some degree of respect on Si Cwan's part. And he had handled himself rather well against the Overlord during the meeting. Si Cwan had barely been able to contain his anger and loathing for the leader of the Redeemers, and Xyon's flamboyant tweaking of the sensibilities of the Overlord had provided Si Cwan with much inner amusement.

And he had saved his sister.

Well, that was the most important thing, wasn't it? As inappropriate as he considered Xyon's obvious interest in Kalinda, there was still the fact that the young man had risked life and limb to protect her, at a time when he barely knew her and had no inkling as to her true nature and status. He had been motivated out of the purity of heroism, apparently. On that basis alone, Si Cwan could, at the very least, be patient with the lad. Perhaps try to connect with him in some manner on an emotional basis. Certainly once he had accomplished that, he could then get Xyon to understand that any sort of romantic involvement with Kalinda was . . . well, it just wasn't appropriate. That was the simplest way to put it. Inappropriate. Now, granted, it was going to take a bit of a leap of faith on Xyon's part to accept that. He was, in essence, going to have to take Si Cwan's word for it. But if he could get Xyon to respect his status and knowledge of such things, then it might go that much easier.

He rang the chime of Xyon's quarters, smoothing the front of his tunic as he waited to see if there was any response from within.

What he heard instead was the sound of whispered voices. And then a voice that was unmistakably Xyon's called out, "Go away! Come back later, okay?"

And there was a giggle. A female giggle. One that Si Cwan recognized instantly. How could he not? All those times out riding, when she was a little girl, and he would hear that same quick, light girlish laughter as they pounded across the surface of Thallon, secure in their nobility and future without a care in the world.

Before he was even aware of it, Si Cwan was shoving his fingers into the connection point where the doors fit together. Within moments he had a fingerhold, and that was all he needed. He grunted only once as he applied his considerable strength, and within moments had overridden the doorlock mechanism through the simple expedient of sheer muscle power. He shoved the doors open, stepped in . . .

. . . and saw exactly what he thought he was going to see.

Xyon, barechested, wearing only his slacks, the rest of his clothes scattered about the room. Next to him on the couch, wrapped around him in an embrace, was Kalinda. She was wearing considerably fewer clothes than Xyon. Only undergarments, and Si Cwan could tell from where Xyon's hands were that even those were not going to be adorning her for much longer.

"Si Cwan!" said an alarmed Kalinda. "Now . . . don't overreact. This isn't—that is to say, Xyon and I—"

"We don't owe him any explanation, Kally," Xyon said, starting to get to his feet. "We're two independent people, and don't have to answer to anyone or anything except our own conscience. And if Si Cwan doesn't understand all that—"

What Xyon didn't comprehend was that Si Cwan's lack of understanding didn't even factor into it. The fact was that he wasn't even hearing any of it. From the moment the door had opened, a haze of fury had descended upon his brain and shut out all words being tossed about with the exception of proper names. He heard his own name spoken by Kalinda. He heard her mention the hated name of Xyon. And he heard Xyon speak the affectionate nickname by which Si Cwan, and only Si Cwan, had addressed her since infancy. That was it. Everything else was swept away by rapidly escalating rage.

Xyon had always been confident in his fighting abilities. Granted, he had experienced a small setback when his father had handled him with relative ease. But since that brief and unfortunate encounter, he had told himself two things. First, that his father had caught him off guard. And second, for crying out loud, his father was M'k'n'zy of Calhoun, the savior of Xenex and the single most formidable warrior in the history of the planet. At least, that was what the legends claimed. Xyon knew he had great skills as a fighter himself, but he wasn't kidding himself. His father was legendary. Competing with a legend is a rather daunting proposition; he knew that, since to some degree he had been doing exactly that his entire life. So he didn't let himself become too disheartened over his quick and definitive loss to Calhoun.

But he was still confident that he could dispatch pretty much any other foe with precision and efficiency.

He had a feeling that Si Cwan might make a move

on him. Certainly the Thallonian was angry enough. His eyes looked like they had glazed over, and his entire body was absolutely dead still and tense, pounding with contained energy. He was standing there in the doorway, having just forced it open with an impressive show of strength.

That was not enough, though, to deter Xyon. He was still confident that he could handle whatever situation presented itself, particularly one that involved some sort of physical conflict.

"I will further remind you, Si Cwan," said Xyon, "that these are my private quarters. You have no business here. So I will ask you to depart at once while Kally and I conduct ourselves as we see fit in the privacy of—"

That was as far as he got.

Later, he would review the incident over and over in his mind, and each time would come to the same conclusion. He had not, for a moment, taken his eyes off Si Cwan. His concentration had never flagged, he had never looked over to Kally in a moment of pride to see how he was doing as far as she was concerned. His focus had remained, unwaveringly, upon Si Cwan.

As a result, he would forever remain unable to explain just how it was that, one moment, Si Cwan was on the far side of the room, standing in the doorway, still unmoving, and the next, Si Cwan was across the room with one hand on the waist of Xyon's pants and the other hand around Xyon's throat. He never saw Si Cwan move. He was just . . . there.

The abrupt proximity of the enraged Thallonian was daunting enough. What further confused Xyon was just how Si Cwan had managed to get such a firm grip on him. Instinctively, he grabbed at Si Cwan's arm to try and pry it off, and was inwardly horrified to find that Si Cwan's arm was a collection of corded muscles that wasn't going to be moved short of the application of explosive devices.

"Si Cwan! Stop!" shouted Kalinda.

Si Cwan, however, was apparently just getting started. For with a quick turn, he threw Xyon straight at the temporarily broken door. Xyon hurtled through, unable to stop, and crashed into the opposite wall in the corridor.

Hands balled into fists, Si Cwan stalked toward him, about as easily deterred as a meteor shower. Xyon's head was spinning, and he knew he had only seconds to pull himself together, if that long.

Fortunately those seconds were provided for him as a passing crewman saw the situation developing and, apparently remembering that Xyon was the son of the captain, decided that the best thing to do would be to stop Si Cwan in his tracks. The crewman threw both his arms around Si Cwan's upper torso, momentarily pinning his arms, in an endeavor to stop him. It seemed to Xyon that the only reason the crewman got that close was because Si Cwan's entire attention was focused on Xyon. When he noticed that the crewman was holding him, he reacted with immediate dispatch. Barely seeming to flex his arms, he nonetheless broke the crewman's grasp, and without even turning to look at him, lashed out with a quick right hand. The blow caught the crewman on the side of the head and he went down.

It had been a delay of only moments, but it was sufficient time for Xyon to get back to his feet. Now Kalinda was behind Si Cwan, shouting to him, but he was seized with such a blind fury that he was paying no attention to her at all. Instead he lunged at Xyon, who got out of the way, but Si Cwan pivoted, cat quick, his hands weaving a fast and exotic pattern. Xyon's attention was drawn to the hand movements, which was apparently precisely what Si Cwan wanted, because he suddenly lashed out with his foot and caught Xyon squarely in the pit of the stomach. Xyon doubled over, gasping, and Si Cwan straightened him up with a blow to the chin that Xyon actually partly managed to dodge; if it had landed squarely, it would have broken Xyon's jaw.

Xyon was operating entirely on instinct, as he dodged this way and that, trying to stay out of Si Cwan's way while he recovered his wits. Si Cwan gave him no time to think at all, coming at him with a series of quick leg kicks. Xyon stayed out of their way, mostly by luck, while calculating a plan of attack, and then he launched it. When Si Cwan lashed out with a side kick, Xyon actually vaulted over it and came in fast with a series of lightning strikes to Cwan's head and upper torso.

He certainly launched the blows in a quick and efficient manner. The problem was, not a single one of them landed. With quick parries, Si Cwan brushed every one of them aside with his forearms. He did so in a manner so unhurried, so unruffled, that it was clear to Xyon that Si Cwan felt himself in no danger at all. He was about to take umbrage at that when a sudden leg sweep from Si Cwan knocked Xyon's feet out from under him. The young man fell again, hit the floor, and this time before he could try and stand up, Si Cwan's booted foot was squarely atop his rib cage.

"Si Cwan! Stop!" howled Kalinda, and she was pulling at his arm. But no matter how much she yanked at him, all she managed to budge was his arm. The rest of his body was so unaffected that one would have thought he was simply ignoring the fact that he had an arm at all, much less someone attached to it.

Si Cwan started to apply pressure, and Xyon couldn't catch a breath. It was at that point that it truly began to dawn on him that he was in serious, mortal danger. Si Cwan was implacably fixed on doing him, presumably, sufficient damage to make sure that he never went near Kalinda again. At that point, however, Si Cwan's restraint was non-existent.

Suddenly, just like that, the pressure was gone from Xyon's chest. He gasped in lungsful of air and felt a sharp stabbing pain. He wondered if he had a broken rib.

Si Cwan was bellowing in fury, and small wonder. Zak Kebron was standing directly behind him, and he had lifted Cwan clear of not only Xyon, but the floor. Si Cwan pounded on the massive arms, snarling, "Release me! Right now!" but neither the blows nor the commands were having the least effect on Kebron, who held him in place and seemed about as vulnerable as a small mountain.

"Idiot," said Kebron.

And then, to Kebron's clear surprise, Si Cwan was no longer in his grip. Si Cwan had wiggled free, leaving Kebron grasping only his tunic. Dropping low, Si Cwan threw both his arms around Kebron's left leg, right at the joint of the knee, and pulled. The movement overbalanced Kebron, and Zak fell backward with a crash so pronounced that it caused reverberations throughout the entire deck.

Si Cwan spun once more . . .

. . . and Mackenzie Calhoun was there.

No one quite knew where he had come from, but he was simply there, standing between Xyon, who was just starting to get up, and the enraged Si Cwan. His arms at his sides, he looked utterly relaxed and totally undaunted by the Thallonian.

"Out of my way, Captain," Si Cwan grated.

"Move me," replied Calhoun.

Si Cwan took a step forward . . . and then his gaze locked with Calhoun's for a long moment . . . and then he took a step backward.

"Very wise," was all Calhoun said. Then, apparently having faith that Si Cwan would not attack someone whose back was to him, Calhoun very deliberately turned away from Si Cwan and extended a hand to Xyon. Xyon hesitated only a moment, then took the hand and allowed Calhoun to pull him up. He was surprised that Calhoun brought him to his feet with so little effort that Xyon might as well have weighed nothing. "Are you all right?" he asked.

"I'm fine," said Xyon stoically.

"Really." Calhoun looked him up and down as if he had x-ray eyes, and suddenly prodded the area of Xyon's chest where he had felt the sharpness. Xyon gasped, even though the pressure had been relatively gentle. "Go get that looked at," he said. "Sickbay. Now. Take her with you," he said, inclining his head toward Kalinda.

"I'm not hurt, Captain," she said.

"Yes, I know. I just think some distance will better serve all concerned. As would some additional clothes on your part."

She looked down and remembered that she was relatively scantily clad at that point. She nodded, darted into Xyon's quarters and re-emerged with her clothes hastily tossed onto her. By this point any number of curious crewmen had shown up and were standing there, gawking at the odd scene before them.

"Return to your quarters," Calhoun ordered them in the time-honored tradition of law enforcement officers throughout the centuries. "Nothing more to see here. Show's over. Lord Cwan . . . I invite you to return to your quarters and stay there."

"Are you confining me?" Si Cwan said stiffly.

"At this point, no. I am asking you to stay put. And if you ignore my request, then I will shoot you out the nearest photon torpedo tube. But I'm not confining you."

"I appreciate your consideration," said Si Cwan.

Kebron was on his feet by that time, and he was helping up the crewman whom Si Cwan had knocked down.

"You're damned right it's consideration. You just assaulted a crewman, my head of security, and my son. I could stick you in a cell until you're old and pink. And if anyone here wants to press charges, I won't stand in their way."

He looked around at the others. The crewman, Hudson by name, simply rubbed his jaw and said, "The sooner I forget about how easily he took me out, the better."

"What charges?" rumbled Kebron. "He got lucky, that's all."

"Funny how I always get lucky when we go head to head, isn't it, Kebron?" said Si Cwan.

"I wouldn't push my good fortune right now if I were you, Cwan," warned Calhoun. He turned to Xyon and said, "Well?"

Xyon rubbed his chest and then pulled on the shirt

that Kalinda had handed him. "It's a private matter, sir," he said after a moment. "I regret that it spilled out into the corridor and involved others. It should not have. In any event, I see no reason to clutter your time, or anyone else's, with the fallout."

"Very well," said Calhoun. "Sickbay, then. Si Cwan, your quarters. The rest of you," and he gestured that they should go on about their business.

Si Cwan did not move, however. He remained exactly where he was, his gaze never leaving Kalinda and Xyon as they walked away together, she with her arm around his waist, helping him along.

First he paced his quarters for a time, and then when he came to the realization that pacing didn't make the quarters any bigger, Si Cwan sat in one place and stewed. He remained that way until he heard a chime at his door. "Come," he said.

To his utter astonishment, Robin Lefler was standing there. Her face still looked a bit puffy, but she seemed in slightly better shape than she was earlier. Perhaps the medicine was having some effect.

"What are you doing here?" he asked.

"What am I doing? What are you doing, is the better question." She sniffed and walked forward. The door shut behind her and she leaned against the wall.

"Would you care to sit?" he asked.

"That probably wouldn't be wise, seeing as I would most likely fall asleep," she informed him. "I want to know if you've gone crazy."

"I want to know if the world has gone crazy," replied Si Cwan. "We are helping the Redeemers, have you heard that?"

"Yes, I've heard."

"Madness!"

"From the way I've heard it, the captain has no choice."

"And now this. Kalinda's involvement with . . . with . . ."

"With Xyon. You can say it. He has a name. 'Xyon.' "

"I know his name. I know, to some degree, I should be grateful to him. But still . . ." He shook his head, feeling utterly discouraged. "I feel as if I am alone in this matter. As if no one can comprehend how I feel. Nor do I really know why I would expect them to understand. Of everyone on this vessel, I alone am of the nobility. No matter, as others have pointed out, that my line may have ended. That that which I ruled over is gone. Nobility comes from within."

"So does compassion . . . and . . . and . . . and . . ."

"And what?'

Her response was an explosive sneeze that Si Cwan would have sworn had enough force to blast a hole through the bulkhead. By the laws of action and reaction, he would have expected her head to fly off her shoulders as a result.

"Are you all right?" he inquired.

"Fine. I'm fine. Look . . . Si Cwan . . . I think you're gonna have to start exploring just how much of this is your precious nobility . . . and how much is just plain jealousy."

"Jealousy!" He scoffed at the notion. "I am simply concerned with what's best for her, that is all."

"It'd be understandable. I mean, all this time you've been looking for her, and worrying about her. And now she's here . . . and she's ignoring you for Xyon. That must be hard to take."

"Robin . . . you are an intelligent woman, and I've come to respect your advice and counsel. But please believe me when I say that you have misread the situation completely. It is not at all as you have described it. I am only worried about propriety."

"You're saying basically, then, that you feel he's not good enough for your sister."

"It is nothing personal," shrugged Si Cwan. "No one on this ship is."

"And you? Would no one be good enough for you? On this ship?"

"I don't know what you mean."

"Well . . ." Charmingly, she cleared her throat. "Let's get you a 'for instance.' " She leaned forward, her fingers interlaced, and her voice dropped to an almost intimate level. "Let us suppose, for sake of argument, that I said to you, 'Si Cwan, I think I'm falling in love with you. I love your dignity, your nobility. I love the way you conduct yourself, when you're not busy making a fool of yourself. I love your heroism. In short, I find you incredibly attractive, on both an emotional and physical level. I want to take our relationship to a new and more intimate level. Now . . . what would you say to all that?"

He considered it, stroking the narrow beard that lined his chin. "I would be flattered, of course. But other than that, I. . . ."

And then he looked into her eyes. Really looked there. And he saw a depth of emotion, a bottomless pool that seemed to be inviting him to swim within them. He was astounded by the intensity of what he was seeing there, and it was entirely focused on him.

For a moment, just a moment, he forgot about his title and station. Instead all he could see was this woman with her emotions so on the surface, that he wondered just how in the world he could have missed it all this time.

"I . . ."

"You don't know, do you?" she said quickly. Abruptly she sat back, as if she was trying to cover something up as fast as she could. "You see? It's always easy to judge such matters from a distance. But once it's close up, once your own emotions are in play, it's not quite as simple to say, 'Sorry. You two can't be together because of rank.' "

"Robin . . . I see your point, but . . ."

"He makes her happy, Si Cwan." She took his hand, which didn't thrill him overmuch, because she had been coughing into it. But he took some consolation from the fact that she was a human with a human sickness, and therefore the odds were that it wouldn't be able to make the transition to the Thallonian system. "And it's obvious she makes him happy. They're young and they're exploring a universe of possibilities. If you deny it, then . . ." She sat up, apparently seized by an inspiration. "Then you're no different than the Redeemers."

"What?" The criticism stung like no other. "How can you say that? I'm her brother—"

"And they're the self-styled saviors of the galaxy. They're imposing their worldview on others without caring what the others may think, or what makes those others happy. You're displaying the exact same lack of consideration. You would 'redeem' her by making sure that she shares your view of things, whether she wants to or not. Obviously you're not going around taking over planets . . . but the principle is the same. Either you show tolerance in all things, or you don't. Would you ever dream of forcing a world full of strangers to think the way you do?"

"No, of course not."

"Then why are strangers entitled to more consideration than your own sister?"

"You just . . ." He hung his head. "You just don't understand, Robin."

"Actually, I think I do. I'm afraid that you're the one who doesn't. But I'll tell you right now, if you don't understand, and soon . . . you really are going to lose her, and soon. Because the more you try to force them apart, the more they're going to want to stay together, just to spite you."

Slowly he looked up at her . . . and he chuckled.

"Did I say something funny?" she asked.

"Not intentionally," he smiled. "But you have given me something to think about. Something very important. Thank you for that, Robin."

He reached over and embraced her quickly. For an instant he felt her reciprocate in a far more intense fashion that he had imagined she would. He released her and looked into her eyes with a measure of curiosity. "Robin, that 'example' you gave me before. Asking how I would react if you told me you felt . . . a certain way about me. That was simply a hypothetical . . . wasn't it?"

"Of course!" she said, a little too quickly. "Of course it was. I was just trying to get a point across to you. I hope I succeeded."

"I think you did. But Robin . . . if you did have . . . you know . . . feelings of that nature for me, then I—"

"Si Cwan," she said quickly, "you don't have to say anything. It's really not necessary. It was just pretend. I hope you understand that."

"I understand . . . perhaps more than you think I do."

Robin nodded briskly, then sneezed with so much power that she stumbled back and almost knocked herself off her feet. "I . . . goddago," she said and backed out of Si Cwan's quarters, leaving the Thallonian noble thoughtfully considering his options.

# VII.

It took the bridge crew some time to get used to the sight of a Redeemer vessel pacing them. The impulse was to be at battle stations, preparing for a direct assault. Indeed, the captain had told them to remain battle-ready, but the ship had stood down from yellow alert. They were cautious, and Kebron kept a wary eye on any sign that the Redeemers were powering up their weapons. But there was nothing. One would have thought the Redeemers to be the most benign of races in the history of the galaxy.

They reached the Tulaan star system, and Soleta held a brief (over the screen) conference with the Prime One who, along with the Overlord, had returned to the Redeemer vessel. He indicated the point where the far watch points had indicated that the Black Mass had first emerged, and then Soleta—in conjunction with

McHenry—plotted a course that would take them in the direction of the Black Mass so that they could see it first-hand and, hopefully, intercept it.

By that point, Calhoun brought the ship to yellow alert so that they would be ready for anything. Si Cwan was likewise on the bridge as the *Excalibur,* side by side with the Redeemer ship, hurtled in the direction of the Black Mass' last reported position. Although the entity was moving at warp speed, it was nevertheless only in the realm of warp one or two. The starship could move far faster, of course, and therefore could get to the Black Mass long before it got anywhere near Tulaan IV. They would have lots of time to try and deal with the Mass and somehow get it to change course or, preferably, turn around and head back for the Hunger Zone. At the very least, they hoped to re-steer it toward an uninhabited system, of which there were more than a few.

There was none of the usual banter on the bridge as they watched the monitor. Even though they knew that the sensors would inform them of contact well before there was a visual, they couldn't help but strain their eyes studying the screen.

And finally, Soleta—the more experienced sensor monitor—announced, "Captain. I'm getting readings, dead ahead."

"What are they?"

She paused for a long time before finally saying, "I do not know."

"You don't know?" Calhoun tried to keep the surprise out of his voice. "Best guess, then."

"A biological form, moving at approximately warp one point three. Impossible to determine its size, since it keeps changing. Best description is that it is like an amorphous, living cloud."

"Is it one entity?"

"I do not believe so. It appears to be composed of millions of smaller entities, but I am unable to get an individual reading from any of them."

"Put it onscreen."

Calhoun imagined that the collective breath of the bridge crew was being held as the screen shifted for a moment, and then the Black Mass appeared on it.

He didn't quite know what he was looking at, at first. "Highlight it, Lieutenant," he said. Within seconds the screen adjusted so that the rest of space dropped out and the pulsing Black Mass was the only thing on it.

"My God," whispered Shelby.

It was not the most professional thing she had ever said, but Calhoun could fully understand it. In his memoirs, James Kirk had written of a time when the *Enterprise* had encountered a gigantic, space-going amoeba. Calhoun had often wondered what it must have been like to be on the bridge of that legendary ship, to encounter something as incredible as that and know that somehow, it had to be dealt with. But it wasn't as if he had wondered about it so much that he had a compulsion to actually find out. As it happened, though, that was exactly what was happening.

And not only that . . . but the Black Mass seemed bigger than the amoeba reportedly was. Bigger . . . and more vicious.

Calhoun had a knack for knowing when danger was near, a sort of sixth sense that warned him and had helped him to survive during his days as the Xenexian warlord. Never in his life, though, had this survival instinct been less necessary, because never had the danger been more obvious.

"Suggestions?" Calhoun said.

"I don't suppose dropping the Redeemers a nice good-bye note and getting the hell out of here would be an option," suggested McHenry.

"Actually, that's already crossed my mind. Si Cwan . . . tell me specifically what your people did against it."

"Everything," said Si Cwan. "Everything . . . and nothing." He was staring at the screen with what seemed to Calhoun an almost haunted expression. "We threw everything we could at it, and not only didn't we slow it down . . . it didn't even acknowledge us."

"All right," Calhoun said slowly. "Mr. Kebron, open a hailing frequency, broadest possible band. Let's see if we can talk to it."

"Talk to it?" Cwan was shaking his head and he turned to Calhoun. "You still don't understand, Captain. Let me make it clear to you. The battle between our forces and the Black Mass was the single most humiliating experience in the history of the Thallonian Empire. My uncle took his own life because he could not stand living with the disgrace . . . nor was he capable of surviving in a galaxy where the Thallonians were that inferior to another being. All we can reasonably do is leave the Redeemers to their much deserved fate and leave."

"Because we don't care about the Redeemers."

"Correct."

"And the Fennerians?"

"They have my sympathies," said Si Cwan, "but they are casualties of war. Such things happen, regrettable as that may be. And in this war, we are at least on the verge of having one of our greatest enemies wiped out by a force that no one and nothing can stop. Let us be satisfied with that and be done with it."

"And if next time the Black Mass swarms," Shelby said, "it's toward a system or world that we do care about? Understandable, Ambassador, that we have no desire to extend ourselves for the Redeemers. But if twenty, thirty years hence, another world, another system dies because of the Black Mass . . . and we could have stopped it here, now . . . then are we not, in some small way, responsible for that as well?"

"You can't stop it," Si Cwan told her. "The most—the very most—that you will be able to do is get its attention. And if you do that, we may very well all die."

"No response to the hail on any frequency, Captain," Kebron said. He did not sound surprised.

Truth to tell, neither was Calhoun. They might have had as much luck trying to strike up a conversation with a comet. "Are you sure this thing is sentient?" It was a general question, aimed at whoever might be in a position to answer.

"Captain, at the moment I am not entirely sure of anything except that it is moving on its projected course," said Soleta.

And Si Cwan added, "I wouldn't venture to say what it is at all."

"All right. Inform the Redeemer vessel that we're going to be arming weapons. Bring shields up, go to red alert."

"Red alert, aye."

Within moments the klaxon was sounding throughout the vessel. Everyone was bracing for what promised to be a very daunting proposition. Word was out throughout the ship of just what it was that they were facing, and as screens throughout the ship brought the Black Mass into focus, crewmembers were shaking their heads in astonishment.

In her quarters, Kalinda looked at the screen mutely. She had heard so many stories about the thing from her brother, but seeing it here, now . . . it was like having a childhood nightmare suddenly come to life right in front of you.

Her door chimed. "Come," she said.

She suspected the identity of the person on the other side of the door, and she was correct. It was Xyon. Immediately she was up and in his arms, and they kissed passionately. "I can't believe," she whispered in between kisses, "that I ever thought you were some sort of arrogant, know-nothing slime."

"And I can't believe I thought you were a standoffish, self-centered brat," he whispered back.

They continued to kiss for a moment, and then she broke off and stared at him. "You thought that about me?" she said in surprise.

"Well . . . remember," Xyon said, obviously thinking quickly, "you weren't yourself. So the personality I had a problem with . . . probably wasn't yours anyway."

She smiled in amusement. "All right. Fine. I'll let you get away with that one." He started to lean forward to bring their lips together once more, but she moved easily away from him and instead went to her computer screen, which was at that point tied in with the other screens throughout the ship. "Have you ever seen anything like this?"

He walked over and gaped at it. "Looks like a science experiment gone berserk. So that's the dreaded Black Mass, huh."

She nodded.

*"Grozit.* Someone should just dump it in a black hole or something and be done with it. There is one, actually, not too far off the Black Mass' path, as I recall."

"Sounds good to me. Maybe you should suggest that to your father."

"He's got plenty of people to suggest options to him. He doesn't need me."

He paused, and Kalinda looked at him with a raised eyebrow. "Isn't this the point where you're supposed to say, self-pityingly, 'He never needed me?' "

"You think it's funny?"

"No. I don't. But I'll tell you what I do think," and she took his hand. "I lost my birth mother and father . . . and then there was a woman on Montos who I thought was my mother . . . except all those memories were false. I feel like I have a piece missing out of my life. With all those losses . . . it makes me all the more aware of how important it is to value something when it's there."

"Such as a father."

She nodded. "It's obvious that he's wanted to connect with you. And let's be honest, Xyon . . . you could have left by now. Your ship is sitting down in the shuttle bay, but it's fully repaired. There's nothing keeping you here."

"Don't underestimate yourself," said Xyon.

At that, she laughed lightly. "Somehow, I don't think I'm the reason. I'm not an idiot, Xyon. You're a . . . a man of the cosmos. You've been around. Am I supposed to seriously think that you would stay in any one place for any one female?"

"Why are you so quick to dismiss the notion, out of hand?" he asked. "Why is that concept so unthinkable?"

"Because I . . ." She looked down.

He took the tip of her chin and brought her face up so that he was looking into her eyes. "Because you what?"

"Because I don't dare think that you might stay for me . . . want to be with me . . . because that will get my hopes up and I don't want to be disappointed."

"Kalinda . . ."

And suddenly his head whipped around. He frowned. "Did you hear that?"

"Hear what?"

He went quickly to the computer, checked the screen. "I was right."

"Right about what? I don't understand."

He looked up at her and said, "We're firing on the Black Mass. The battle is joined."

Xyon wasn't precisely correct in his assessment.

"Any reaction to the warning shot, Mr. Kebron?"

"None," said Kebron. "Still no reply on any hailing frequencies."

"McHenry—?"

Mark McHenry didn't even need the rest of the question framed. "No deviation from the current path that it's following. The shot across its bow . . . or whatever you'd call it . . . hasn't caused it to alter its course."

"All right," said Calhoun. "Tell the Redeemer vessel to hang back. I want to draw closer and see what happens when we uses phasers directly on it."

"Nothing will happen," said Si Cwan confidently.

"You know, Ambassador, you're becoming annoyingly one-note," Calhoun told him.

"You've trusted me in the past when I've told you about things in Thallonian space," Si Cwan replied. "If you wish to disbelieve me now, or simply desire to find out for yourself, it is of little consequence to me."

"Awaiting targeting order, Captain," said Kebron. "The Redeemers have pulled back."

"Let's go for broke, Mr. Kebron. Target dead center . . . or at least what passes for dead center at the moment. And . . . fire."

The *Excalibur* cut loose with its phasers, firing straight into the heart of the Black Mass.

"No discernable effect," said Soleta from her scanners.

Si Cwan made a "told you so" grunt. "See? It's invulnerable."

"Not necessarily," Soleta corrected him. "We did not hit it."

"Are you questioning my marksmanship?" asked Kebron. He sounded mildly amused that anyone could conceivably do such a thing.

"You struck where you aimed. But you did not hit the Black Mass."

"Impossible."

"You will find," Si Cwan said with a sanguine air, "that you will use that word a great deal when dealing with the Black Mass."

"The creature—if such it is," Soleta said, "morphed itself around the shots. It happened so quickly that it would have been undetectable to the eye. It simply sensed the phaser blast, and opened a hole within itself, allowing the shot simply to pass right through. Our weapons might be useful against it . . . presuming we can get it to stand still."

"Full phaser spread and photon torpedo array, Mr. Kebron," said Calhoun. "Let's see just how much simultaneous fire power it can handle."

Within moments the *Excalibur* had unleashed a full-blown assault on the Black Mass. And even as the ship cut loose with everything it had, Calhoun was starting to get the uncomfortable feeling that Si Cwan had been right in his relentless declarations as to the Black Mass' invincibility.

The phasers hammered at it, the photon torpedos slammed through it with their destructive payload. Nothing. Wherever the weaponry was, the Black Mass wasn't. Calhoun couldn't fathom it. Phasers, by definition, moved with the speed of light. Dodging them with such facility should have been an impossibility, for the moment that the Black Mass saw the phaser beam coming at it, the phaser beam was—to all intents and purposes—there.

And no matter what they did, the Mass continued unswerving on its course.

"We're receiving a hail," said Kebron.

Calhoun turned in surprise. "From the Black Mass?"

"No. From the Redeemers. They want to know if they should join the battle."

"I don't see any point to it at this time," Calhoun admitted. "So far, we—"

"Captain!" Soleta said. And there was something in her voice that was about as close to alarm as the Vulcan science officer ever came. "I think we got its attention!"

This visibly startled Si Cwan. "What? Are you sure? We fired on it twenty years ago with everything we had and it never even noticed us."

"But you did so while it was eating," Soleta pointed out. "At least that is what you told us. It may be that, while heading for its nourishment, it's more inclined to be aggressive defensively and offensively."

Shelby moved over to the science station, looking over Soleta's shoulder. "What is it, Lieutenant? What makes you think we got its attention?"

"Look for yourself. A section of it is splitting off . . . and coming right for us."

It was true. A small part of the Black Mass—although small was a relative term, considering that it kept changing in size from one moment to the next—was on a direct intercept course for the *Excalibur.*

"And it is moving very quickly," Soleta said. "When separated from the rest of the Mass, it is apparently capable of even greater speed than the Mass as a whole. It is presently moving at approximately warp four."

"Mr. Kebron, inform the Redeemers we're embarking on a strategic retreat. Mr. McHenry, kindly move us somewhere that isn't here."

And suddenly it was right there.

Calhoun had no idea how such a thing could possibly be. Seconds before it was still a safe, albeit rapidly closing, distance. And suddenly, there had been a ripple of space—he had been certain he had seen such an effect from the corner of his eye—and then the Black Mass was right on top of them.

And suddenly the screen went completely black.

"It's all over us, sir!" Soleta called out. "It's completely enveloped the shields!"

"Is it eating them somehow?" demanded Calhoun.

"Negative, sir!"

"Burgoyne to bridge!" came the alarmed voice of the chief engineer over the intercom.

"Bridge, Shelby here," said the first officer.

"What the hell is going on up there? We've got readings off the shields that I've never seen in my life!

Whatever's doing this, could you kindly get it the hell off my ship?"

"We're working on it. Shelby out."

Calhoun was studying the Black Mass thoughtfully. "Mr. McHenry, get us out of here, full impulse. We're going to try and shake that thing loose."

McHenry didn't move. He was staring, stunned, at the blackened screen.

"McHenry!"

"I . . . I can't," McHenry said.

"What do you mean, can't?" Calhoun was out of his command chair, standing next to McHenry, looking down at him in surprise. "I've seen you fly this ship virtually blindfolded. You piloted her without instrumentation. You're the one who's constantly in tune with his environment. This shouldn't be any different for you."

"Captain . . . it's . . ."

"It's what?"

He had never seen McHenry look so lost. "Sir, something about its motion . . . it's disrupting space/time. I feel completely disoriented. I'm not sure why it's happening, but I can't get any sort of . . . of mental lock on where we are and where we should be. I don't know which way to take us. I could fly us into a star or crash us right into the Redeemer craft. I could—"

"I get the picture, Mr. McHenry."

Soleta said. "We are starting to lose integrity of our force fields. It's not draining them, it's simply . . . pushing them aside. Estimate breeching of the shields in two minutes."

"Bridge to engineering."

"Engineering, Burgoyne here. Give me good news, Captain."

"Actually, you're going to have to give it to me, Burgoyne: You've got sixty seconds to get up here with something that will enable Mr. McHenry to penetrate some sort of space/time distortion field that the Black Mass has around the ship."

To Calhoun's surprise, Burgoyne said, "Mitchell's on his way."

And that was an understatement. Inside of fifteen seconds, Lieutenant Craig Mitchell had materialized on the bridge, Burgoyne having arranged for Mitchell simply to be beamed up. Naturally the transporter didn't work ship to ship while the deflectors were up, but there was nothing to prevent intraship beaming.

Mitchell was Burgoyne's second-in-command in engineering. Although ensigns Yates, Beth and Torelli had frequently worked with Burgoyne, it was to Mitchell that they actually reported. Mitchell was a heavyset man, although he had lost some weight recently and was planning to lose more. He had a head of brownish black hair, and a thick beard that Burgoyne told him to shave so often that it had become something of a running joke between the two of them. He also had a tendency to make the worst jokes of anyone on the ship . . . an attribute which Shelby had once commented ed on as "going some."

Without any sort of explanation, Mitchell immediately walked over to McHenry and draped an odd-looking device over his head and eye. "And this would be?" asked McHenry.

"An exographic targeting scanner," Mitchell said. He had a tendency to rumble when he spoke; his voice was only slightly less deep than Kebron's, and when Kebron spoke it tended to sound like a rockslide. "Adjusted for use when the viewscreen becomes inoperative for some reason. We've never had to worry about using them before as long as wonder boy here was at the conn. Good thing we kept it handy, though. So what happened, McHenry? Lose the old touch?"

"My touch is just fine, thanks," said McHenry, although it was evident that he was rather put out over the fact that he had to use some sort of supplement. He strapped it over his face while Mitchell stayed nearby in case the device needed adjustment. Then McHenry sat there for a long moment, taking in readings which he in turn fed directly into the navigational computer. "Okay," he said after a few moments. "Okay . . . I've got it. I still feel like I'm wearing a sack over my head, but I've got it. Where to, Captain?"

"I'm still blind, Mr. McHenry. I'm not wearing an ETS. Just move us away from the Black Mass at maximum impulse. We need a straight line of movement, because we're going to try something."

"What are we trying, sir?" Shelby said, sounding a bit worried.

He glanced at her. "Trust me."

Smiling gamely, she replied, "Why did I have a feeling you were going to say that?"

Within moments, the *Excalibur* was cutting through space at full impulse speed.

"What are you trying to do, Captain? Get the high winds to blow it off?" inquired Si Cwan.

"I assume, Lord Cwan, that you're familiar with the notion that objects in motion tend to stay in motion. Well, we're in motion, and so is the Black Mass. When we stop . . . with any luck, the Black Mass keeps going. Mr. McHenry, get ready to hit the brakes on my order. And . . . full reverse. Now!"

The *Excalibur* slammed to a halt. If it had had tires,

and been on a road, there would have been skid marks. Theoretically, once the starship came to an abrupt halt, the organism surrounding them should have slid right off.

It was, in fact, an excellent theory. Unfortunately, the fact did not cooperate with it. The viewscreen remained black.

"It's still there, Captain," said Soleta.

"So I noticed," said Calhoun.

Burgoyne's voice crackled up from engineering. "Captain, we're seeing a drain from the exhaust!"

"The what?"

"The exhaust from the impulse engines! The hydrogen plasma! Something's consuming it! It's not hurting us any, but it's damned weird!"

"It's eating the hydrogen plasma? Why?" said Calhoun. He looked to Soleta, who shook her head.

Burgoyne, however, had heard the comment. " 'It?' Can I assume safely from that report, sir, that some part of that Black Mass is still in residence around our shields?"

"That would be a very safe assumption, yes."

"Can we get it off, please?"

"We're working on it, Burgy. Bridge out."

"We can only assume," Soleta now said, "that consuming the hydrogen plasma is adding to the creature's strength. That's how it's managing to remain attached to us."

"That and the inertial damping field. When we decelerate at impulse, the IDF is helping to keep the thing in place," said McHenry. When he turned and looked at them with the ETS on his face, he bore a disconcerting resemblance to a Borg.

"You're suggesting we try the same stunt at warp

speed," said Calhoun. "The IDF will have less time to adjust, and the lag time in the adjustment might be what's needed to kick the thing loose."

"Whoa, hold it." It was Lieutenant Mitchell who had spoken up. He had been silently observing the entire exchange, but now he stepped forward. "I hate to bring this up," said Mitchell, "but you're pushing the specs on this ship. You bring this vessel to a sudden halt while at warp speed, you risk tearing the ship into pieces. The structural integrity field might not keep us together. To say nothing of the fact that what the IDF can't adjust for on the outside of the ship, it also is going to be slow adjusting for on the inside. We could be scraping crewmen off the bulkhead with a spatula. There's got to be a better way."

"Captain, the Mass is beginning to penetrate our shields."

"You know, I always liked this slam-to-a-halt plan," Mitchell continued smoothly. "In fact . . . this could be the greatest plan ever made."

"I'm glad you approve," Calhoun said. "Mr. McHenry, take us to warp six. Bridge to engineering."

"Engineering, go ahead," came Burgoyne's voice.

"Burgy, we're going to accelerate to warp six and then stop abruptly in hopes of shaking the Black Mass loose."

"Has Lieutenant Mitchell informed you that you could tear the ship apart in doing so?"

"He has brought it to our attention, yes."

"So we're on record then . . . presuming our record isn't destroyed."

"That's correct. In case we shred ourselves, your warning has been duly noted."

"Good. I wouldn't want to be in trouble with Starfleet in the event we all die."

"Commendable, Burgy. Calhoun out. McHenry, on my countdown: Three . . . two . . . one . . . warp factor six, now!"

The *Excalibur,* like a gazelle flushed out into the open by hunters, leaped into warp. It coasted up the warp scale, accelerating and hitting warp six in no time at all. Everyone on the bridge was tense, leaning forward, their collective breath held. All accept Calhoun, who seemed utterly confident and, indeed, even a bit blasé about the unorthodox maneuver.

"Captain, we're at warp six and holding steady."

"And the Black Mass?"

Soleta scanned it. "We are moving at a far higher warp rate than it is accustomed to. And it no longer has the hydrogen plasma from the impulse engines to sustain it. I believe it is . . . uncomfortable."

"All right, Mr. McHenry," Calhoun said slowly, methodically. "Get ready to bring us to a halt. Ladies, gentlemen . . . in the event that we're all sucking vacuum in a moment, may I say it was a pleasure working with you."

"A pure delight," deadpanned Kebron.

Calhoun began to count down from ten. The countdown seemed endless, the tension building with each descending number. For a moment, Shelby wondered whether Calhoun had started so high just to build up the drama.

Finally it came down to "Three . . . two . . . one . . . and . . . full stop!"

McHenry took a deep breath that was most likely a prayer, and slammed the ship into reverse in order to bring it to a halt.

The sudden lack of movement was so abrupt that Calhoun nearly skidded out of his chair. McHenry slammed up against the conn panel, and Boyajian—sitting in for the under-the-weather Robin Lefler—got the ops control in the pit of his stomach. Soleta barely managed to maintain her position, and Shelby would have tumbled clean out of her chair if Calhoun hadn't managed, with one hand, to grab the back of her uniform and hold her in place even as he fought to stay where he was. Si Cwan, who wasn't sitting, fell forward. However, being Si Cwan, he turned it into a deft forward roll and came up on his feet.

Kebron, naturally, didn't budge an inch.

Calhoun actually fancied that he could hear the creaking of metal, the stress upon the structure of the ship itself. For a second he was positive that it had not worked; that the ship was, indeed, ripping itself apart. He had to admit to himself that engineers were always predicting the worst, because that was their job to a degree.

It felt as if the ship was elastic, stretching like a massive rubber band . . . and then snapping back. It was in that snap that he was suddenly sure the vessel was going to tear apart, and then, just like that, the disorienting sensation was gone.

And so was the Black Mass. The stars were visible once more. And there, not far off, to starboard, was the section of the Black Mass which had, until very recently, been clinging to the shielding of the ship. It actually seemed confused, undulating back upon itself as if it were looking around for something. Probably the *Excalibur.*

"I knew it'd hold together," Mitchell said proudly, and patted the nearest railing.

"McHenry, take us out of here, warp six. Plot us a roundabout course that will bring us back to Tulaan IV, and let the Redeemers know that we're still in one piece. Barely, but in one piece. All sections report in. Boyajian, crew assessment. Was anyone in the ship hurt?"

"I'm getting reports of some serious bumps and bruises, several fractured ribs, a couple of broken arms and legs, one concussion."

"Poor bastard," rumbled Kebron.

"I think it was more than one crewman who sustained the injuries, Zak," said Soleta. "Not one person with bumps and bruises, fractured ribs, broken limbs and concussion."

"That's a relief."

"Soleta, is the Black Mass coming after us?"

"No, sir," she said looking at the scanners. "It appears to be following the most direct course back to the . . . parent body, for lack of a better word. Its ability to warp space around itself is continuing to make it difficult to get reliable readings off . . ."

Her voice trailed off then, and that was more than enough to grab the attention of everyone on the bridge. "What's wrong, lieutenant?" inquired Calhoun.

"Sir . . . I'm still getting a reading on the Black Mass."

"But you said they were moving off . . ."

"They are. I'm picking up something else, still attached to our deflectors. A couple of them are still attached to us."

"How much? How large, I mean, or how many . . . actually, I'm not sure what I mean at this point," Calhoun admitted. "What are we looking at?"

"A small readout near by the starboard nacelle. Only a

foot or so across. I almost missed it; I wouldn't have noticed it at all if I hadn't been doing a scan of the vessel's exterior, looking for something like this, just in case."

"Take two gold stars out of the ship's stores, Lieutenant, you've earned them. I want you to feed the coordinates directly to Watson in the transporter room. Calhoun to sickbay."

"Sickbay, this is Selar. Are you quite through tossing the ship around, captain? My fetus was quite perturbed."

"My apologies to you and your unborn associate. I need you to have your people ready a stasis tank. We have a life form we're going to want to keep as harmless as possible."

"How large a tank?"

"Three by five feet should suffice," Soleta whispered to Calhoun. "That will give it room to move about so that we can observe it."

"Three by five," said Calhoun. "As soon as it's ready, bring it to transporter room A and be ready. Calhoun out. All right, Kebron," he said, turning to the Brikar at the tactical station. "When everything is in place, I want you to lower the shields. At that point, Soleta, you coordinate with Watson and get that thing aboard here and beamed directly into the stasis tank. I want to see up close just what it is we're dealing with. And once we know that . . ."

"Then we can stop it?" said Shelby.

"Either that," Si Cwan commented, "or else be able to tell the Redeemers just exactly the nature of the creature that is going to wipe them out."

"I'm sure that, if the Redeemers know precisely what it is that's going to devour their world and their star, they can die happy," said Calhoun.

"I certainly can tell you that if I know what's going to eat the Redeemers' world and their star, I can die happy," said Si Cwan.

"If we're fortunate," said Calhoun, "we'll all have our wish." He then focused his attention on the depths of space and watched Si Cwan's expression as the Thallonian tried to figure out whether he had just been insulted or not.

# VIII.

CALHOUN LEANED IN CLOSE to the stasis tank and
shook his head in slow amazement. "Remarkable," he
said for what seemed the umpteenth time. "Just remarkable."

His astonishment was understandable. The sight was,
in fact, remarkable.

It had turned out that there were apparently four of
the Black Mass entities clinging to the ship's shielding.
Apparently they had managed to hold on when the ship
had made its abrupt start and stop. For their troubles,
they had been left behind, and were little more than sitting ducks when the *Excalibur* dropped its shields and
brought them aboard.

They reminded Calhoun vaguely of Trill symbionts,
although they seemed to be no kin of that race. They
were wormlike in appearance, solid black of course. It

had taken Calhoun some minutes to determine, as Soleta already had, that there were four of the creatures in the stasis tank. They stayed so close together, so utterly intertwined with one another, that it was difficult to have any clear idea immediately of just how many of them there were.

The thing that Calhoun noticed most prominently—and that which he found probably the most daunting—were their mouths. One end of their nauseating wormlike bodies was nothing more than a perpetually open mouth. The mouths would flutter closed every so often, but would open once more a very short time later. They did not have teeth.

"Remora," said Soleta. She was standing next to Calhoun, and she appeared to be making notes on her science tricorder.

"Who's she?" asked Calhoun.

"Remora," Soleta repeated. "Any of several marine fishes, native to earth, of the family Echeneidae. They attach themselves to larger creatures such as sharks or whales via a sort of sucker disk. These remind me of them."

"Are they sentient? Individually so, I mean?"

"I simply do not know," Soleta said. "If they are, they have certainly resisted every attempt to engage in any sort of meaningful dialogue. They would appear to have about as much intellectual prowess as a goldfish."

Standing nearby, Kebron said warningly, "Watch it. I have goldfish. They challenge my intellect daily."

Soleta didn't even glance at him as she commented, "I am not certain whether that is more of a commentary on the fish or you."

"You're cold, Soleta."

"I am Vulcan, Kebron."

"Same thing."

They were grouped in sickbay, watching the four animated fragments of the Black Mass moving about. Shelby was there as well, and she was shaking her head in amazement as she watched. "They're never still. Do you notice that? They just keep on moving and moving, twisting and turning back on each other constantly. When was the last time you ever saw such a constant, unceasing writhing of flesh?"

Calhoun, without hesitation, replied, "Graduation night at the Academy."

Despite the seriousness of the circumstances, Shelby actually laughed at that. "I knew you went to more interesting parties than I did."

"They never spend any time at all out of contact with each other," observed Selar, apparently not caring one way or the other about the respective quality of parties attended by anyone else in the room. "We've tried a variety of ways to separate them, just to see what would happen, but nothing has been successful thus far. We're hoping that—ah."

The "ah" was in response to the entrance of Burgoyne. S/he was carrying some sort of bizarre-looking device that Calhoun had not seen before. "Where should I set it up?" asked Burgoyne.

"Right over here," said Soleta.

As Burgoyne moved in from one direction, however, Doctor Selar moved in from the other. "Soleta . . . a moment of your time, please."

Soleta nodded and walked over to Selar, who stepped away from the group to provide them with a minimal degree of privacy. "May I ask how much longer this will be going on?" she inquired. "This is my sickbay, after all. Not a science lab."

"I had thought to make matters convenient for you, Doctor," replied Soleta .

"Yes, but this has been going on for longer than anticipated."

"This is a new species and a matter of science, doctor. There is never any period of time 'anticipated' in such instances. We study, research and test until we have answers, however long that may take. I am surprised that you would even question that."

"All right, Soleta. Fine. You . . ." It sounded as if Selar was in pain. Then she put fingers to either side of her temples and, taking a deep breath, appeared to calm somewhat. "You . . . do whatever is required. However, I would request that, at the very least, you do so as quietly as possible. I am possessed of a headache at the moment."

"Yes. Of course." Soleta looked at her askance, but Selar said nothing further, merely turned on her heel and went back about her business.

"Lieutenant. Ready when you are," called Burgoyne. Soleta turned and saw that Burgoyne, although s/he had the device set up, was watching Selar as she walked away. Soleta shook her head and rejoined the group.

"So what have we got here?" asked Calhoun. His purple eyes were glittering slightly. Soleta had to admit that she couldn't remember the last time she had dealt with a captain who expressed such intense joy and interest in the sheer act of discovery. "It appears to be a sound device of some sort."

"That is precisely correct," replied Soleta.

"Very good, Captain," Shelby said approvingly. "Obviously you were paying attention in science classes.

Apparently the Academy wasn't entirely extended parties of writhing flesh."

"Shame, that," said Calhoun wistfully.

"To continue," said the unflappable Soleta, "it's a harmonic dissonance generator. Very small scale, of course. I'm interested to see if there's any manner in which our shields or deflectors can be used against it somehow. Considering the manner in which it adhered to the shields, I do not hold out much hope, but . . . we must try all options. Are you ready, Lieutenant Commander?"

"Whenever you are," said Burgoyne cheerfully.

The generator was right up against the stasis tank. "Activating on three . . . two . . . one . . . and activated," said Burgoyne.

The effect was immediate, if puzzling.

The creatures stopped.

For the first time since they had been brought aboard, the samples of the Black Mass which they had lucked upon ceased their internal movement. It was as if they were trying to figure out just what it was that they were being exposed to.

And then they went berserk.

"Perfect," said Soleta upon observing the subsequent small-scale chaos, and Calhoun was struck by just how apt Kebron's description of her had been. She really was cold, because what they were observing was difficult for anyone to watch, despite the inherently destructive nature of the creatures before them.

The four black wormlike entities thrashed about wildly, as if they had suddenly gone blind (although where their eyes were at all was still a matter of some debate) and then, just like that, they split apart from one another. As if driven apart by the pounding of a surf or hauled apart by raging currents, the four entities lost contact with one another, driven to the four far ends of the stasis field.

"Better than we could have hoped," Soleta said approvingly.

"You were expecting this?"

"No, Captain, merely hoping for it. The harmonic dissonance is forming, for them, the equivalent of a small-scale deflector wave. If it were magnetic, it would be the equivalent of like charges repelling. I've introduced a vibrational frequency to them to which they are all responding on a molecular basis. Under those conditions, it becomes insurmountably painful for them to be in touch with one another. If they do, they encounter vibrations so violent that they feel as if it is going to tear them apart, and so they have no choice but to keep separate from each other. Watch. They will try and draw close to one another again, but they will fail."

Soleta was absolutely right. Each tentative move the creatures made toward one another was rebuffed by the waves of sound. Indeed, it was almost pathetic to watch.

"Are they being hurt in any other way?" asked Shelby.

"No. They're not even really being hurt as it stands," said Soleta, "as long as they remain separate from one another. Individually, they're vibrating at high speeds molecularly, but that in and of itself is not particularly painful. They'd be aware of the vibration, certainly, but there is no discomfort. It is only when they come in contact that they sense discomfort and end up moving apart from each other."

Then Calhoun leaned forward, frowning. "Is that supposed to be happening?"

The creatures were starting to droop. Until that point, they had been continuing in their futile endeavors to get near each other. Now, however, they were ceasing motion altogether.

"Doctor Selar," Soleta called, as she began checking readings on her tricorder. "A moment of your time, please. And bring your medical tricorder, if you would."

Selar approached them with her by-now-standard lack of grace. She was holding her tricorder and she did not seem pleased that her presence was required. "Yes. What?"

"Could you scan the creatures, please, and compare them to the readings you took when they were first brought on board."

The doctor nodded and began inspecting the creatures in her customary brisk, straightforward manner. By that point, they had stopped moving altogether. Selar continued to study her readings, and soon there was an unmistakable frown on her face. "These two," she pointed to two of the creatures on opposite sides of the stasis field, "are dead."

"Are you sure?" said Shelby.

Selar fired her a look.

"Sorry. What was I thinking?"

"I do not know. As I said . . . these two are dead . . . and these other two are dying. What have you done to them?"

"Nothing. Aside from keeping them apart, nothing."

"It may be," speculated Selar, "that saying you're doing nothing 'aside from keeping them apart' may be the equivalent, as far as they're concerned, as saying that you're doing nothing but keeping someone from breathing."

"Shut off the generator. Now," said Calhoun.

Immediately Burgoyne shut down the harmonic dissonance generator. The two dead creatures, naturally, did not move. The two remaining, however, immediately began to twitch and writhe about. As if rediscovering each other from a very great distance, they hurtled toward one another, intertwined, and stayed that way.

"All vital signs returning to normal," Selar said. "They will live. Am I done here?"

"Yes, thank you, doctor," said Soleta.

Selar nodded stiffly and walked off, swaying as she went. But she was stopped in her tracks by Soleta, who called, "Oh, doctor. Since we have two dead specimens, dissecting them might be helpful. Might I count on your assistance for that?"

"Of course. I cannot think of anything I would rather do," said Selar, and she walked off.

"Good lord, she's in a bad mood," muttered Shelby to Calhoun under her breath.

"I heard that, Commander," came Selar's voice from across the sickbay.

Shelby winced. "Vulcan ears, Commander," Calhoun reminded her, sounding sympathetic. "What can you do?" Then, becoming all business, he turned to Soleta. "I want a full report on the biological make-up of these things inside of two hours, Lieutenant."

"Captain, it will take me at least three hours to do the job to the fullest of my capabilities," Soleta told him.

"I want a full report on the biological make-up of these things inside of an hour, Lieutenant."

Soleta opened her mouth to protest, then closed it again. "One hour it is, sir."

"I knew I could count on you, Lieutenant."

"That is very encouraging, sir, considering that if I had voiced another protest, you might well have given me a deadline of last week."

"That's the secret of our success, Lieutenant. Our ability to communicate. It's not quite up there with theirs, granted, but it works for us."

The "theirs" he was referring to meant, of course, the two surviving creatures, still intertwined with one another and apparently oblivious to the rest of the world.

Kalinda and Xyon were intertwined with one another and apparently oblivious to the rest of the world. At least, so it seemed to Si Cwan while he was standing outside Kalinda's quarters, waiting for them to acknowledge the chime.

"Would you mind coming back later?" Kalinda's voice came from the other side.

With effort, Si Cwan said, "Not at all. Kindly continue . . . whatever it is you were doing." And with that, he started walking down the hallway.

Very.

Slowly.

It was more than enough time for Kalinda to make it to the door and stick her head out. She was wearing a dressing gown and she called, "Si Cwan? Are you all right?"

"All right?" asked Si Cwan, turning back to face her.

"Yes, all right. You sounded . . . odd just then."

"I am sorry," Si Cwan said politely. "I was unaware I sounded any way in particular. I simply wished to speak with you."

Xyon appeared just behind Kalinda. He was tucking the edges of his shirt into the tops of his slacks. "Look, I'll just be going, if the two of you want to talk . . ."

"No, that's quite all right," Si Cwan said quickly. "Not necessary at all."

"I'm not looking for trouble right now, that's all."

"Nor will you have any," Si Cwan said with his most winning smile. "There are things that must be said, to Kalinda . . . and to you. And now, my children, is as good a time as any to say them."

" 'My children?' " said Xyon suspiciously.

"Come. Come," and Si Cwan draped an arm around either of them, escorting them back into Kalinda's quarters. He made an endeavor not to stare at the rumpled sheets on the bed. "Sit down, please. No, now you don't have to sit on opposite sides of the room," he laughed. "That's quite all right. You can sit next to each other. You don't have to worry about sparing my feelings or some such nonsense. We are all adults here, after all. Well . . . some of us are younger adults than others, but the concept remains the same, correct?"

"Correct," said Kalinda, shifting uneasily in her chair. "So . . . what is it, Si Cwan? What did you want to talk about?"

"Why, the two of you, of course," Si Cwan said expansively. "I have been giving the matter a good deal of thought, and have also been listening closely to the advice of people whom I respect. And I believe that I have been handling this matter inappropriately."

"I thought trying to kill your sister's lover *is* appropriate behavior where you come from?" Xyon said sarcastically.

"Well, actually it is," Si Cwan told him with all seriousness. "In a case involving a princess and a commoner having a dalliance, yes, absolutely. Not only would my trying to kill you in such an instance be appropriate, it would be considered absolutely mandatory. So you see my problem. My instincts and training are sending me in one direction, whereas the new mores and standards under which I am expected to live are sending me in another. It is something of a predicament."

"I should think so," Xyon said, trying to look understanding. "And may I ask what conclusions you've come to?"

"There's only one possible conclusion, really," Si Cwan said. "One reasonable conclusion, in any event. I must live in the present, not in the past. Thallon is nothing but rubble now, the empire fallen. I cannot and should not expect Kalinda to adhere to bloodlines that no longer exist.

"The point is, I do not wish to be unreasonable or intransigent. It is clear to me that the two of you make each other quite happy. I cannot reasonably put forward a protest on this matter based upon a social order that no longer exists. I think . . . perhaps most of my difficulties stemmed from my simple reluctance to acknowledge that. I was raised as part of the Thallonian Empire, and part of me still does not want to admit that those times are gone. I am afraid, Xyon, that you were the victim of a good deal of personal fall-out on my part."

"Well . . . no harm done, then," Xyon said.

"I am glad that you feel that way. Ultimately, all either of us cares about is Kally's happiness."

"Absolutely."

"Good. It's settled, then," Si Cwan said, slapping his knees and standing. "When would you like me to do it?"

There was a moment of confused silence. "It? Do what? What 'it' are you supposed to do?" asked a puzzled Xyon.

"Why, the marriage, of course."

"Marriage." Xyon's voice was flat.

"Of course. The environs in which I once lived may be gone, but I still hold my status and rank. And as a high noble of my family, I am empowered to perform marriages. Oh . . . but I see that, once again, I have misread the situation. I simply took for granted that you, Xyon, would act in the manner of a Thallonian noble. There is that antiquated class structure in my head once more. Rather than lower, in my own mind, Kalinda to the status of commoner, I elevated you in my thinking to that of nobility. So that you would be, in my mind, 'good enough' for my sister. That was foolish, I suppose." He laughed. Xyon laughed as well, although rather uncomfortably.

"Now a Thallonian noble," continued Si Cwan, "were he in the sort of relationship with a princess that you are now enjoying . . . why, marriage would simply be the natural order of things. Any other action or attitude toward his beloved would be . . . well, unthinkable. But it is, once again, inappropriate to hold you to an outdated, outmoded standard. The fact is, I'm sure, that you have absolutely no intention of doing the noble thing and marrying my sister. Is that not right, Kalinda?"

"Why are you asking me?" said Kalinda. "I cannot speak on behalf of Xyon's feelings."

Xyon looked at her in surprise. "Well, of course not, but you can speak on behalf of yours. Remember what you were saying earlier? About how you'd never expect me to stay for you?"

"Of course. But that doesn't mean I wouldn't want you to. I just . . . I wasn't expecting it."

"Nor should you," Si Cwan said, sounding quite defensive of Xyon. "I would hope, Kally, that you do not make the same mistake I did and hold Xyon to an impossible standard of devotion and—"

"Now hold on! Are you saying I can't be devoted?"

"Am I giving offense again?" Si Cwan said, sounding sincerely apologetic. "It was not at all my intention."

"Are you saying I'd be unwilling to marry Kalinda?"

"Truthfully, I do not know you all that well, Xyon. I do not know what you would and would not be willing to do. I was simply trying to give you the benefit of the doubt, that's all. Far be it from me to put any sort of pressure upon you."

"Well, you are!"

"How?"

"By saying that you don't expect me to marry your sister!"

Si Cwan and Kalinda exchanged looks, and then Kalinda said gently, "Xyon . . . I hate to admit it . . . but even I'm not quite following what you mean."

"Kalinda!" and Xyon pointed accusingly at Si Cwan. "Don't you see what he's doing!"

"I will tell you what I'm doing," said Si Cwan. "I am leaving. Apparently, in my efforts to make certain that you two are happy, I've instead simply stumbled upon a sore subject. Kalinda, obviously, is not at all put off by the notion of marriage. You, Xyon, are. She will not force you into any such permanent bond . . . and you, Xyon, are not quite certain of where your mind is in the matter. Perhaps it would be best if I simply kept my distance for the time being so that I do not give any additional offense. Good day to you."

"Si Cwan, wait . . ." Kalinda started to say.

"No, no . . . I would not want to risk any further disruptions. Good day, I said." And with that, Si Cwan exited into the corridor. He stood there for a moment, reviewing in his mind everything that had just transpired . . .

. . . and then he laughed to himself, softly and with great satisfaction.

# IX.

IN MANY WAYS, CALHOUN HATED CONFERENCES, particularly when there was as much on the line as there was with this one. It made him feel . . . vulnerable in a way. After all, there he was at a table surrounded by everyone whose advice in a given situation might be of value. He was expecting them to provide him with useful information. They, in turn, would anticipate his being able to develop a strategy and put it into effect.

The problem was that the distribution of responsibility did not go equally both ways. For it was entirely possible that his people could come to him at any given time of crisis and say, "Sorry, Captain . . . we've no idea what to do." At which point it would be up to him to come up with something. As the old earth saying went, the buck stopped with him. Admittedly, it was not a saying that Calhoun completely understood. He had heard it once in passing from an older professor at the Academy, and had endeavored to research it to understand its meaning. The only relevant information he'd been able to turn up, however, indicated that a buck was an adult male deer. He was at a loss to comprehend how the apparent hunting metaphor worked, but rather than try to figure it out, he had been more than willing to chalk it up as yet another one of those simply incomprehensible things about humans and just let it go.

Burgoyne, McHenry, Soleta, Selar, Shelby and Si Cwan were grouped around the table in the conference lounge. Calhoun toyed with the notion of announcing, in a very serious tone, that they had entirely too many people whose name began with the letter "S" on hand, and some of them were simply going to have to go. But he decided, wisely, that it was neither the time nor place. "All right," he said. "What have we got?"

"We have completed the autopsy on the two creatures which died," Selar said. "Computer: File Mass 1 Alpha."

A detailed chart of the disassembled creature appeared on the computer screen. "And just before lunch, too. Most appreciated, Doctor," said Calhoun.

Ignoring the comment, Selar said, "It does not have a standard brain as we understand it. Instead of one central cerebral organ, it appears to have a network of brain tissue throughout its body. Its skin is not a normal epidermis, showing a remarkable capacity for elasticity. It is little wonder that the creature, as a whole, is capable of such drastic shifts in its proportions. A conservative estimate indicates that the creature can swell to approximately five times the size it was here. Conservative estimate, as I said. It could possibly become even larger."

"But what causes it to change in size?"

"Its stomach."

Calhoun leaned forward, frowning. "I beg your pardon?"

"At rest," Soleta stepped in, pointing to the appropriate organ on the screen, "the creature's stomach is rather small. No larger than the size of the average fist. But its stomach has the capacity to expand immensely."

"Caused by its eating. What does it eat, though?"

"As near as we can determine, just about anything. It draws nutrients and energy from anything it consumes, and excretes the waste material," said Soleta.

"Here's another interesting thing," McHenry spoke up. "I decided to do some research into the migratory paths of the Black Mass . . ."

"You did?" said Calhoun.

"Very heads-up of you, Mr. McHenry," Shelby said approvingly. "You're usually not quite so . . . aggressive."

"That thing," McHenry said with uncustomary heat, "blinded me. Shut me down. I take that very, very personally."

"Good," Calhoun replied. "So what have you got?"

"Well, the problem is that a good deal of information about the Black Mass is anecdotal, as we know. So some of this is guesswork. Although it is solid guesswork. Some guesswork involves more guessing than others, and that of course could possibly undercut the reliability of the research. So I guess you could say—"

"Mr. McHenry . . . the point, please," Calhoun said with remarkable patience.

"Oh, right. Right. Okay, here's the thing: As near as I can tell—best guess—"

"Mark!" said an exasperated Burgoyne.

"They always travel a route with a pulsar on it."

Si Cwan blinked in confusion. "A pulsar? What would that be?"

There were soft chuckles from around the table. "Si Cwan, the knowledgeable guide around Thallonian space, doesn't know what a pulsar is?" asked Shelby.

"I'm unfamiliar with the term."

"Admittedly, it's not used much outside of earth," said Soleta. "It's a name for a type of neutron star— dense stars composed mostly of tightly packed neutrons."

"That is something I've heard of," said Si Cwan, sounding a bit defensive. "But a 'pulsar' . . . ?"

"A term coined by earth scientists in the twentieth century. A pulsar is a neutron star surrounded by an extremely powerful magnetic field," McHenry explained. "The magnetic field produces a strong electric field that rips protons and electrons from the surface of the neutron star. The rotation results in detectable bursts, or pulses, of radio waves. Those pulses are what prompted scientists to term such stars 'pulsars.' "

"So what's the significance of all this, then?" asked Calhoun.

"We've put together a hypothesis," said Soleta. When she spoke, her hands moved in slow, lazy gestures as if she were painting a portrait with her fingertips. "The Black Mass resides in the Hunger Zone, like . . . like a great serpent which has devoured a cow. It sits there digesting its meal, a process that takes many years. Eventually, however, the food supply in the stomach of the Black Mass dwindles to a noticeable degree. At that point . . ."

"They swarm?" said Si Cwan.

"Correct," Selar stepped in. "By discharging energy

plasma, they are able to move quite quickly. At first, this rapid—albeit utterly normal—speed served the needs of the creature. But the Black Mass consumed all the usable stars and systems in its immediate vicinity over the centuries. And so it developed a new means of propulsion to get about."

"By all means, don't keep us in suspense," said Shelby.

"In the heart of the Hunger Zone," said Soleta, "it is our theory that there is very likely either a pulsar or neutron star. The way that the Black Mass is able to move at faster-than-light, as an entity, is that they essentially surf the event horizon of the pulsar and, using a modified version of the slingshot effect first pioneered by the starship *Enterprise,* move off at warp speeds. By this means, they find a useful system and eat the planets first. This provides them with needed mass. They then regurgitate the mass into the star, consuming the star in its entirety as well, thus giving them the plasma they require. Their stomachs now massive, they move through space by discharging the plasma."

Selar's and McHenry's heads were bobbing in agreement. Calhoun managed to keep a poker face, but Si Cwan could not keep the incredulity out of his expression. "Let me see if I understand this correctly. This creature, this Black Mass—the single most feared entity in all of Thallonian space, a monstrosity that has been used to scare recalcitrant children into going to bed—you are sitting here and telling me that, in essence, it gets around by . . . by . . ."

"Passing cosmic gas, yes. Mildly amusing, I suppose."

"Oh, I'm sure the notion will provide hours of hilarity for the billions of beings who have died because of it," said Si Cwan.

"To continue," Soleta said, clearly not wanting to dwell too heavily on the Black Mass' means of propulsion. "the Black Mass maintains its course until it comes upon another pulsar, which it then uses to whip around once more and hurtle back to the Hunger Zone . . ."

McHenry picked up the narrative. "We think their need to 'hang together' stems from evolution. Not all of the Black Mass can get to a particular destination, you see. Some of the unit sacrifices itself in order to get the rest of the Mass to a given point. Biologically co-dependent, over the centuries they've become linked at such a core level that it's become a biological imperative. They cannot exist individually."

"I get it," said Shelby, leaning forward. "They need to function as a unit. They can split into smaller units and function independently, but if they're split from one another into individuals . . . they die."

"Exactly," Selar said.

"And sound seems to break them apart," Burgoyne pointed out. "You saw the effect the harmonic dissonance generator had on them. So all we have to do is . . ."

Then s/he paused, seeing the problem. Then they all understood it, exchanging glances that underscored the fact that their difficulties were just beginning.

"All we have to do is what?" asked Si Cwan.

"All we have to do," said Calhoun, "is change the laws of physics by getting sound to travel in space."

The High Priest was discovering that he was becoming rather fond of sunsets on Fenner.

In his hiding place, deep in the Fennerian jungle, far away from any of the planet's residents, he had a good deal of time for contemplation, deep thought, and general pondering of the way of things. He felt somewhat aggrieved that the Overlord had given his oath to the inhabitants of this world that they would be forever "safe" from being redeemed. A tragic concept, that. It was like being safe from one's own heart. Nevertheless, it had been the Overlord's decision to make, and so not open to question.

But Xant would have liked this world. That much the High Priest was quite certain of. The jungle was indeed lush, the local animals quite harmless. And that sunset . . . undoubtedly the single most beautiful that he had ever seen. He couldn't get over it. Who would have thought that a planet such as this would be possessed of such a remarkable sunset? The way that the rays filtered through the horizon, and in turn illuminated the flora and fauna surrounding him.

He hoped he wouldn't have to annihilate everyone on this world.

That would be a sad thing, truly a sad thing. After all, the Fennerians actually had the opportunity to witness the sunsets as well. If they were all dead, why . . . it was almost as if the sunsets wouldn't matter anymore, for who would be there to see them? A thing of beauty is only worthwhile if there is someone there to witness it.

The High Priest had been carefully selected for this duty. He was a very light sleeper, unnaturally so, in fact. As a result, in the event that anyone from Starfleet actually managed to track him down, day or night, he could still take his life and—consequently—end the lives of all those on Fenner. Obviously it was not his first choice, but he would still do it. He also had detection devices in his cabin. If any small vessels came within range, obviously searching for him, he would act on the assumption that his capture was near and, once again, he would kill himself. One did what had to be done.

He heard a rustling in the trees nearby. His dagger was comfortably on his hip, and his hand strayed toward it, just in case.

The brush parted . . . and the most curious creature that the High Priest had ever seen peered out at him. It was large, about twice as big as the High Priest. It was covered with white fur, and had an odd, wrinkled face. It looked anthropoidal.

Considering the size of the thing, the High Priest touched his thigh to make sure that his blaster was secured to it. If the thing rushed him, or appeared the slightest bit hostile, he wanted to be prepared for it.

But instead, far from hostile, the creature seemed genuinely curious and certainly seemed to have no intention of attacking the High Priest. Instead it moved toward the Redeemer, grunting softly, tilting its head with interest. "Ooooff? Ooooof?" it asked.

Still maintaining his guard, the High Priest said, "Well, hello . . . and who are you?"

The creature watched him for a moment more . . . and then backflipped. It turned a somersault right in midair, and then flipped back again.

The High Priest laughed. The creature was trying to entertain him. Certainly it was a simplistic beast, but despite the initial appearance it had, it was obviously harmless.

The white-furred creature did a backward roll, then laughed in an odd grunting fashion and applauded for itself, banging its large padded hands together in clear triumph, pleased at its own cleverness.

"Very good! Very good!" said the High Priest, clapping his hands in approval. Then he laughed again, struck by the amusing irony that the mindless creature had taught him a trick, rather than the other way around. "Can you do this?" The High Priest proceeded to bounce up and down in place.

The creature watched him for a moment, tilting its head quizzically, and then it imitated the bouncing.

"What a sight we must be, eh?" called the High Priest to his newfound friend. They bounced up and down for a few minutes and then the creature placed a hand on the ground and started to run in a circle. It did so with great excitement and another series of "Oooof! Woooof! Woooo ooof oooof!"

Then the creature flopped back onto his hind quarters. It looked a little tired.

"Wait. Wait right here," said the High Priest of the Redeemers. He ran back into his makeshift cabin and emerged a moment later with some foodstuffs. He had no idea whether the thing would consume it or not, but it was certainly worth a try. He held it up, waving it in the direction of the creature's face, and said, "Here. Here. Want to try it? You might like it. Hmm? Like it?"

Clearly the creature, for all its size, was still tentative around the Redeemer. It approached slowly, head cocked, apparently hypnotized by the sight of the food being dangled in front of it. Obviously nervous, but overcome by its hunger, the creature slowly reached up and, ever so carefully, took the food from the High Priest's outstretched hand. It was now seated bare inches from the High Priest.

"Very good," said the High Priest approvingly, "very good." And then, more for his own amusement than anything else—for naturally he didn't expect a reply—the High Priest added, "What do we say?"

The creature looked up at him and said, very clearly, very crisply, "Night night."

"No, we say thank y—"

The High Priest's response was so automatic that it didn't dawn on him at first that the animal had spoken. Then he caught himself in mid-reply and gasped, "What did you say?"

"I said night night. Is your hearing defective?" inquired the creature.

No words were coming out of the High Priest's throat.

"The reason I'm saying night night, by the way, is because I've just jammed a hypo into your leg. I'd estimate another three seconds before it takes full effect. Frightfully sneaky trick, I'm afraid, but then again . . . these are dangerous times, as someone once said."

The truth of what had happened was filtering through the High Priest's brain. He tried to pull out his knife, but his arms weren't functioning. He suddenly realized that his legs weren't working either, and he started to sag to the ground. The white-furred creature caught him on the way down.

"I said 'full effect.' However, even the partial effect is enough to make you harmless to everyone . . . yourself, me, everyone. Oh, but I've been a frightful boar and haven't introduced myself. Ensign Janos, attached to the Starship *Excalibur*. A pleasure to make your acquaintance. I've had the devil's own time tracking you here. You were very well hidden. Very well. So good for you, I suppose, but you know, you couldn't hide forever. Oh . . . oh dear. You seem to have gone all unconscious."

Which he had. The High Priest had passed out. The only thing stopping him from falling was Janos' arm.

Slowly Ensign Janos lowered the High Priest to the ground. Then he walked into the makeshift cottage and discovered transmitting equipment there that the High Priest had been using to keep in touch with the other Redeemers. It would be merely the work of moments to reconfigure it so that Janos could get word to the *Excalibur* and let them know that the planet Fenner was safe. Then something caught his eye. Something quite pretty and, truthfully, rather magnificent. He sat down next to the insensate form of the High Priest and, gazing at the sky, said, "Smashing sunset tonight, don't you think?" And he proceeded to keep up a steady stream of chitchat with the unconscious Redeemer as the sunlight dwindled on the horizon.

## X.

"YOU'VE GOT ME COMPLETELY CONFUSED NOW!" said Xyon.

He was sitting on the deck of his ship, the *Lyla*. Specifically, he was sitting on the floor of the vessel, while Kalinda sat in the pilot seat nearby and regarded him with open curiosity. "Why do I have you confused?" she asked. "What is there to be confused about?"

"This whole situation! The things that your brother said—!"

"What things did he say that were so terrible?" she asked. "He offered to have us be together. Don't you see, Xyon? We won! We have what we want . . ." Then she hesitated. "Or do we? Well, that's really the problem, isn't it."

"No. The problem," said Xyon, stabbing a finger at

189

her, "is that everything was going fine until your brother suddenly started piping in with this business about marriage. That suddenly changed expectations . . ."

"What expectations?" she asked, blinking her eyes like a blinded owl. "I told you what my expectations of you were . . ."

"Yes, you told me. But they changed once you got your brother's encouragement, didn't they. Suddenly—"

"Suddenly nothing," she shot back. "If anyone's changed in all of this, it's you. All of a sudden you're saying I want things that I didn't ask for . . . didn't even think of asking for, because I know you're not capable of giving them."

"How do you know that?"

"Are you saying you are?"

"I'm saying . . ." Xyon moaned and gripped his blond hair on either side as if he were ready to tear it out of his head . . . which he more or less was. "I don't know what I'm saying."

"Well, that much I believe."

"I wasn't thinking ahead, Kalinda. When you and I became involved, I wasn't . . . I mean . . . I never think ahead. You know? Life's too short."

"And it gets shorter if you make a full time profession of risking it," she told him. She slid off the chair and took his hands in each of hers. "You could stay here, you know."

"Oh, yes, of course; starships are always in the habit of taking in strays."

"This isn't just a starship, and you know it. Your father is the captain. And he wants to be more of a father to you, we both know that. He won't turn you away."

"Kalinda . . . I . . ."

"But, of course, think of everything you'd be giving up." She spoke with an edge to her voice, a trace of bitter anger that he hadn't heard before. "Your freedom. Your life of adventure. It's not as if you'd be gaining anything from it—security, me—none of those things matter."

He blew air impatiently through his lips. "Are you going to bother to listen to anything I have to say, or are you simply going to have this entire discussion by yourself?"

"Fine. I'm listening. Go ahead. Say what you want."

He stared at her. "I don't know what to say," he admitted.

She released his hands and stood, shaking her head in a discouraged manner.

"Kalinda, it's just . . . it's a lot to process at one time. A lot to deal with. I don't want to rush into anything, I don't want to make any mistakes, I don't want—"

"Me?"

"Yes, I want you." He tried to sound teasing as he got up, went to her and took her hand. "Haven't I been pretty obvious about that?"

"But you want me on your terms."

"I didn't know any terms had to be set. That was your brother's idea. He's trying to push us into something that neither of us is ready for, in hopes of pushing us apart."

"Tell me something, Xyon. If you were going to leave, right here, right now . . . and I said I wanted to come along with you, be with you. The only 'term' attached is that we be together, for however long it's something we both desire . . . would you want that?"

"Of course," he said without hesitation.

"Think," she said softly, "about what you'd be agreeing to. I'd be there, all the time. You'd have no privacy. You'd have someone else's life intertwined with yours. Anything that you wanted to do, any task you desired to undertake, would have an impact on me. So naturally you would be honor bound to discuss it with me. And if I said 'No, I don't want to risk myself . . . and I don't want you to risk yourself,' why . . . what then, Xyon? So I'm asking you again: If you were going to leave, right here, right now . . . and I said I wanted to come along with you, be with you. The only 'term' attached is that we be together, for however long it's something we both desire . . . would you want that?"

"Of course," he said with a great deal more hesitation.

He tried to speak more, but she put a finger to his lips. "I think," Kalinda said in a very gentle tone, "that if we are to speak of this more . . . and I emphasize 'if' . . . then it should be later. Don't you think that would be a better idea?"

He found himself nodding, and then Kalinda kissed him gently on the knuckles of his right hand and eased herself out the door of the ship.

Xyon was alone.

The Overlord actually seemed excited.

Having been brought over from the Redeemer ship, he sat in the conference lounge with Calhoun and all the senior officers, and listened to the entire description of what the *Excalibur* had discovered in its encounter with the Black Mass. Most of the commentary seemed to be coming from the younger Vulcan woman, Soleta.

He noticed a couple of times that the one called McHenry seemed about to interrupt, particularly when Soleta was describing means of propulsion, but she managed to silence him with a look.

When she was finished, the Overlord sat back, taking it all in. "But where does that leave us, then? Sound cannot travel in space."

"True," agreed Calhoun. "But we believe we've found a way around it. Mr. Burgoyne . . . ?"

The Hermat, Burgoyne, got to hir feet and started to move while s/he spoke. The Overlord suspected that, for some reason, s/he felt more comfortable that way. "Phasers can be rigged," s/he said, "to make them over into, essentially, blasts of magnetic dissonance. Pure magnetic fields wouldn't hurt them or contain them, but magnetically based dissonance blasts will very likely split them apart. If we're fortunate, then it will have the same impact it had on them in sickbay."

"You can do this thing?" said the Overlord.

"Yes. It actually is not that difficult a proposition for us. We suspect you may be able to as well, although we're not quite certain. Your phaser weapons are different from ours, and obviously I'm not familiar with all the working parameters."

"Well, it should not matter whether we can or not," the Overlord told them. "After all, you are here. The Black Mass is still approaching Tulaan IV, but there is time to do what needs be done. And you can . . ."

The Overlord stopped. He found the smiles from around the table to be somewhat disconcerting. He could not, for the life of him, imagine what they might be smiling about.

"Do it yourselves," said Calhoun.

The Overlord's already obsidian face darkened even farther, which would have seemed impossible. "Do not test me, Captain. Do not play this game. My threat to the people of Fenner still stands."

"Actually . . . it doesn't," Calhoun informed him. He seemed remarkably smug about it, too. Of everyone in the room, the Overlord noticed that Si Cwan seemed the most pleased.

Shelby said, "You see, your threat isn't standing; actually, it's sort of . . . Mr. Kebron, what would you say it was doing?"

"Lying down," Kebron said.

"Yes, lying down. Good choice of words. Your threat is lying down, Overlord," said Shelby. "Unconscious. No threat to himself, and certainly no threat to the innocent people of Fenner."

"This is a trick," said the Overlord.

Calhoun shrugged in response. "If it pleases you to believe that, fine. But I assure you that the next time you contact Fenner, one of my people is going to be responding."

"You could not have found him. Nothing could have tracked him there."

"As I said, we have no reason to lie. Check for yourself if it will make you happy. I don't particularly care."

He looked around the room, saw the challenging expressions . . . and he knew then, beyond question, that Calhoun was telling the absolute truth. There indeed was no reason to lie. Any fabrication would be quickly discovered.

"I see," the Overlord said slowly. "So let us say, for the sake of discussion, that you are telling the truth. Am I now to understand that you will abandon the quest against the Black Mass?"

"We have given you some idea of how to defeat it and save yourselves," Calhoun told him. "Whether you choose to or not is entirely up to you. It is not our concern whether you manage it or not, though."

"Have you considered the fates of future races who might find themselves victims of the Black Mass?"

"Absolutely. And if we are so inclined, we can destroy the thing after it has devoured Tulaan IV . . ."

"And you," said Si Cwan, revelling in the notion a bit more than the Overlord would have liked.

"You see, Overlord . . . we are gamblers, you and I," said Calhoun. "You gambled that I would care enough about the predicament you put upon the Fennerians that I would aid you. I gambled that one of my people, on his own, would be able to find and incapacitate your High Priest. So in a sense, we both won. Chief engineer Burgoyne here will be happy to provide you with the specs as to how you may be able to convert your phasers over, and you can take that information against the Black Mass . . ."

"Or take it to your grave," Si Cwan suggested.

"That's enough, Ambassador. I think the Overlord gets the point."

"Oh, I do. I do. But there is a point that you still do not seem to 'get.' "

"Really," said Calhoun. "And what would that be?"

"That I will not have my word gainsayed. Prime One . . ."

The Overlord's red eyes blazed with cold satisfaction, and he was pleased to see the momentary unease in the conference lounge as they tried to determine just what he meant by that . . . and why he was calling for his second-in-command when Prime One was, in fact, not there.

Suddenly there was the sound of a Redeemer transport device. The Overlord had noticed that the sound of the Redeemer transport mechanism was somewhat different from that of the *Excalibur.* He could only surmise that it was because the Redeemer's technology was so far superior to, and more powerful than, the Federation's. Of course, even the Redeemers' transporters couldn't penetrate shielding . . . but the starship's shields weren't up at that moment.

Heads whipped around as everyone leaped to their feet, uncertain just what was happening. Everyone, that is, except Chief Engineer Burgoyne 172, and Doctor Selar. The two of them shimmered out of existence in a transporter haze. The only things there that marked their former presence were their uniforms, along with comm badges, left in crumpled heaps.

Calhoun was around the table so fast that the Overlord had barely blinked before the captain was right in front of him. "Where are they!" he demanded. "What did you do?!"

"You remember the blessing I bestowed upon them?" said the Overlord, not at all intimidated by the angry Calhoun. "When I placed my hands upon them? While doing that, I encoded them with my personal DNA trace. This entire meeting has been monitored by Prime One from back on my ship, through a communications device on my person. He has served me well, this Prime One, and when I spoke his name after he heard all that had transpired here, he knew precisely what to do."

"What . . . did he . . . do?", said Calhoun, looking as if he was ready to snap the Redeemer's neck.

But the angrier Calhoun became, the calmer the Overlord grew. "Our world is called Tulaan IV for a reason. There are, in fact, eight planets in this system. We are simply the fourth one away from our sun . . . although, as poor fortune would have it, the one whose orbit takes us straight into the Black Mass' path. Aside from our homeworld, there are two other worlds that are habitable. Three worlds; a good deal of territory to search . . . plus, for all you know, we have created underground refuges on one of the uninhabitable worlds. So you do not have overmuch time in which to look around for your departed officers. This is not to say that you could not find them, of course. A very lengthy, prolonged sensor sweep should do the job. A week should suffice, I think. Perhaps two, at most. A pity that the Black Mass will not provide you with that much time."

There was dead silence in the conference lounge then. The Overlord revelled in it.

"The abduction of your people, captain . . . was my back-up plan. Do you . . . have a back-up plan? Because if you do, now would be an excellent time to employ it."

"We have you," said Calhoun, "as hostage."

"True. And I will happily remain here. Kill me or do not kill me, as you see fit. It is of no consequence to me. If my system dies, I die anyway. But then again . . . so do your people. It is entirely up to you. I do not personally care if your people are doomed or not. But you might very well care. Do you, Captain? Care, I mean?"

Calhoun said nothing. After a time, he simply nodded.

"I can take that to mean that you will continue in your assistance of our plight?"

"I want my people back, alive and unharmed."

"And you will have them . . . when we are alive and unharmed."

For a long moment, Calhoun didn't speak. Then he said, "There was a time . . . not that long ago, in fact . . . where I would have let them die. Where I would have thrown out any life rather than let myself be dictated to by monsters such as you. You are very, very fortunate . . . that you did not encounter me in those days."

"I daresay your crewmen are fortunate as well."

"But I want you to know," Calhoun said stiffly, "that after we do this . . . all bets are off. And I will not rest until you, and everything you stand for, is wiped out of Sector 221-G."

"Are you threatening me with war, Captain? And here I had hoped that we would be able to become allies."

With a low growl, Calhoun said, "Mr. Kebron . . . place the Overlord in the brig."

The Overlord stood and bowed slightly. "I will go quietly . . . although I will request that, in the unfortunate happenstance that you fail, you return me to my world so that I may die with the others of my race."

"Gladly."

"Oh, and Captain . . . one more thing."

"I," said Calhoun, "have had more than enough of your dictates."

"Not a dictate; merely a suggestion. While you are fighting the Black Mass . . . which is, by my calculations, approximately eighteen hours away from us . . . I do not suggest you leave shuttles behind to sweep the area, hoping to stumble over your missing crewmen. I regret that I have left instructions aboard my ship that any such vessels are to be shot down on sight. I do apologize for the inconvenience."

Xyon found it odd: He had become used to the solitude. He had even come to enjoy it. Yet now, for some reason, the vessel felt . . . empty. He felt empty. But it was not such an overwhelming, keening sensation that he felt any great drive to do something about it.

It had been some time since Kalinda had left him in his ship. From the time that she had departed until now, he hadn't budged an inch.

"Lyla," he said.

The entity which lived aboard the ship, and was permanently merged with the inner workings of the vessel, said promptly, "Yes, Xyon."

"Lyla . . . do you ever feel lonely?"

"No, Xyon. It is impossible for me to feel lonely."

"Why is that?"

"Because it is not part of me."

Xyon looked around as if he could actually see Lyla, tucked away in the ship's inner workings. "What do you mean? How can it not be part of you?"

"Xyon . . . as you know, I'm an engram computer. I do not see other creatures, do not touch them or interact with them in any way save for my voice. If I possessed the normal socialization capabilities of other creatures, I would lose my mind. I would go insane. That would certainly not leave me of any significant service to anyone."

"Okay, I understand that, but—"

"So when I was installed as part of this ship, any part of me that would have been a triggering device for socialization was removed."

Xyon hadn't known this. "So you were just . . . lo-botomized? They carved pieces out of your personali-ty? That's what you're telling me?"

"Yes, but only because you asked."

"Lyla, that's . . . that's terrible . . ."

"Is it, Xyon? Is the inability to feel loneliness . . . all that more terrible than actually feeling it? I will always be complete unto myself. The work done on me here in the starship simply expedited a repair program that I could have instituted myself via the nanotech that is part of my maintenance programming. It would have taken more time, but I could have done it. I do not need—"

"Me?"

"Of course I do not need you, Xyon. I am a ship. You are humanoid. I do not need you in particular to exist any more than you need me in particular to travel through space." She paused a moment and then added, "But that does not mean that I do not like spending time with you. That I would not rather spend time with you than with other beings. You were speaking, howev-er, of necessity and absolutes. Those are always very difficult questions to answer."

"Yeah. I know. And they don't seem to get any easier no matter how many times you ask them."

"Xyon."

The deep male voice was so unexpected that Xyon actually jumped slightly. He looked around and saw Mackenzie Calhoun standing in the doorway.

"Captain," he said, acknowledging his presence.

"Xyon," Calhoun said again. He stepped fully into the ship, through the irised doors, and then stood there for a moment, looking and feeling somewhat awkward. Xyon had trouble envisioning an awkward Mackenzie Calhoun.

"This is somewhat difficult, but there's no other way to put it: I was hoping I could borrow your ship."

"Borrow my ship," Xyon said blankly. "Why should I lend you my ship?"

"Two of my people are missing. The Overlord arranged for their disappearance. They're on one of the worlds in this system, and those worlds are being watched by Redeemer vessels. Your ship, however, has a cloaking device, so I'm told."

"You're told correctly," Xyon replied. "But if anyone told you that I'm in the habit of loaning out my ship, then in that you were misinformed."

"No one told me that. But I was hoping that—"

"Captain, if you need help . . . if your people need help . . . then I'll help. That's what I do. But I'll do it my own way, by myself."

"Why?" Calhoun stepped forward and sat on the edge of the pilot seat. "Why do you do this? This . . . going about the galaxy, trying to help people, being a hero."

"Why do you?" countered Xyon.

Calhoun allowed a small smile. "Good point. So are you saying you're trying to be like me? Live up to the legend?"

"No. I'm trying to be like me. I just . . ." His hands moved in vague patterns. "I just haven't figured out . . . exactly who I am yet. How much of me is you, how much is mother . . . and how much is just me."

"Don't worry about the first two," said Calhoun. "Just worry about being the best you possible, and everything else will come in time."

"Did they teach you that at Starfleet Academy?"

"In a sense. The gardener there said it to me one

time. You have to learn to take wisdom wherever you can get it." He hesitated and then said, "Are you sure you want to do this? Check out the planets, see if you can turn up my crewmembers."

"Which ones? Oh, *grozit,* tell me it's not Si Cwan."

"No, no," chuckled Calhoun. "It's Burgoyne, my chief engineer, and Selar, my CMO."

"Oh. Well, they're okay, those two. Sure, I'll do it. I can . . ." He looked off in the general direction that Kalinda had gone. "I can use the distance. The time on my own."

"Xyon . . . is there anything you'd like to talk about?"

Xyon laughed softly. "It's too late, Captain. Anything I wanted to talk about . . . it was a long time ago. I was somebody different then."

"No. You were never different. You were always my son."

"Believe it or not, I know that. I was all too aware of it. And when I was here . . . you stood up for me. Helped me out."

"I wish I could have been there more for you . . ."

"No. You don't. Because you wouldn't have given up all this," and he gestured in a manner that took in the starship, the stars, all of it, ". . . you wouldn't have given up all this for anything. And . . . I think I understand that a little."

"Do you?" He seemed amused by the concept.

"Yes. I do. I mean, don't get me wrong. I'm still mad at you."

"Oh, of course. That goes without saying," Calhoun said. "A lifetime of anger doesn't disappear in so short a time."

"But there are . . . other things. Things that . . . well, it's not important. It's just that I see there are . . . possibilities I hadn't considered. And it's like you said: it's hard to know anything for sure. Even yourself."

"I know one thing for sure," said Calhoun.

"Oh, *grozit,* you're not going to say you love me, are you? I mean, we've been over this . . ."

"No. No, I wasn't going to say that at all. As I've said to you before . . . it's impossible to love someone that you don't really know. But I'm . . . I'm pleased that I've had the chance to meet you. And I hope that, once this business is over . . . perhaps you'll stay a while longer. What's happening with you and Kalinda, by the way."

"The same thing that happened with you and mother."

"Oh." He paused. "And how is it going to turn out this time?"

"I don't know. I wish I did."

"Do you love her? Does she love you?"

"Oh, come on, Captain. You know our type. We never get to know anyone enough to love them."

"I'm not sure about that," Calhoun said slowly. "I've been thinking that might not be true."

"Don't tell me that, Captain. You'll destroy my entire view of the universe."

"All right," said Calhoun. "It can wait until later."

"Until later. I'll power up my ship, make a few last minute preparations, and be on my way." He looked in annoyance at his father. "These missing crewmen . . . the Redeemers are holding them over your head so that you'll cooperate and help save their miserable planet, right?"

"Right."

"And if you stop the Black Mass, they'll survive."

"Right."

Xyon shook his head. "Life isn't fair. Then

again . . . I suppose I've always known that. That's why I go around trying to even the odds wherever I can."

"Now," said Calhoun approvingly, "you're starting to understand." He extended a hand. "Good luck."

After staring at the hand for a moment, Xyon took it and gripped it firmly. "You too, Captain."

Calhoun started to leave, then stopped and said, "Xyon . . . before you go . . . could you tell me where your mother is? I . . . I would like to say hello to her. Try and catch up with her, just . . ."

"She's dead, father."

"What?"

Xyon looked down. "She's dead. She passed away two years ago. That's why I left. I had nothing to stay there for."

"Why didn't you tell me?"

"Because," and he brought his gaze up level with Calhoun's own, "her last words were, 'Don't tell your father. He'll grieve, and he's had enough grief in his life.' She kept track of you, you know. Kept up with your career, such as it was."

"So why tell me now?"

"Because you deserve to know. And because she deserves to have you grieve for her."

Calhoun sighed heavily. Suddenly he looked a lot older. "You're right. On both counts. Thank you for telling me. And Xyon . . ."

"If you tell me you're sorry, you can go look for your own crewmen."

"All right. I won't say," and he paused just long enough to give space between the first half of the sentence and the last: ". . . I'm sorry."

Calhoun walked away then, leaving Xyon alone to

prepare for his departure. He ran a final systems check, then left the ship, made a quick stopover at sickbay for a couple of items, and—shortly thereafter, fully cloaked—the good ship *Lyla* departed the *Excalibur* on a mission that was even more of a longshot than the one Janos had embarked upon earlier.

## XI.

IT WAS DIFFICULT TO BELIEVE that Tulaan V could be any more inhospitable than Tulaan IV was, but indeed that was the case. And that was something, in the midst of a cold desert where wind howled along the plains, that Burgoyne and Selar were quickly discovering firsthand.

When they had first materialized naked and cold on the dark and fearsome surface, the wind cutting through the air had almost been enough to dispose of them right then and there. However, a small package of protective clothing had been left waiting for them. Obviously the Overlord tended to think these things out well ahead of time. The clothes were barely enough to shield them from the initial ravages of the planet's surface, heavy and lined as they were, but the condition of this world was such that there was no way they would be able to survive unless they found shelter, and quickly.

Fortunately, that was immediately attended to, for there was a series of caves nearby. They were not small, and they were not particularly glamorous, but at least they were functional. The only problem was, even though they were a short distance away, Selar seemed unable or unwilling (or both) to get to them. The loose clothes hanging over her bulging body, Selar staggered under the assault of the winds and it was only Burgoyne's determination and stubborn refusal to acknowledge the likelihood that they were dead that kept them going.

"Leave me!" shouted Selar over the shrieking of the wind.

"You don't seriously think I'm going to follow that suggestion!"

"Why should you!? You never listen to me any other time!" Then she said nothing more, simply grunted under the weight of her upper body and the pressure of the wind.

Burgoyne, on the other hand, kept up a steady stream of chatter. For the most part, it was intended as steady encouragement for Selar. In point of fact, all it did was annoy her, which Burgoyne would have known had s/he looked into Selar's eyes. Fortunately, Burgoyne was too busy trying to see, hir eyes narrow slits against the wind, hir free arm in front of hir face as s/he kept them moving forward, always moving forward. That was because s/he was concerned that, if they stopped moving, they wouldn't be able to start again.

Closer and closer still they drew to the caves, and finally they were right there, just a few feet away.

And it was at that point that Selar collapsed. The distance didn't matter. She could have been five feet or five hundred feet, she simply couldn't move another step.

And the bothersome thing to Burgoyne was that s/he was beginning to feel a good deal of pain. S/he wasn't sure why. The chill from the pounding wind, that s/he was prepared for, that s/he was capable of withstanding. But this was something else, a general cramping, a feeling of unease that s/he couldn't attribute to anything in particular. But Burgoyne was disciplined when it came to pain management. S/he pushed it aside, focused on what needed to be done, and then put one arm around Selar's back, and the other under her legs. Burgoyne took a deep breath, which in and of itself was dangerous and a problem because it stung hir lungs viciously, and then s/he hoisted Selar into the air. S/he grunted under the formidable weight as s/he staggered the final steps to the nearest cave and practically tumbled in. S/he did not, however, allow Selar to fall. Instead s/he took the brunt of the impact with hir knees, and s/he felt the jolt throughout hir entire body. Hir legs were aflame with agony as s/he allowed Selar to slide out of hir arms and onto the floor.

For all hir pain, the first words out of hir mouth were, "Are you . . . all right?" S/he still had to speak loudly, for the sound of the wind was slightly diminished but still deafening.

On the floor, Selar started pushing herself back toward the far end of the cave, letting her legs do most of the work. "I am . . . sufficient," she said through gritted teeth. "Thank you . . . for helping me . . ."

"Not a problem."

Panting, Selar looked up and said, "Why do you

say . . . that?" Her breath sounded ragged in her chest. "It is not logical. Obviously it was . . . a problem . . ."

"Just trying to be polite," said Burgoyne.

"Burgoyne," Selar said, "we have been transported . . . against our will . . . to a hostile planet . . . where we will very likely die. This is the sort of . . . situation . . . that does not truly require social niceties." She paused and stared at Burgoyne, who had an odd expression on hir face. "What is it?"

"Do you think you could call me Burgy. Just once?"

"I am Vulcan. Vulcans do not do diminutives."

"Oh, for crying out loud . . ."

"Be satisfied that I address you as something other than Lieutenant Command—"

And then she screamed.

And so did Burgoyne.

It was precisely the same cry, at precisely the same time, for precisely the same period. Selar fell back, gasping, taking in deep lungfuls of air. Then she stared at Burgoyne, who was halfway across the cave. When the pain had hit hir, s/he had literally leaped backward as if stabbed. Since s/he was not weighed down, and retained hir catlike reflexes, naturally s/he was far more nimble. S/he was not, however, in any less pain.

Selar fixed hir with a look that seemed to contain cold fury. "That . . . was not funny."

"What?" Burgoyne's eyes were bleary as s/he looked back at Selar. "Fuh . . . funny?"

"Imitating . . . my pain . . ."

"I didn't imitate anything! I felt it!"

"Burgoyne, if you are attempting some pathetic source of humor . . ."

"I'm not. I swear." Hir face, hir manner, made it

clear that s/he was not kidding. "Whatever hit you just then, I felt it too . . ."

"Whatever hit me? You mean the labor pain?"

Burgoyne went dead-white. "You're kidding."

Selar stared at hir.

"You're not kidding. Of course you're not kidding. But . . . but why did I . . . ?"

"Because we have an empathic link."

"If we have an empathic link, then why are you so nasty to me?"

"Because we have an empathic link!" Selar said with barely contained exasperation. "You are not exactly the sort of individual a Vulcan would choose to have a deep mental and spiritual bond with, Burgoyne! Do you understand? You are loud. You are overdemonstrative. You are flamboyant. You are—"

"The father of your child, and in love with you."

"In love."

"Yes."

"With me."

"Yes."

Selar shook her head. "Burgoyne . . . to your other attributes . . . I think it would be best if I added 'insa—' "

She did not manage to get the word "insane" out, for another wave of agony hit her, far worse than the previous. It hit Burgoyne as well. Burgoyne let out a yowl that Selar thought would deafen her.

"There is no pain," she whispered, and stepped out of herself. She brought her mind far, far away from what she was feeling, refused to acknowledge it, shunted it away into a deep part of herself that was so far away from her consciousness, she would never need to feel it. That done, she steadied herself, calmed her breathing, slowed her racing heart. She told herself that she was having trouble maintaining her control and discipline thanks to the circumstances into which she had been thrust, and the distracting and onerous link she had with Burgoyne. But she would not let it overwhelm her. She was Vulcan. She could handle it. "There is no pain," she said again.

"Like hell there isn't!" Burgoyne said through gritted teeth. "All that pain you've been suppressing? Well, I found it for you! It's linked right over to me!" S/he took deep, panting breaths.

As Selar steadied herself, so did Burgoyne's writhing ease. Within moments they were both lying on the floor of the cave, panting like long distance swimmers. Slowly Burgoyne propped hirself up on one elbow. Hir voice hoarse, s/he said, "This is fun. We have to do this more often."

Selar said nothing.

Burgoyne pulled hirself over to Selar and said, "So how long does it take . . . ? Vulcan labor, I mean. Once the labor pains have begun."

"We Vulcans may be a precise people, but even for us, some things are not an exact or precise science. I do not know how long it will take. I will try to shield you from as much of what I am feeling as possible." She was starting to sound like herself. She found that encouraging. "It may be less and less possible as the labor progresses. These are not ideal conditions. And the increase in intensity of the pains will likely intensify the strength of our link."

"So the more you feel, the more I'll feel."

Selar looked up at Burgoyne with genuine contrition. "I am . . . sorry, Burgoyne. It is not right that you should be put through this."

"And it's right that you should? You said it yourself: here you were, minding your own business, and suddenly the Vulcan perpetuation drive kicks in and your life is made to stand on end. That doesn't seem particularly fair to me." Burgoyne stood up then, half-hunched over to accommodate the low ceiling of the cave. S/he shoved hir hands under hir arms and, forcing a smile, said, "We don't get to pick and choose what happens to us all the time. Sometimes you just have to deal with what's been given you."

"That is very profound."

"No, it's not."

"You are right. It is not. That was simply me being polite again."

And then the next wave hit her, and however much she thought she had prepared herself for it, it wasn't enough by half. She did everything she could to contain it, to redirect it, to send it to a place where the two of them would be untouched by it. Ultimately, however, she could not defeat all of it, and what she felt, Burgoyne felt.

Burgoyne had never experienced anything like it in hir life. Despite hir reflexes, despite hir grace, s/he hit the ground hard and curled up, clutching hir belly even though there was nothing out of the ordinary in there. S/he kept trying to tell hirself that it was literally all in hir mind, that there was no physical reason for hir to feel the way s/he was feeling. S/he was not remotely successful, and all s/he could do was hang on and try to keep focus until the waves of anguish passed hir by.

S/he lay several feet from Selar, and they fixed each other with looks of sheer exhaustion. And part of that weariness came from the knowledge that their difficulties had only just begun.

"So . . . let's recap," Burgoyne managed to say. "Trapped on an alien world . . . no supplies . . . just the clothes on our backs . . . freezing . . . in labor with both of us feeling it . . ."

"Is there some . . . point to this recitation?" inquired Selar.

"I was just figuring . . . that things couldn't get worse."

In the near distance, there was a roar. It was not the roar of a wind. It was deep and powerful and was coming from the throat of something that sounded rather angry and certainly very hungry.

Selar stared at hir as Burgoyne moaned. "Tell me, Burgoyne," she inquired just before the next labor pain hit. "Do you ever tire of being right all the time?"

When Shelby walked into the captain's ready room, Calhoun was sitting at his desk, studying his sword. The weapon, which he had kept with him all these years, lay gleaming and polished on the desk top.

"We'll be within range of the Black Mass in ten minutes, Captain," said Shelby. She glanced at the sword. "Planning to challenge it to a duel?"

He picked the sword up, hefted it. "Tell me: do you think that I should go down to the brig and cut off the Overlord's head?"

"Absolutely," Shelby said immediately. "Then, if you want, I can organize a soccer game down in the holodeck. We can use the head as the ball."

"You're joking."

"Yes."

"I'm not."

"I know." She paused. "What do you expect me to say, Mac? Great idea, fearless leader. Head right down to the brig and murder, in cold blood, a prisoner."

"A blackmailer, a mass murderer . . . he tried to kill my son."

"You can't do it, Mac."

He laid the sword down gently and shook his head in disgust. "What good is being the captain of a ship if you can't rid the galaxy of the occasional monster?"

"That's what we're trying to do with the Black Mass."

"Stop one monster, empower another." He placed the sword back on the wall.

"We do have options, you know," said Shelby. "The Overlord has committed crimes. Crimes in the eyes of the Federation. Once this is done, we can bring him back to Federation space. Have him tried . . ."

"And risk a full-blown war between the Federation and the Redeemers? You notice, Elizabeth, that we haven't seen much of the Redeemer fleet since this all started?"

"Yes, I had noticed, now that you mention it."

"Why do you think that is?"

She considered it a moment. "They're in hiding somewhere?"

"In hiding. Or lying in wait. Being kept in reserve in the event that they're needed. Who knows how much firepower they've got stashed away. But I can make a guess as to what purpose they intend to put it. In fact, I wouldn't be the least bit surprised if, presuming we try to leave Thallonian space with the Overlord, we suddenly find ourselves staring down the gun barrel of every ship in the Redeemer fleet. I like a challenge as much as the next man, Eppy . . ."

"More."

"More than the next man," he admitted. "But there are certain odds that even I would prefer not to take on if I can help it. One of the first things I learned as a warlord was that knowing what fights to stay out of was as important as knowing which fights to fight."

"I know how angry you are over the situation, Mac. The simple, hard truth is . . . sooner or later, the Black Mass would have to be dealt with. By somebody. So it turned out to be sooner, and it turned out to be us. The reasons really shouldn't matter."

"They do matter. To me."

"Meaning what?" she said, her arms folded. "That your pride is hurt?"

"Eppy, I love you."

"So what you're saying . . ."

Then his last words penetrated, and her eyes widened. "What?"

"You heard me."

"But . . . but I . . . it . . . but . . ." She was trying to find something to say, and then a way to say it. "What do you mean? Where did that come from?"

"From the heart. I'm sorry, Eppy, but the conversation we were having . . . it sounded old. We've had variations on it for as long as I've been in command. It was time to try something different."

"Wait . . . wait . . ." She shook her head as if trying to shake off a dream. "So you're saying you told me you love me . . . just as some sort of conversational gambit? Or is this something that you're going to wind up apologizing for tomorrow?"

"Tomorrow. Eppy, who knows if there's ever going to be tomorrow. Who knows . . . anything? About anything?"

"I always thought you did, Mac. I've never seen anyone so utterly confident that he knew so many answers to so many questions."

"Eppy . . ." He was careful to keep a distance from her, as if afraid that he did not trust himself in proximity. "There is no one else on this ship that I feel as close to as I do to you."

"What about XO Mueller?"

The words slipped out before she could think better of it, and the moment they had been voiced, she wished she could have taken them back.

But Calhoun did not seem upset. Instead he actually smiled. "I should have known. How long have you been aware?"

"Long enough. Mac, it's none of my business . . . forget I asked."

"Mueller is . . . a fine officer," Calhoun said. "A good woman . . . a good friend. And we . . . had another aspect of our relationship. But she isn't you, Eppy. She never could be."

"Mac . . . you and I, we're too different . . ."

"That's fortunate. If we were too much alike, we'd probably kill each other."

"And what am I supposed to do?" she demanded. She had no idea how to react. Conflicting emotions were tumbling about wildly in her mind. "How am I supposed to handle this? Dammit, Mac, we had an agreement. An understanding."

"Things change. Even me."

"And what am I supposed to do now?"

"You could," Calhoun suggested, "tell me if you feel the same way. After all we've been through, after all the difficulties we've come through together . . . do you, Elizabeth Paula Shelby, feel the same way about me that I do about you?"

She didn't know what to say. Her mind was completely frozen. She tried to find the words, tried to sort out the emotions that were at war with each other . . .

And then the door to the ready room slid open. McHenry was standing in it. "Sorry to disturb you, Captain, but . . . it's showtime."

"All hands, battle stations," said Calhoun briskly. He was out the door before Shelby could formulate another sentence, or even frame another word. She followed him onto the bridge, unaware of the fact that she would never set foot into the captain's ready room again.

# *XII.*

SI CWAN, ANXIOUS TO SEE THE END of the Black Mass after it had haunted his darkest nightmares for more than twenty years, was on his way to the bridge when Kalinda fell into step next to him. "Where are you going?" he asked.

"The same place you are. The bridge. To watch this end."

"Shouldn't you be with Xyon? At a time like this . . ."

"He's gone."

Si Cwan slowed, stopped and faced her. "Gone?"

"His vessel is gone. No one would tell me where or why." Her face was immobile, impossible to read. "He left without even saying good-bye."

"I'm sure he had a reason. And I'm sure that—"

She walked past him then, and into the nearest turbolift. He stepped in next to her, and she turned and looked up at him. "Did you mean those things you said? About Xyon and me getting married? Or was it some elaborate psychological trick to drive a wedge between us."

"If what you have with Xyon is solid . . . is real . . . then nothing I could possibly say or do could ever drive a wedge between you."

"You didn't answer my question."

He looked away from her. "All I want for you, Kally, is for you to be happy."

"On whose terms?"

"It doesn't come down to terms . . ."

"Doesn't it? Doesn't it, Si Cwan?"

"I didn't feel he was right for you, but I would have come to deal with it, given time . . ."

"It wasn't for you to deal with, Si Cwan. It was for you to embrace. My happiness. You should be celebrating it, accepting it. Not dealing with it. 'Dealing with it' is what you do when an enemy attacks, not what you do when your sister is in love."

"Kalinda," he sighed, "you're too young to know what love is."

"And you're too tall to know what love is."

He stifled a laugh. "What? What does height have to do with understanding the true nature of love."

"As much as youth. Although maybe I'm more accurate. From your lofty height, you look down on something that you can't even begin to understand."

The turbolift slowed and opened onto the bridge, and the two of them walked out in silence.

There was no sound on the bridge. No one spoke. No one even seemed to be breathing.

The Black Mass was still coming, not more than nine hours away from the Tulaan system. Nine hours away from putting an end to the Redeemers . . . and also ending the lives of Burgoyne and Selar, wherever they might be.

Robin Lefler was back at her post. She was sniffing slightly, but otherwise was not giving any indication of the flu which had hammered her earlier. She nodded an acknowledgment to Si Cwan and Kalinda when they stepped onto the bridge, but otherwise focused her attention completely on the looming Mass.

When Calhoun spoke, it was the picture of icy calm. If she had not been there herself, Shelby would never have believed that, mere moments before, the man was coming as close to opening his soul to her as he ever had. "Mr. Mitchell," he said. "Are we ready to go?"

Down in engineering, Craig Mitchell, acting in Burgoyne's stead, turned to Ensign Ronni Beth who was studying the controls. She turned to him and gave him a confident "thumbs up" gesture. "Ready on this end, Captain," he said. "Phasers are realigned to fire pure blasts of magnetic dissonance."

"How long can we sustain each blast?"

"Without overheating? Twenty seconds each."

"So the only way to do this is a steady series of barrages. Soleta," and he turned toward his science officer. "Will it be enough to drive them apart?"

"And why won't the Black Mass be able to dodge around it, as it did with our previous attack?" asked Si Cwan.

"Because a phaser is a pinpoint blast of concentrated light," explained Soleta. "We're not dealing with light here. By reconfiguring the phasers, we're essentially creating fields of dissonance. Far more wide-spread, and they should theoretically affect the entire area that they hit. By continued and sustained fire, there's a chance that it will cause the Black Mass to dissolve into components, and those individual components will die."

"I notice an excessive number of 'theories' and 'perhaps' in your explanation there, Soleta."

"Simply trying to be as accurate as possible, Captain."

"Let's hope that we're dealing in more than theory. Mr. Kebron . . . target all phaser banks on the Black Mass. Sustained barrages of magnetic dissonance in alternating twenty-second intervals."

"Phasers locked and ready, sir," said Kebron.

"And . . ." Calhoun held his breath for a moment, and then said, "Fire."

The phaser banks cut loose, and the Black Mass was under attack.

"If any piece of it comes toward us, reconfigure phaser lock and fire on that instead," ordered Calhoun.

"Aye," was all Kebron said, concentrating on the phaser array before him.

Into the heart of the Black Mass stabbed the phasers of the *Excalibur*, giving it everything they had. In engineering, Mitchell and Beth watched the readings with apprehension, making rapid-fire adjustments to keep the flow of energy steady and not risk any diminishment in the ship's attack.

Long minutes ticked by without any outward sign of anything happening. And then Soleta said, "Sir . . . Black Mass is breaking apart."

A startled cheer went up from the bridge crew.

"Quiet!" snapped Calhoun in an uncharacteristically sharp tone. His gaze had not wavered from the screen. He was clearly not going to relax his guard until the Black Mass had, once and for all, been stopped.

The Black Mass surged, rippled, fought against the magnetic dissonance of the phasers. Even from their distance, they could see it trembling, fighting to maintain its integrity. "They're having an effect . . . they're definitely having an effect," said Shelby.

"Engineering to Bridge. Captain, I'm not sure how much longer we can maintain this barrage," came Mitchell's voice.

"Do your best, Mr. Mitchell, so that we can do our worst."

"Aye, sir," said Mitchell. And then he was suddenly heard to mutter a string of imprecations that appeared to question both Calhoun's competence and his parentage.

Smothering a grin, despite the gravity of the situation, Calhoun said, "Mr. Mitchell, you've still got an open line here."

"Oh. Sorry, sir." The comm link immediately went dead, and Calhoun shook his head. Pretend you thought the comm link was closed and then speak out of turn "accidentally." A nice way to let the captain know exactly what he thought of the present situation without opening himself up to charges of insubordination. A very old stunt . . . and one that Calhoun could recall pulling himself once or twice in his career.

More time went by, and now even Kebron was reporting of the strain to the phaser array. In the meantime, the Black Mass continued to fight back. It rippled, it wavered . . .

"There it goes!" said Lefler excitedly. "It's going!"

The Black Mass, under the sustained pounding of the ship's weaponry, fell apart . . .

. . . and regrouped.

It happened so quickly that it almost didn't register on them. Within seconds, the Black Mass had reformed itself, become smaller, tighter, more determined than ever to make headway.

"Sir!" came the call from engineering without any preamble. "We're going to have to shut down or we're going to blow out the phaser banks!"

All eyes turned to Calhoun. He could have been carved form a block of marble.

"Cease fire," he said quietly. "Mr. McHenry, give us some distance . . . just in case the Black Mass couldn't take a joke."

"A joke?" Si Cwan obviously couldn't believe it. "That was our entire strategy . . . our plan of attack . . . and you refer to it as a joke?"

"Soleta did warn us, repeatedly, that it was theoretical. I appreciate your candor, Lieutenant."

"It was only appropriate, sir."

The Black Mass, shaking off the last lingering effects of the phaser barrage, moved off. The immediate threat from the *Excalibur* ended, and with the ship clearly not intending to press an attack, the Black Mass resumed its previous course. Apparently it had even managed to absorb and digest some of the energy unleashed by the phasers, because it was discharging that same energy and picking up speed.

"Why isn't it coming after us, the way it did before?" asked Kalinda.

"Are you knocking it, princess?" inquired McHenry.

"Obviously not. I'm just curious."

"My guess is that we did it some degree of damage,"

Soleta said. "And it feels the need to keep the entirety of itself together, just in case there are further attacks. It doesn't want to split its resources."

Si Cwan came down and around to face Calhoun. "And now," he said with forced calm, "what do we do?"

There was, once again, dead silence on the bridge.

It was Kalinda who broke it. "Someone should just dump it in a black hole or something and be done with it," she said.

"An excellent idea," said Soleta, "provided there was a black hole in the area."

"Xyon said there was one. Not far off the Black Mass' path."

"Xyon said . . ." Calhoun looked at her. "When did he say this?"

"The other day."

"Why didn't he suggest it to me?"

"He said you had other people to give you advice and didn't need his."

"You're all fired," Calhoun said immediately to the entire bridge crew. "Mr. Kebron, punch me up some star maps of the area, now."

"If you're rehiring me, Captain, we'll need to discuss salary increases."

"Now, Kebron."

Kebron had already brought up star charts of the entire area. All eyes on the bridge scanned it.

"Nothing," Soleta said after a few moments. "There is no indication of any black hole on any of the star charts. If it's here, it's unrecorded, and Xyon stumbled onto it on his own."

"Where is Xyon? Let's get him up here, have him point it out to us," suggested Shelby.

"He's unavailable," Calhoun said quickly, and Shelby saw a glance exchanged between Calhoun and Kalinda. She had no idea what was going on, and had the uncomfortable feeling that this was yet another one of those times when Calhoun was up to something that he wanted as few people as possible to know about. Without giving Shelby time to inquire about it, Calhoun said, "Ambassador . . . is it possible that a black hole could be in this area without appearing on any star maps?"

"Quite possible," said Si Cwan. "Remember, we're roughly in the heart of Redeemer territory. Even at the height of our influence, this was not an area that the Thallonians ventured into a great deal."

"Mr. Kebron, have security escort the Overlord up here. It's about time he served some sort of purpose other than threatening us."

It took only a few moments to have the Overlord brought up to the bridge. It was somewhat annoying to see that a stay in the brig had not diminished his sense of authority or fundamentally arrogant air one bit. The way he walked around the bridge made it seem as if he considered everyone there as objects to serve his whim, rather than people with their own minds or concerns.

"A black hole. In this general area," Calhoun said, indicating the section that was on the star map. "Do you know of any?"

"Of course," said the Overlord. "It is here." And he pointed to a specific section.

"Mark that location, Soleta," ordered Calhoun, and obediently a glowing indicator flashed onto the screen right where the Overlord had said.

"Why didn't you tell us about it?" asked Calhoun.

"Tell you about it?" The Overlord looked stunned that the notion was even broached. "Why would I? Of what possible relevance is it? You are needed to deal with the Black Mass, not to visit sacred sites of the Redeemers."

"Sacred sites? A black hole?" Calhoun looked to Si Cwan, who shrugged. "Why would a black hole be a sacred site?"

"We call it the Beyond Gate. It is said that it is the place where Xant went beyond. It is from there that he will re-emerge, when he is ready, and return to Tulaan IV."

"If your Xant went into there," Soleta advised him, "I would not be lighting candles in the window waiting for him to come home. No one comes out of a black hole."

"Including space-going swarms of hungry creatures," Calhoun said meaningfully.

The Overlord could not have looked more stunned. "You are not seriously thinking of trying to send the Black Mass into the Beyond Gate . . . ?"

"If we can figure out a way, you bet we will."

"But . . . but that is impossible! Unconscionable!" The Overlord was clearly becoming incensed. "First, the Beyond Gate is not along the path of the Black Mass. You cannot cause the Mass to deviate from its course. Your task is to destroy it altogether . . ."

"Our task, which you have inflicted upon us, is to stop it, period, and we will use any and all means to do so," Calhoun advised him. "As for not being able to get the Black Mass to deviate: the thing is an animal, Overlord, not the force of nature that you claim it to be. As an animal, it has instincts, and instincts can be misled if you're clever enough."

"But to send a creature such as that into the Beyond Gate . . . Xant would not approve! It is a holy relic, do you hear me?" He was becoming very agitated. "A holy relic! You cannot, must not, do this thing!"

"The fact that it has you this upset is more than enough for me," said Calhoun. "Mr. Kebron, have the Overlord escorted back to his temporary home, would you, please?"

The Overlord was visibly trembling with rage as security guards appeared on either side of him. He said nothing, merely fixed them with fearsome looks from his blazing red eyes. Although the Overlord was, at this point, powerless to all intents and purposes, there was still something there that Shelby found extremely disconcerting. Without a word, maintaining his dignity, the Overlord followed the guards out.

"All right," Calhoun said briskly. "Now that I've talked tough to the Overlord, let's not make a liar of your intrepid captain. The black hole is about three hours distant. We have that much time to figure out how in hell we get that thing to shove itself into a black hole and out of our lives."

"The creatures must have a highly evolved sense of color," said Soleta.

"How do you figure that?" asked Calhoun.

"Because they're drawn through the color band to the types of stars that would be attractive to them," Soleta said reasonably. "The magnetic dissonance settings of the phasers had some effect on them, although it did not come close to stopping them. If we can disorient them again, we can lay a path of tri-cobalt flares as a lure that they might be confused enough to follow. That path of flares, in turn, would lead to a field of tri-cobalt flares in the general vicinity of the black hole. If we use the flares to draw the Black Mass close enough, then it will be pulled in."

"A black hole for the Black Mass. It has a certain attractive symmetry to it," said Calhoun. "Let's do it, people."

# XIII.

BURGOYNE DID NOT KNOW what to attend to first: hir own agony, the impending birth of the child, or the slow approach of whatever was out there on the surface of the planet.

It did not take hir long to determine that Selar's condition was the first priority. The Vulcan doctor had withdrawn to some sort of odd state of mental distance, staring up at the cave roof and gasping at certain moments. Burgoyne was more than able to tell when those moments were, because s/he felt them even more sharply in hir gut than Selar did.

The simple fact was that, from a biological point of view, Burgoyne was completely unequipped to deal with the sort of sensations that s/he was experiencing. Hermat birth was actually fairly painless. An already existing flap was eased open and the Hermat child was brought into the world by the gentle hands of a Hermat medical practitioner. Not a problem, not a fuss, not even much muss. So for a Hermat, any Hermat, to have to experience the level of pain that Selar was experiencing, just for the purpose of producing a child, was unprecedented in Hermat medical lore and an utter departure for Burgoyne or any other Hermat.

"Steady . . . steady . . ." Burgoyne said, hir fangs clenched. S/he felt another wave of discomfort and nausea flooding over hir. Selar moaned somewhat belatedly; Burgoyne was already staggering enough for both of them. S/he sank to hir knees, leaning over Selar as s/he did so, trying to focus on the job at hand. The pain was coming faster now, and although the contractions were less sustained now, they were harsher and sharper when they did hit. Burgoyne felt as if stars were exploding behind hir eyes, and it was all s/he could do not to pass out.

"Come on, Selar . . . get it done already," whispered Burgoyne, fighting back yet another swelling of the agony. "And keep it down. We don't need that whatever-it-is coming—"

"Coming . . ." Selar's eyes were now wide open. She had been doing all she could to deal with the pain via mental discipline, but with the apparent advent of the child, and the disconcerting awareness of Burgoyne's mental proximity, it was too much for Selar. "It . . . is coming . . . it is . . ."

And she let out a scream, her focus slipping completely away. The moment the pain hit her, it rebounded through Burgoyne via their link, and Burgoyne was likewise twisting about on the ground. All s/he wanted to do was shove out of hir the small intruder within hir body, except there was nothing in there. Nothing but the pain which was paralyzing hir, putting hir brain on fire . . .

Lying on the ground several feet away from Selar, trying to get to the Vulcan so s/he could aid her in the final moments of the birth process—that was when Burgoyne saw it.

The creature was in the mouth of the cave. It was snarling at the occupants.

It was large, at least eight feet from tip to tail. It possessed a single eye, blinking implacably at Burgoyne, clearly not the least bit interested in backing out of the cave and going about its business elsewhere. Above the eye, on its forehead, was a horn, long and pointed like a unicorn's or some other fanciful beast. It was slung low to the ground, poised on all fours like a gigantic warthog. Most remarkable were the small wings on the creature's spine. They were moving, twitching, and they seemed far too small to be of any use. The entire monstrosity was covered with a coating of thick purple fur.

"All right," Burgoyne said slowly as s/he came to a crouch. The pain was too overwhelming for hir to fully stand. "All right, just . . . back out of here. Okay? Just get out of here. We're trying to have a child here, and you're not doing anyone any good by . . ."

Selar cried out. The shout was actually a mild warning, giving Burgoyne about a split second's notice before she was hit with the same pain. S/he staggered, falling . . .

. . . and that was the moment that the creature chose to charge.

Remarkably, its wings actually seemed to perform some mild function as the creature took a quick running start, leaped, and sailed through the air at Burgoyne, letting loose with a roar designed to paralyze its victims.

It was unnecessary in Burgoyne's case. S/he was paralyzed already; paralyzed with the pain of the labor contractions smashing through hir, playing havoc with her mental balance. With the pain exploding in hir head, s/he was barely able to react in time as the monster angled straight toward hir.

A phaser would have made short work of it. A knife might also have proven handy. What s/he did have, however, were hir claws. That, and a determination that s/he was not going to end her existence in the belly of some creature in the middle of nowhere.

Burgoyne let out a scream that matched the creature's, in ferocity if not in volume. S/he rolled out of the way and lashed out with hir feet, the claws on hir toes fully extended. S/he sliced across the creature's midsection, ripping out a good chunk of its side and eliciting a fairly satisfying screech of pain from the creature.

It spun in place, ready to charge again, and then another wave of pain struck Burgoyne. S/he gasped, unprepared for it, and that was when the purple creature came at hir, jaws wide, ready to bite hir in half. It scooped up Burgoyne in its mouth, enveloping hir entire upper torso, and proceeded to bite down.

The only thing that stopped Burgoyne from being bitten in half was that s/he had one arm braced against its upper jaw, one arm securing its lower jaw, and s/he was doing everything s/he could to hold them apart. Hir arms were quivering with tension, s/he was panting from the effort, and then the worst pain of all hit hir. It made all the others seem mild in comparison.

And instead of succumbing to the pain, which was

what s/he was most tempted to do, s/he did the opposite. S/he focused it, used it, summoned it to hir and took all the agony, all the anguish, and instead of allowing it to debilitate hir, s/he forced it to strengthen hir. S/he let out a shriek that, instead of acknowledging the pain, served as a war cry. S/he shoved the jaws of the beast wider and wider apart . . .

. . . and then s/he heard a most satisfying snap.

It was the sound of the creature's jaws breaking.

Now it was the monster's turn to be in pain as it bellowed hideously and flopped over. The impact threw Burgoyne clear, and the Hermat pivoted in place and charged, leaping across the intervening space, propelled by hir powerful limbs. S/he skidded right under the creature's belly and hir claws lashed out, slicing the creature right up the middle and rolling out the other side.

The creature blinked its one eye furiously and came at Burgoyne with its horn. Burgoyne snagged the horn just before it would have lanced straight through hir chest, and the creature pushed hir halfway across the cave floor, dragging hir all the way. It roared right in her face.

That was the moment when the incisions that Burgoyne's dextrous claws had made finally did their job. The cuts ripped open, the skin no longer able to hold together, and the creature's innards spilled out onto the cave floor.

The monster let out a yelp of surprise, its eye rolling around, trying to see what was happening under its belly. It knew it smelled something, and its ears perked up when it heard something that sounded like a wet, splashing noise. Then it came to the realization that the animal guts it was detecting, through smell and sound, were its own.

It tried to get away from Burgoyne at that point, but it was too late. Too late for itself in terms of its own survival, and too late in the hope of retreating from Burogyne who smelled victory. Burgoyne came in from the side, and this time when pain hit hir from the contractions, s/he used the energy of it to push off from hir feet and practically fly over the distance to the creature, sinking hir fangs into its throat and tearing out a piece of the jugular vein. Blood fauceted from it and s/he revelled in it, letting out a scream of triumph that was louder than anything the creature had unleashed thus far. The great beast took only one more step, and then toppled over. It hit the ground heavily and didn't move, its final breath rasping in its throat.

Burgoyne took no time at all to revel in hir triumph. Instead s/he shoved the creature's carcass aside and rolled over toward the Vulcan. "Selar," s/he whispered, surprised at the hoarseness of hir own voice. "Selar, it's okay . . . it's going to be okay n—"

And then Burgoyne flipped completely over. S/he fell next to Selar, whose eyes were wide, and together they bore down, and together they felt it coming, and they gasped in synch, and they pushed together, and cried together, and when the child's head emerged Burgoyne felt it as much as Selar. Gasping, s/he pushed the pain aside, and crawled, hand over hand, over to where the child was emerging. "I have it . . . I have it . . ." s/he managed to get out, tears rolling down hir face, and there it was with the most elegant little pointed ears, and close-cropped blondish hair, and then Burgoyne's guts convulsed as s/he pushed the child out with Selar. And then the child was nestled in Burgoyne's arms. Burgoyne couldn't believe it. S/he laughed and sobbed simultaneously.

"Your . . . fault," came Selar's voice, raspy and tired.

"What . . . would be my fault . . . precisely," inquired Burgoyne, sounding no less exhausted.

"I would have been . . . far more dignified . . . in the labor . . . less histrionics . . . without link to you. You made it . . . difficult for me to focus . . . less controlled . . ."

"Sorry," Burgoyne said contritely.

Selar paused a moment, and then said, "Do not worry about it . . . Burgy . . ."

Burgoyne laughed softly. Then s/he saw that Selar was starting to sit up, and said quickly, "I wouldn't if I were you. Just stay put. Relax. You've earned it. I think . . . we both have."

Selar was staring at the fallen monstrosity at the side of the cave. "What . . . is that?" she said.

"Couldn't tell you. It sure looks strange to me, though."

Selar could only nod in agreement. Then she focused on the bundle in Burgoyne's arms. She did not smile, of course. The edges of her mouth, however, did turn upward slightly, which for her was a tremendous advancement. "What is it? Is it a boy . . . or a girl . . . or . . . ?"

Burgoyne had automatically torn a piece off hir own ragged clothing and wrapped it around the child. "I think it's more in the 'or' category."

# XIV.

The Black Mass knew hunger.

The Black Mass knew exhaustion.

This had been a particularly difficult migration for the Black Mass. It had known assault. It had known discomfort.

Now it wanted to know sustenance, and it wanted to know it soon. It sensed sustenance not far off, and it hoped, at the most fundamental core of its being, that there would not be more noise.

(It did not actually know noise as noise, of course. Until then, it had known largely silence. Noise was a concept it could not begin to grasp as such. It simply knew it as a negative sensation, something that had hurt it, something that was unnatural.)

It tired of noise, tired of something trying to hurt it. Was it not simply trying to survive? To exist? Was it

236

*not simply going about its business, as it had for as long as any part of it could possibly recall? What right did the noise have to interfere, to try to drive it apart. No right. None at all. It should just leave the Black Mass alone, it should . . .*

*It was there.*

*The noise.*

*Was there.*

*The Black Mass felt it, just as it had earlier. It pushed it away, and still the noise came. It ran, and still the noise came. And all of us, we creatures, we pull together and it will not hurt us, it will not stop us, we are the Black Mass, felt at a primal level, fighting for survival, attacking us, hurting us, and we will hurt it, we will make it stop, but we are so hungry and have no idea which way to look first . . .*

*. . . and then it stopped.*

*We, the Black Mass, let out a collective silent sigh of relief. We have held together. We are not alone, no member is alone.*

*But we are angry.*

*We have not attacked before. We have been patient. We have cared about food, only food, but now it must be made to stop, it must stop, it will come at us again and again . . .*

*Light.*

*Light . . . from . . . a star?*

*We had not detected it before, but there it is . . . light . . .*

*Go . . . there . . . go and eat . . . see . . . must have . . . light . . .*

*Eat . . . eat . . . eat . . .*

\* \* \*

"It's going for it!" called Soleta, sounding remarkably excited for a reserved Vulcan.

And indeed, that was exactly what was happening. Slowly, steadily, the Black Mass was following the trail of the tri-cobalt flares that the *Excalibur* had strung in preparation for the creature's advance.

In the distance was the Beyond Gate, the black hole that would ideally serve as the creature's final resting place. Once there, it could never hurt anyone again . . . except in the unlikely event that it happened to run into Xant on his way out.

"Come on," said Shelby in an encouraging whisper, as if the thing could actually hear her. She was on the edge of her seat. Other members of the bridge crew were likewise positioned forward on their chairs. "Come on . . . go for it, you oversized oil slick."

Each of the cobalt flares snuffed out of existence as the Black Mass rolled over it, trying to absorb what it perceived as energy from a star, drawn by the light, coming up empty but pulled inexorably to the next one, and the next, searching for sustenance. Closer and closer . . .

"Thirty seconds until it reaches the event horizon," Soleta reported. "Twenty-nine . . . twenty-eight . . . twenty-seven . . ."

"You're very fond of countdowns, aren't you?" McHenry asked her.

"Yes," was her straightforward reply.

The countdown continued. The Black Mass' approach toward the black hole continued as well. Closer and closer it drew, the final flares beckoning to it . . .

*Something . . . is wrong . . .*

*No star. No food. Look . . . but not touch. See . . . but no feel.*

*We are hungry. This star . . . not enough . . . need food . . .*

*Must eat . . . eat . . . eat . . . this is . . . not enough . . . must eat . . .*

"It's slowing down."

"No," whispered Calhoun upon hearing Soleta's pronouncement.

"It's definitely slowing down. It's on the edge of the point of no return . . . but it's not going all the way over. It's hesitating . . . maybe it suspects something . . ."

The Black Mass began to surge, moving about, thrashing this way and that, as if trying to sense something . . .

"Ready phasers," said Calhoun. "Let's see if we can push it over the edge . . ."

"Captain!" Soleta's increased volume put across the gravity of the situation. "It's coming after us!"

"You mean it's heading this way?"

"No, I mean it is coming straight for us!"

*Food . . . there . . . the thing which made the noise . . . we want it . . . we want it . . . food . . . food . . .*

It was their last stand. Calhoun knew there was no time to try anything else. This was their last, best shot. If they couldn't get the creature into the black hole, there would be no stopping it. But it wasn't going for the flares, and the only chance they had was to try and pummel it once again, break it apart, send its components hurtling into the gravity well of the black hole. "Engineering! Phasers on line!"

"Captain," came back Mitchell, "we've pushed it too far already. I can't give you bursts for more than five seconds each."

"That won't be remotely enough, Mr. Mitchell."

The thing was coming straight toward them. Space was warping around it, and Calhoun knew that within seconds it would be upon them. They could still outrace it, still get out of its way . . . but that wouldn't stop the Black Mass. It would just get them to safety. There had to be another way, there—

"Captain!" Kebron suddenly said. "Detecting a small vessel, moving fast, straight toward the Black Mass."

"Onscreen!" ordered Calhoun.

Somehow, he knew. Before he even saw it, he knew. He knew whose ship it was going to be.

"Give me a hailing frequency," he said. His voice sounded very distant, very cold.

"You're on, Captain," said Kebron.

"Xyon," he addressed the small craft with such calm that one would have thought he was scolding a cranky child on a playground. "You're on a collision course with the Black Mass. Pull back."

Deep down, he hadn't been expecting an answer, but he got one anyway. "This was my idea. Just helping see it through."

"You're not supposed to be here."

"I know. But I came anyway. Did some checking at Tulaan IV, made sure justice was done, then came here. I'm doing my job. You wanted to make sure they were safe; so I'm making sure."

"Xyon, veer off!" There was greater urgency to Calhoun's voice. "Now! Kebron, tractor beam."

"Out of range, sir," said Kebron.

"Xyon!" It was not Calhoun who had spoken. It was Kalinda, standing there on the bridge, calling out to him. "Xyon, don't do it!"

"Came back for you, Kally. Wanted to make sure . . . you were all right." His voice was crackling over the link now, beginning to break up. "This is the way to do it. Si Cwan . . . you punch like a girl. Dad . . . see if you can improve his punch. He needs all the help he can get. We . . . all do . . ."

Calhoun mouthed his name, mouthed words . . .

"Don't you dare say I love you," warned Xyon, and then the crackling overcame his communications beam, and his voice was lost.

But the visual was there, for all to see.

Xyon's ship hurtled straight and true, directly into the Black Mass. There was no hesitation, no slowing down, and as a result the ship was through the far side of the Black Mass before the entity fully understood that something had thrown itself into it.

What it did fully understand, however, was hydrogen plasma . . . the type being emitted by the impulse drive of Xyon's ship. It knew the taste . . .

As one, the millions of creatures that comprised the Black Mass wheeled around and went right for Xyon's ship. The plasma lured it, and it came, and kept coming . . .

*Eat eat eat eat eat eat eat eat . . .*

And then it was right there, right there, crossing the event horizon of the Beyond Gate.

The black hole, a bottomless pit of reality, drawing in light and gravity and anything else, impossible to see except through instrumentation, a thing that was a blend of science and legend, hanging there in space.

Nothing meant anything to a black hole, for it sat there, God's kitchen drain, pulling in anything that got within range . . .

. . . pulling in the Black mass.

*What is happening to us?*

*We are being pulled apart, but we must not, we must stay together, we are the Black Mass, do not leave us alone, we must be together, not separate forever, stay together, do not go, do not go . . .*

At the last second, it seemed to realize that something was wrong. It tried to reverse itself, tried to pull out, and the Black Mass began to shred. Half of it was being pulled away, the other half endeavoring to escape, and for one horrific moment the bridge crew thought that part of the Mass was going to get away. Even a part of it could be devastating if it managed to find a way to continue on its course.

But then that part which was on the verge of escaping . . . stopped trying. Instead it hurled itself toward that which was already caught, reforming, coagulating into its magnificent whole once more and spiralling down, down . . .

It stretched, elongated, twisted down and away, the Mass black against the black hole, and Soleta could have sworn . . . could have *sworn* . . . that somewhere in the inner recesses of her mind, where her sensitivity to other minds was at its greatest, somewhere in there she sensed some sort of hideous collective scream, as if something had realized its fate at the last moment and had been horrified by it. And then it was gone, just like that, leaving her to wonder if she had imagined it . . . and hoping that she had.

They stared in silence at the place where the Black Mass had vanished. So formidable had the creature been, that they almost expected it somehow to make a miraculous return from the maw of the Black Hole. But there was nothing. There were certain constants of the universe that nothing—not even the Black Mass—could overcome.

"Mr. Kebron," Calhoun said tonelessly, in a voice as still as death, "scan the area. Is there any sign of Xyon's ship?"

"No, sir."

"Scan it again."

"Sir, there is no sign of—"

"Scan it . . . again."

"Yes, sir."

"You too, Soleta."

"Aye, sir."

For the next ten minutes, the sensors of the *Excalibur* swept the area, probing and searching.

And finding nothing.

Xyon was gone.

# XV.

SELAR AND BURGOYNE HUDDLED close to one another as the temperature in the cave dropped. It seemed to Burgoyne that the wind was only getting stronger, and the meager clothes with which they had been provided were becoming less and less effective with every passing moment. Obviously night on this damnable world was going to be even worse than day . . . and of course there was no telling just how long night was going to be.

Selar was holding the child close to her bosom. She had nursed the child earlier, although her own hunger was interfering with her ability to do so. But she had done the best she could, and the child was resting comfortably. Still, Burgoyne had no idea how long the child's comfort was going to last. How long, indeed, any of them would last.

"I hope you plan to be involved with the rearing of the child," Selar said. "It would be best. . . ."

"Do you really hope that?" Burgoyne was tired, hungry, and not a little fed-up with the entire situation. "Do you really hope that I will be around? Because it's difficult for me to be sure. You see, all I've ever been is nice to you. And sometimes I think you're being responsive, and sometimes not. I never know where I stand with you. To be blunt, Selar—and this may not be the best time and place, but it's not as if we have a choice—to be blunt, you are the single most aggravating individual I have ever met."

"You have just summarized my sentiments about you as well."

"Good. I'm glad."

They sat there for a moment longer, huddled in the cave, and then Selar said in a low voice, "Perhaps . . . we deserve each other."

Slowly Burgoyne turned to look at her. "What . . . do you mean?"

"I mean . . . precisely what I just said. Perhaps we deserve one another. Perhaps we are the only ones . . . who can possibly stand each other. That may not be such a . . . terrible thing. After all, to be alone . . . is not logical."

"Be careful what you say," said Burgoyne. "For all we know, you'll change your mind again once we're off this rock."

"That is quite possible. However, there is every likelihood that we will not 'get off' this rock, as you say. For, to be blunt, I do not see how anyone can . . ."

And then, to their shock, there was the unmistakable, tell-tale humming of a transporter. Before it had even fully registered upon them, the cave had dissolved around them and they found themselves sitting on the transporter deck of a Redeemer vessel.

Standing in front of them was the Redeemer known as Prime One. He regarded them with open curiosity, his attention particularly drawn to the small child clutched tightly to Selar.

"I see you have been busy," he said.

The Overlord was not happy.

He had been escorted from the brig to the transporter room, and from there he was to be sent over to his ship which had moved to within range of the *Excalibur.* Captain Calhoun and Commander Shelby had been waiting there for him, as well as Si Cwan. "You," he said stiffly to Calhoun, "have transgressed on holy ground. By using the Beyond Gate to dispose of the Black Mass, you have forever sullied one of the purest, the greatest religious sites of the Redeemers."

Calhoun looked at him with a gaze that seemed capable of drilling through the back of his head. "Overlord," he said—very soft, and very deadly—"you have no idea at the moment just how fortunate you are, and how lightly I am letting you off. Your High Priest, who was captured by my crewman, has been returned to your vessel. You are also being returned to your vessel . . ."

"As we are returning your doctor and chief engineer," the Overlord reminded him.

"Whom you kidnapped. The long and short of it is, Overlord . . . you have absolutely no idea how lucky you are. It is requiring every ounce of willpower I have at the moment not to kill you where you stand. I could do it, in a heartbeat, with absolutely no compunction or remorse."

"Then why don't you?" The Overlord didn't sound particularly challenging when he spoke. Indeed, he seemed more curious than anything.

"Because," said Calhoun, "unlike the Black Mass . . . I do not always operate on instinct, lest I be pulled down into something from which I can never return."

"Very wise," said the Overlord. "Understand, Captain . . . I cannot forgive you your transgression. However . . . the inescapable truth is that you did save Tulaan IV. You have saved my race."

"I know." His lack of enthusiasm was quite evident.

The Overlord turned and stepped up onto the platform. When he looked back at Calhoun, he said, "Be aware that, as far as the Redeemers are concerned . . . there is a truce between us."

"Which will last exactly as long as it takes for another helpless world to call to us, begging us to aid them against you."

"I have given the matter some consideration, actually. You see . . . much has happened as a result of both your intervention in this sector of space, as well as in your aid against the Black Mass. These events require thought, contemplation. We must consider quite thoroughly all the ramifications, and how we may best serve Xant as a result. Therefore . . . we will not be redeeming any worlds for at least a year. We will simply reside on Tulaan IV . . . and think. We do not seek peace, you understand . . . but neither do we mindlessly pursue war. We, too, you see . . . are capable of giving thought to matters rather than acting on instinct. Good day to you, Captain . . . Commander . . . Ambassador." He bowed slightly.

"Energize," said Calhoun.

The Overlord shimmered out of existence, and a moment later, Selar and Burgoyne appeared on the platform.

"Thank God. Get yourselves down to sickbay," said Shelby. "You look like you've been through . . ." She stopped, stared. "Is that . . . what I think it is?"

"That depends. What do you think it is?"

"A baby."

"Oh, good. I'd have been worried otherwise."

Shelby and Si Cwan moved forward to get a better look. "Congratulations," said Shelby. "I'd guess it wasn't exactly the best conditions to have . . . him? Her?"

"Him," said Selar a bit too quickly.

"What is his name?" asked Si Cwan.

"Well," Burgoyne said, "under ordinary circumstances, my child's name would be Burgoyne 173."

"Except I was not especially sanguine about that," said Selar. "There was some dispute between us. But then we learned—that is to say, the Redeemers told us—of the sacrifice made by the Captain's son. And so, if it is agreeable with him, we wanted to name the child Xyon."

"I think that's very sweet," said Shelby, visibly moved. "Captain, what do you think about—?"

They all turned and saw that Calhoun was no longer there.

Shelby went to his quarters to tell him the answer to his question—the one he had posed in the ready room—was "yes." But he was not there.

She went to Ten Forward. He wasn't there either.

She called up to the bridge. They had not seen him there, either. Beginning to get worried, she checked with the computer, which assured her that, yes, Captain Calhoun was definitely on the ship.

Tapping her comm badge, she said, "Shelby to Captain."

There was a pause, and then she heard Calhoun's voice. He sounded very distant. "Calhoun here."

"Mac . . ." She didn't know how else to phrase it. "Are you okay?"

"I'm fine."

"Do you want to talk?"

"Not right now."

"All right, well . . . if you do . . . you know where to find me."

"Thank you. I appreciate that. Calhoun out."

She told herself that, really, she shouldn't have been surprised. In many ways, Calhoun was still a loner. He tended to internalize everything, particularly grief. It made perfect sense that he would find somewhere small, private, isolated—and handle his mourning there.

There were things she wanted to say to him, things that needed to be said. But they could wait until a time that he was ready to hear them. They had time, after all. All the time in the world.

No words had been necessary. That was the wonderful thing about her.

Calhoun sat in her quarters, staring off into space. Mueller rested a hand on the back of his shoulders and said nothing. Nothing at all.

He should have gone to Shelby, he knew that. He should have been able to pour out his heart to her, to grieve to her. But he did not want to appear weak to her. Somehow he felt that it would lower her opinion of him, make him less in her eyes. He could not bring himself to risk that. How could she love him if she saw him that way? That wasn't the Calhoun she knew, or the Calhoun she would want to know. She needed . . .

He needed . . . he. . . .

Kalinda stood in the observation deck, looking out at the stars. She didn't even have to glance to her side to see that Si Cwan had walked up next to her.

"I'm sorry," he said. "I know that does not make much of a difference at this point . . . but I am sorry."

"Why?" she asked.

"Because . . . I misjudged him. Because you were able to see him in a way that I was not . . . that my upbringing, my instincts, would not let me see. I should have been able to rise above my instincts. Gotten to know him . . ."

"No one knows anyone. Not really," she said.

"Yes, so I hear. But you knew him . . ."

"No. I didn't. When he came back—came back because of me—I was the most surprised person on that bridge." She looked out at the stars. "I had absolutely no faith that he would return. None at all. But he did. I didn't know him, either. And now . . . I'll never get to."

"I know. That is what I feel the most sorry about. I really did want you to be happy."

"I know you did," she sighed. "You just didn't know how to go about it."

"It will not be a mistake I make again. The next time . . ."

"Next time?" She looked up at him and laughed bitterly. "There won't be a next time. I'm never going to love again. It's too difficult, it's too painful, it's . . ." She shook her head. "It's not worth it."

He rested a hand on his shoulder and said, "Yes. It is."

"Oh, and you know this? You know this from personal experience?"

"No," he admitted. "But I have it on reliable authority."

She hit him on the upper arm. It didn't hurt him at all, but he felt obliged to say "Ow" just to make her feel better.

Tears began to trickle down her face, but she wiped them away. Then she wrapped her hands around Si Cwan's arm and they stared out at the stars together.

Dr. Maxwell paced sickbay nervously. He was not looking forward to what he was going to have to tell Dr. Selar. This was not news that she was going to be happy about hearing.

How could they have vanished? How was it possible?

The doors to sickbay hissed open and Ensign Beth walked in. He crossed quickly to her and said in a low voice, "What have you found?"

"Nothing."

"Are you sure?"

She nodded. "Positive. Mitchell and I have run a complete scan of the entire ship. There isn't a centimeter we left uncovered. Wherever those things are, they're not on the vessel."

Maxwell sagged into a chair. "I don't know whether to be upset or relieved. But if they're not here . . . where are they?"

"I couldn't tell you. But, you know . . . we were

dealing with an alien life form. Who knows what its capabilities are. Maybe when the rest of the Black Mass vanished into the black hole, the things just . . . discorporated."

Maxwell stroked his chin thoughtfully. "You know . . . I like that. I like that a lot. It almost makes sense."

"Don't say I never did anything for you," said Ensign Beth, as she turned and headed back down to engineering.

Meantime, feeling somewhat relieved, Dr. Maxwell looked once more at the empty stasis tank, from which the only two remaining creatures that had once been part of the Black Mass had disappeared. He rolled the notion around on his tongue. "They just . . . discorporated." It sounded better and better.

It certainly sounded a lot better than, "I have no idea where they disappeared to."

Xyon stared out at the stars through the viewport of the *Lyla* and, even though he couldn't see the *Excalibur,* he imagined that Kalinda was looking back at him.

It had been a near thing. Using the energy to switch to "cloak" at the last second, barely pulling away from the black hole before it had pulled him in. A very near thing. He couldn't help but feel that he had escaped it for a purpose. And that purpose did not involve returning to the *Excalibur.*

"It's better this way," he said.

He had not been addressing Lyla, but she wasn't terribly good at discerning random comments which weren't directed at her. "What is, Xyon?" she asked.

"They probably think I'm dead. That I was pulled

into the black hole. I mean, of course they know that I have cloaking technology at my disposal, but it would very likely not occur to them that I would survive and then not let them know."

"Why? Because they wouldn't think you that insensitive?"

"Insensitive?" He scoffed. "No, just the opposite. I'm being very sensitive to their needs. My father is Mackenzie Calhoun, dammit. Tough as nails, smart, unsentimental. Having me around . . . it was making it difficult for him to function. I could see it in his eyes; he was losing his edge. That wasn't fair to him, and to the others who served with him, who need him in top form. And Kalinda . . . poor kid. Torn between me and her brother. Not knowing what she wanted. Why should she have had to make a choice between a life with him, on a bustling starship, and an uncomfortable hand-to-mouth existence with me?"

"Because she wanted to make that choice?" suggested Lyla.

"It's good to want things," said Xyon. "But it would have been practically indecent of me to insist that she have to choose. But one of us was going to have to, so I chose for her. Believe me, it's better this way. All around."

He was silent for a long time then. Finally Lyla said, "Xyon . . . are you all right?"

"I will be," he sighed. "Sooner or later, I will be."

"It was not an easy decision, was it?"

"Sure it was," he lied. "Easiest decision in the world. Well . . . not the easiest."

"No?"

"No. The easiest decision," and he grinned like a just-satisfied predator, "was deciding what to do with the Black Mass creatures I liberated from sickbay. That decision was no challenge at all."

And he laughed. And Lyla, having no idea why, but feeling that it was the right thing to do, joined in.

On the surface of Tulaan IV, the Redeemers went about their business and planned for their future.

In the meantime, on the other side of their world, two small, black, wormlike entwined creatures contentedly chewed on the planet's surface . . . and started to grow . . .

# *XVI.*

THE NORMAL LOW LEVEL BUZZ of conversation on the bridge tapered off as Captain Calhoun stepped out from the turbolift.

He had missed an entire shift, which was unprecedented for him. Everyone understood, however, and no one knew quite what to say to him when he did reappear.

He went to his command chair, took his seat, and when he looked around at the respectfully silent crew, a smile played across his lips. It was a sad smile, but a smile just the same.

"Captain," began Shelby.

"Commander . . . it's all right," he interrupted. "All of you . . . really . . . it's all right. The important thing . . . the thing I'm not going to lose sight of . . . is that he went out like a warrior."

There were nods from all around.

"It was very . . . Xenexian of him, believe it or not. The notion of dying in one's bed is anathema to my people. To die in combat, on the other hand, is very much to be desired . . . and to die in combat while saving others is the highest, most noble passing that anyone could wish for. I will miss him . . . and regret the time that we did not spend together, and the time we will not have . . . but the bottom line is, he died heroically. All of us . . . should only be so fortunate as to have that opportunity," said Mackenzie Calhoun, five minutes before the *Excalibur* blew up . . .

**OUR FIRST SERIAL NOVEL!**

*Presenting, one chapter per month . . .*

**The very beginning of the Starfleet
Adventure . . .**

**STAR TREK
STARFLEET: YEAR ONE**

**A Novel in Twelve Parts**

**by
Michael Jan Friedman**

**Chapter Four**

# *Chapter Four*

As Connor Dane slipped into an orbit around Command Base, he saw on his primary monitor that there were still a handful of *Christophers* hanging around the place. He glanced at the warships, observing their powerful if awkward-looking lines.

"Can't hold a candle to you, baby," Dane whispered to his ship, patting his console with genuine affection.

Then he punched in a comm link to the base's security console. After a second or two, a round-faced woman with pretty eyes and long dark hair appeared on the monitor screen.

"Something I can do for you?" she asked.

"I believe I'm expected," he said. "Connor Dane."

The woman tapped a pad and checked one of her monitors. "So you are," she noted. "I'll tell the transporter officer. Morales out."

With that, her image vanished and Dane's view of the base was restored. Swiveling in his seat, he got up and walked to the rear of his bridge, where he could stand apart from his instruments. After all, the last thing he wanted was to materialize with a toggle switch in his belly button.

Before long, the Cochrane jockey saw the air around him begin to shimmer, warning him that he was about to be whisked away. The next thing he knew, he was standing on a raised platform in the base's transporter chamber.

Of course, this chamber was a lot bigger and better lit than the ones he was used to. But then, this was Command Base, the key to Earth's resounding victory over the Romulans. It didn't surprise him that it might rate a few extra perks.

The transporter operator was a stocky man with a dark crewcut. He eyed Dane with a certain amount of curiosity.

"Something wrong?" the captain asked.

The man shrugged. "Honestly?"

"Honestly," Dane insisted.

The operator shot him a look of disdain. "I was wondering," he said, "what kind of man could see a bunch of birdies invade his system and not want to put on a uniform."

The captain stroked his chin. "Let's see now . . . I'd say it was the kind that was too busy popping Romulans out of space to worry about it." He stepped down from the platform. "Satisfied?"

The man's eyes had widened. "You drove an escort ship? Geez, I didn't—"

"You didn't think," Dane said, finishing the man's remark his own way. "But then, guys like you never do."

Leaving the operator redfaced, he exited from the chamber through its single set of sliding doors. Then he looked around for the nearest turbolift.

As it turned out, it was just a few meters away, on the opposite side of a rotunda. Crossing to it, Dane went inside and punched in his destination. As the doors closed and the compartment began to move, he took a deep breath.

He would get this over as soon as he could, he assured himself. He would satisfy his curiosity. Then he would get back in his Cochrane and put as much distance between himself and Command Base as he possibly could.

The lift's titanium panels slid apart sooner than he had expected, revealing a short corridor shared by five black doors. Dane knew enough about Command protocol to figure out which one he wanted.

Advancing to the farthest of the doors, he touched the pad set into the bulkhead beside it. Inside, where he couldn't hear it, a chime was sounding, alerting the officer within that he had company.

With a rush of air, the door moved aside. Beyond it stood a broad-shouldered man in a black and gold admiral's uniform, his hair whiter than Dane remembered it.

Big Ed Walker's eyes narrowed beneath bushy brows. "Connor," he said. He indicated a chair in his anteroom. "Come on in."

Dane took the seat. Then he eyed the admiral. "I'm glad you recognize me, Uncle Ed. For a moment there, I thought you were confusing me with someone who had some ambition to be a Starfleet captain."

Walker chuckled drily as he pulled up a chair across from his nephew. "Funny, son. But then, you always did have a lively sense of humor."

"I'm glad I amuse you," said Dane. "But I didn't come here to crack jokes, Uncle Ed. I came to find out how my hat got thrown in the ring. I mean, you and I haven't exactly been close for a good many years now, so I know it wasn't a case of nepotism."

The admiral nodded reasonably. "That's true, Connor. But then, you can't call that my fault, can you? You were the one who chose to leave the service and strike out on your own."

"I had no desire to be a military man," Dane tossed back. "No one seemed to believe that."

Walker smiled grimly. "I still don't. What you accomplished during the war, the reputation you earned yourself . . . that just proves you had it in you all along. You're a born officer, son, a natural leader—"

"So are dozens of other space jockeys," Dane pointed out, "guys who'd give their right arms to join your star fleet. But you picked me instead." He leaned forward in his chair, deadly serious. "So tell me . . . what's the deal, Uncle Ed?"

Alonis Cobaryn grunted softly to himself as he studied the scale hologram of the *Daedalus*-class prototype. Somehow, the two-meter-long hologram had looked more impressive in the darkened briefing room where he had seen it the day before.

Here at the center of Earth Command's primary conference room, a grand, solemn amphitheater with gray seats cascading toward a central stage from every side, the hologram seemed small and insignificant. And with two dozen grim, lab-coated engineers occupying a scattering of those seats, already making notes in their handheld computer pads, the Rigelian had to admit he was feeling a little insignificant himself.

He saw no hint of that insecurity in the other captains standing alongside him. But then, Hagedorn, Stiles and

Matsura were used to the soberness of Earth Command environments and engineers. And while neither Shumar nor Dane could make that claim, they were at least Earthmen.

Of all those present, Cobaryn was the only alien. And while no one in the facility had done anything to underline that fact, he still couldn't help but be aware of it.

For some time, the Rigelian had been fascinated by other species. He had done his best to act and even think like some of them. However, after having spent an entire day on Earth, he was beginning to wonder if he could ever live as one of them.

Abruptly, Cobaryn's thoughts were interrupted by a loud hiss. Turning, he saw the doors to the amphitheater slide open and produce the slender form of Starfleet Director Abute.

As the dark-skinned man crossed the room, the engineers looked up from their pads and gave him their attention. No surprise there, the Rigelian reflected, considering Abute was their superior.

"Thank you for coming, ladies and gentlemen," the director told the lab-coated assemblage, his voice echoing almost raucously from wall to wall. "As you know, I have asked the six men who are to serve as captains in our new fleet to critique your work on the *Daedalus*. I trust you'll listen closely to what they have to say."

There was a murmur of assent. However, Cobaryn thought he heard an undertone of resentment in it. Very possibly, he mused, these engineers believed they had already designed the ultimate starship—and that this session was a waste of time.

However, Abute disagreed, or he wouldn't have called this meeting. The Rigelian found himself grateful for that point of view, considering he was one of the individuals who would have to test the engineers' design.

The director turned to Matsura. "Captain?" he said. "Would you care to get the ball rolling?"

"I'd be happy to," said Matsura. He took a step closer to the hologram and pressed the flats of his hands together. "Let's talk about scanners."

It seemed like a reasonable subject to Cobaryn. After all, he had some opinions of his own on the matter.

Matsura pointed to a spot on the front of the ship. "Without a doubt, the long-range scanners that have been incorporated into the *Daedalus* are a big improvement over what we've got. But we can go a step further."

Abute seemed interested. "How?"

"We can devote more of our scanner resources to long-range use," Matsura answered. "That would allow us to identify threats to Earth and her allies with greater accuracy."

The engineers nodded and made notes in their pads. However, before they got very far, someone else spoke up.

"The problem," said Shumar, "is that additional long-range scanners means fewer short-range scanners—and we need that short-range equipment to obtain better analyses of planetary surfaces."

Cobaryn couldn't help but agree. Like his colleague, he was reluctant to give up any of the advantages Abute had described the day before.

Matsura, on the other hand, seemed to feel otherwise. "With due respect," he told Shumar, "you're equating expedience with necessity. It would be nice to be able to get more information on a planet from orbit. But if we could detect a hostile force a fraction of a light-year further away . . . who knows how many Federation lives might be saved some day?"

Shumar smiled. "That's fine in theory, Captain. But as we all know, science saves lives as well—and I think you would have to admit, there's also a tactical advantage to knowing the worlds in our part of space."

Matsura smiled too, if a bit more tightly. "Some," he conceded. "But I assure you, it pales beside the prospect of advance warning."

Cobaryn saw the engineers trade glances. Clearly, they hadn't expected this kind of exchange between two captains.

Abute frowned. "Perhaps we can table this topic for the moment." He turned to the engineers. "Or better yet, let's see if there is a way to increase both long- and short-range scanning capabilities."

Grumbling a little, the men and women in the lab coats made their notes. Then they looked up again.

The director turned to the Rigelian. "Captain Cobaryn? Can you provide us with something a bit less controversial?"

That got a few chuckles out of the engineers, but not many. They seemed to the Rigelian to be a rather humorless lot.

As Matsura stepped away from the hologram, looking less than pleased, Cobaryn approached it. Glancing at the crowd of engineers to make sure they were listening, he indicated the hologram's warp nacelles.

"While I am impressed," he said, "with the enhancements made in the *Daedalus*'s propulsion system, I believe we may have placed undue emphasis on flight speed."

Abute looked at the Rigelian, his brow creased. "You mean you have no interest in proceeding at warp three?"

His comment was met with a ripple of laughter from the gallery. Cobaryn did his best to ignore it.

"In fact," he replied diplomatically, "I have *every* interest in it. However, it might be more useful to design our engines with range in mind, rather than velocity. By prolonging our vessel's ability to remain in subspace, we will actually arrive at many destinations more quickly—even though we have progressed at a somewhat slower rate of speed.

"What's more," he continued, "by shifting our emphasis as I suggest, we will be able to extend the scope of our operations . . . survey solar systems it would not otherwise have been practical to visit."

Stiles chuckled. "Spoken like a true explorer," he said loudly enough for everyone to hear him.

Cobaryn looked back at the man. "But I *am* an explorer," he replied.

"Not anymore," Stiles insisted. "You're a starship captain. You've got more to worry about than charts and mineral analyses."

Abute turned to him. "I take it you have an objection to Captain Cobaryn's position?" he asked a little tiredly.

"Damned right I do," said Stiles. He eyed the Rigelian. "Captain Cobaryn is ignoring the fact that most missions don't involve long trips. They depend on short, quick jumps—at ranges already within our grasp."

"Perhaps that is true now," Cobaryn conceded. "However, the scope of our operations is bound to grow. We need to range further afield for tactical purposes as well as scientific ones."

Stiles looked unimpressed with the argument. So did Hagedorn and Matsura. However, Stiles was the one who answered him.

"We can worry about the future when it comes," he advised. "Right now, more speed is just what the doctor ordered."

There was silence for a moment. Without meaning to do so, the Rigelian had done exactly what Abute had asked him not to do. Like Matsura, he had become embroiled in a controversy.

"Thank you, gentlemen," the director said pointedly. "I appreciate the opportunity to hear both your points of view."

Cobaryn saw Stiles glance at his Earth Command colleagues. They seemed to approve of the concepts he had put forth. But then, that came as no surprise. It was clear that they were united on this point.

"Since Captain Stiles seems eager to speak," Abute added, "I would like to hear his suggestion next."

"All right," Stiles told him. He came forward and indicated the hologram with a generous sweep of his hand. "Two hundred and thirty people. Entire decks full of personnel quarters. An elaborate sickbay to take care of them when they get ill." He shook his head. "Is all this really necessary? Our Christophers run on crews of thirty-five—and most of the time, we don't need half that many."

"Your Christophers don't have science sections," Shumar pointed out abruptly, his arms folded across his chest. "They don't have laboratories or dedicated computers or botanical gardens or sterile containment chambers."

It was a challenge and everyone in the room knew it. Stiles, Shumar, the other captains, Abute . . . and the gathering of engineers, of course. Their expressions told Cobaryn that this was much more entertaining than any of them might have expected.

Stiles lifted his chin, accepting the gauntlet Shumar had

thrown down. "I read the data just as you did," he responded crisply. "I heard the argument for all those research facilities. My question is . . . how much of it do we need? Couldn't we cut out some of that space and come up with a better, more maneuverable ship?"

Shumar shook his head. "Maybe more maneuverable, Captain, but not better—not if you consider all the capabilities that would be lost if the *Daedalus* was sized down."

"And if it's *not* sized down," Stiles insisted, "the whole ship could be lost . . . the first time it engages the enemy."

Again, Director Abute intervened before the exchange could grow too heated. He held up his hand for peace and said, "I would say it's your turn, Captain Shumar. To make a suggestion, I mean."

Shumar cast a last baleful glance at Stiles. "Fine with me," he replied. Taking a deep breath, he pointed to the hologram. "As we learned yesterday, we've improved our tactical systems considerably. Thanks to all the extra graviton emitters on the *Daedalus,* we've now got six layers of deflector protection—and as someone who's been shot at with atomic missiles, I say that's terrific."

Cobaryn hoped there was a "but" coming in his colleague's declaration. He wasn't disappointed.

"But what if we were to covert one or two of the extra emitters to another use?" Shumar suggested. "Say . . . as tractor beam projectors?"

Matsura made a face. *"Tractor* beams?"

"Tightbeam graviton projections," Hagedorn explained, his voice echoing easily throughout the amphitheater. "When their interference patterns are focused on a remote target, they create a certain amount of spatial stress—

which either pulls the target closer to the source of the beam or pushes it farther away."

Shumar nodded approvingly. "That's exactly right."

"However," said Hagedorn in the same even tone, "tractor beams are very much in the development stage right now. Some people say it'll be a long time before they can be made practical . . . if ever."

The Rigelian saw some nods among the engineers. It wasn't a good sign, he told himself.

Shumar frowned. "Others say tractor beams will be made practical in the next few months. Those are the people I prefer to put my faith in."

Hagedorn shrugged with obvious confidence. "I was simply putting the matter in perspective, Captain."

"As we all should," Abute said hopefully.

"Is it my turn now?" Hagedorn asked.

The director shrugged. "If you like."

Hagedorn began by circling the hologram in an almost theatrical fashion. For a few seconds, he refrained from speaking . . . so when he began, his words had a certain weight to them.

"You've made some interesting improvements in the ship's transporter function," he told the assembled engineers. "Some *very* interesting improvements. For instance, it'll be a lot easier to shoot survey teams and diplomatic envoys to their destinations than to send them in shuttles.

"But frankly," he continued, running his hand over the *Daedalus*'s immaterial hull, "I don't think these enhancements will be of any use to us in combat. As we proved during the war, it's impossible to force-beam our personnel through an enemy's deflector shields."

"Not everything is intended to have a military application," Director Abute reminded him, anticipating an objection from Shumar or Cobaryn.

"I recognize that," Hagedorn told him, as expressionless as ever. "However, transporters *can* have military applications. Are you familiar with the work of Winston and Kampouris?"

Abute's eyes narrowed. "It seems to me I've heard their names . . ."

So had Cobaryn. "They are military strategists," he stated. "They have postulated we can use transporter systems to penetrate deflector shields by sending streams of antimatter along their annular confinement beams."

Shumar made a sound of derision. "Talk about being in the development stage," he said. "Transmitting antimatter through a pattern buffer is and always will be suicide."

Hagedorn shrugged. "Not if the buffer has been built the way we might build a warp core?"

"In which case it would have to *be* a warp core," Shumar insisted. "The same elements that would protect the pattern buffer would make it impermeable to matter transmission."

"Not according to Winston and Kampouris," Hagedorn remarked.

But this time, Cobaryn observed, the engineers seemed to rule in Shumar's favor. They shook their heads at Hagedorn's comment.

Taking notice of the same thing, Abute scowled. "Which leaves us at another impasse, I take it."

Shumar eyed Hagedorn, then Stiles and Matsura. "I guess it does."

The director turned to Dane. "We have one more captain to hear from. Perhaps he can put forth a design recommendation on which we can all agree before we call it a day."

He didn't sound very optimistic, the Rigelian noted. But in his place, Cobaryn wouldn't have been very optimistic either.

Like everyone else in the amphitheater, he looked to Dane. The man considered Abute for a moment, then glanced at the engineers. "Communications," he said simply. "You say you can't do anything to improve what we've got. I say you're not trying hard enough."

The director seemed taken aback—but not nearly as much as the crowd of engineers. "I've been assured by our design team," he replied, "that nothing can be done at this time."

Dane regarded the men and women sitting all around him in their white labcoats. "I've got an assurance for your engineers," he said. "If they don't come up with a quicker way for me to contact headquarters, they can find themselves another starship captain."

Cobaryn had to smile. The Cochrane jockey had not shown himself to be a particularly charming individual. However, he did seem to have more than his share of vertebrae.

Abute looked at Dane for a second or two. Then he turned to his engineers. "You heard the man," he told them. "Let's see what we can do."

There was a rush of objections, but they died out quickly. After all, any engineer worth his degree relished a challenge. Even Cobaryn knew that.

"Thank you again," the director told the people in the gallery. "You may return to your work."

Clearly, that was the engineers' signal to depart. The Rigelian watched them toss comments back and forth as they descended to the level of the stage and filed out of the room. Then he turned to Abute, expecting to be dismissed as well.

But Abute wasn't ready to do that yet, it seemed. He regarded all six of his captains for a moment, his nostrils flaring. Finally, he shook his head.

"Gentlemen," he said, "we obviously have some differences. Honest ones, I assume. However, we must make an effort to seek common ground."

Cobaryn nodded. So did Shumar, Hagedorn, Stiles and Matsura—everyone except Dane, in fact. But the Rigelian knew that Dane was the only one who was being honest with the director.

After all, there was a war raging. The first battle had been fought to a standoff there in the amphitheater, but Cobaryn didn't expect that it would be the last.

# Look for STAR TREK Fiction from Pocket Books

## Star Trek®: The Original Series

**Star Trek: The Next Generation®**

**Star Trek: Deep Space Nine®**

**Star Trek®: Voyager™**

*Flashback* • Diane Carey
*The Black Shore* • Greg Cox
*Mosaic* • Jeri Taylor
*Pathways* • Jeri Taylor
*Equinox* • Diane Carey

#1  *Caretaker* • L. A. Graf
#2  *The Escape* • Dean W. Smith & Kristine K. Rusch
#3  *Ragnarok* • Nathan Archer
#4  *Violations* • Susan Wright
#5  *Incident at Arbuk* • John Gregory Betancourt
#6  *The Murdered Sun* • Christie Golden
#7  *Ghost of a Chance* • Mark A. Garland & Charles G. McGraw
#8  *Cybersong* • S. N. Lewitt
#9  *Invasion #4: The Final Fury* • Daffyd ab Hugh
#10 *Bless the Beasts* • Karen Haber
#11 *The Garden* • Melissa Scott
#12 *Chrysalis* • David Niall Wilson
#13 *The Black Shore* • Greg Cox
#14 *Marooned* • Christie Golden
#15 *Echoes* • Dean W. Smith & Kristine K. Rusch
#16 *Seven of Nine* • Christie Golden
#17 *Death of a Neutron Star* • Eric Kotani
#18 *Battle Lines* • Dave Galanter & Greg Brodeur

**Star Trek®: New Frontier**

#1  *House of Cards* • Peter David
#2  *Into the Void* • Peter David
#3  *The Two-Front War* • Peter David
#4  *End Game* • Peter David
#5  *Martyr* • Peter David
#6  *Fire on High* • Peter David
#7  *The Quiet Place* • Peter David
#8  *Dark Allies* • Peter David

**Star Trek®: Day of Honor**

Book One: *Ancient Blood* • Diane Carey
Book Two: *Armageddon Sky* • L. A. Graf
Book Three: *Her Klingon Soul* • Michael Jan Friedman
Book Four: *Treaty's Law* • Dean W. Smith & Kristine K. Rusch
*The Television Episode* • Michael Jan Friedman

**Star Trek®: The Captain's Table**

Book One: *War Dragons* • L. A. Graf
Book Two: *Dujonian's Hoard* • Michael Jan Friedman
Book Three: *The Mist* • Dean W. Smith & Kristine K. Rusch
Book Four: *Fire Ship* • Diane Carey
Book Five: *Once Burned* • Peter David
Book Six: *Where Sea Meets Sky* • Jerry Oltion

**Star Trek®: The Dominion War**

Book 1: *Behind Enemy Lines* • John Vornholt
Book 2: *Call to Arms . . .* • Diane Carey
Book 3: *Tunnel Through the Stars* • John Vornholt
Book 4: *. . . Sacrifice of Angels* • Diane Carey

# STAR TREK
## THE EXPERIENCE
### LAS VEGAS HILTON

Be a part of the most exciting deep space adventure in the galaxy as you beam aboard the U.S.S. Enterprise. Explore the evolution of Star Trek™ from television to movies in the "History of the Future Museum," the planet's largest collection of authentic Star Trek memorabilia. Then, visit distant galaxies on the "Voyage Through Space." This 22-minute action packed adventure will capture your senses with the latest in motion simulator technology. After your mission, shop in the Deep Space Nine Promenade and enjoy 24th Century cuisine in Quark's Bar & Restaurant.

- - - ✂ - - - - - - - - - - - - - - - - - - - - - - - - - - - - - - - - - - - - - - -

# Save up to $30

**Present this coupon at the STAR TREK: The Experience ticket office at the Las Vegas Hilton and save $6 off each attraction admission (limit 5).**

CODE: 1007                                    EXPIRES 12/31/00.